THE OLD DUCKS' HEN DO

MADDIE PLEASE

Boldwood

First published in Great Britain in 2023 by Boldwood Books Ltd.

Copyright © Maddie Please, 2023

Cover Design by Head Design

Cover Photography: Shutterstock

The moral right of Maddie Please to be identified as the author of this work has been asserted in accordance with the Copyright, Designs and Patents Act 1988.

Every effort has been made to obtain the necessary permissions with reference to copyright material, both illustrative and quoted. We apologise for any omissions in this respect and will be pleased to make the appropriate acknowledgements in any future edition.

A CIP catalogue record for this book is available from the British Library.

Paperback ISBN 978-1-80483-719-1

Large Print ISBN 978-1-80483-718-4

Hardback ISBN 978-1-80483-720-7

Ebook ISBN 978-1-80483-716-0

Kindle ISBN 978-1-80483-717-7

Audio CD ISBN 978-1-80483-725-2

MP3 CD ISBN 978-1-80483-724-5

Digital audio download ISBN 978-1-80483-722-1

Boldwood Books Ltd
23 Bowerdean Street
London SW6 3TN
www.boldwoodbooks.com

To Jane, who has been there every step of the way.

1

'Denny, I have the most exciting news. I'm getting married!'

I put my tea down on the worktop and stared blankly into the far distance for a second. But of course I knew that voice, I recognised that chuckle. It was just the message that confused me for a moment.

'Juliette!' I said at last. 'Did you really say you're getting married?'

She laughed again. I could almost imagine my sister – well, stepsister if I was being accurate – with her feet up on her leopard-print sofa, a gin and tonic in one hand. My much-married mother had left both chaos and the two of us in her wake when she ran off with her fourth husband.

'Yes, me! Married!' Juliette said. 'Isn't it amazing? You have to be there. I won't take no for an answer.'

'Married to Matthew,' I said, 'just to be sure I'm up to speed?'

You never really knew with Juliette. In the past, she had been a first-class flirt, which meant the man of the moment might be consigned to history the next.

'Of course I'm getting married to Matthew, you twit! You know how lovely he is, despite the tweeds and the shooting stick. And the bristly moustache. There are only two men on the planet with a moustache who are attractive, in my opinion, and Matthew is one of them.'

'And who is the other?'

'Tom Selleck, of course.'

'Oh, yes, of course. Well, this is incredibly exciting,' I said, 'when did this happen?'

Juliette gave a little squeak of delight. 'Last night. I know we make an odd couple, but oh, Denny, I'm so happy!'

'You sound it,' I said, smiling. 'And when is the big day? Are you off to Vegas? Or a beach in the Caribbean? Oooh, you need to be careful, it's hurricane season there in the summer, but you might get lucky and avoid them.'

'Don't be daft. This is me and sensible Matthew, not me and some random celebrity with too many tattoos and a drug habit. We're hoping to book a day in June, because he's heard the church has had a cancellation. There are benefits to being the church warden. Lucky for us, eh? Although not so lucky for the local farmer whose fiancée stayed on in Brixham after her hen weekend. Who knew trawler captains could be so gosh darned attractive? But that's not the only reason I'm ringing. I'm already planning a hen weekend. Well, a hen week, actually. More like a hen ten days. Let's just call it a hen holiday. Last night, as soon as I said yes, I started looking through the internet and this morning I have found the most glorious villa to rent on Mallorca. Sea views, a pool and level walking distance to restaurants. Four bedrooms, four bathrooms. My treat. And I want you to be there. You have to be there. You're one of my closest relations left now. Do you realise *we* are now the older generation? The ones who normally get stuck on the boring table at weddings talking about our ailments? Well, that's not going to happen this time, I'll make sure of that. It wouldn't be the same without you there. Do say yes.'

Juliette rambled on for a while, telling me about the villa on the Mallorcan coast, the date, the first ten days in April, and the flight possibilities. She wanted to fly from Birmingham, which was incredibly convenient and anything that avoids a trip to Luton or Stanstead is a plus in my opinion.

I had to admit that her enthusiasm was infectious, but also a bit unsettling. All the years we had both been – for various reasons – effectively single, we'd been able to commiserate with each other about the various men with whom we had been in and out of relationships. Now she was moving on, to a new place which I couldn't really understand. Of course I was happy for her, but even so, I felt a bit – well – left out, I suppose.

I gave myself a mental slap for my rather selfish thoughts, and focused back in on what she was saying.

'And we will each have our own bedroom, and from the pictures on the website there isn't a dud one with bunk beds, a box of Lego under the bed and a loo in the cupboard that doesn't flush properly. Villa Gloriosa is right in the middle of the cutest little fishing village. Cobbled streets, ancient church, boats, sea views, the lot.'

'It does sound wonderful,' I said when she stopped to draw breath.

I hadn't done anything exciting for months and the winter seemed to be going on forever. This sounded like a terrific opportunity for some fun before Juliette dived back in to married life.

'I'll send you the link,' Juliette said. I could hear her fingers tapping away on her laptop and a moment later there was a corresponding ping from my inbox.

'Oh, my goodness. It looks fantastic! Who else is coming?'

'The other Old Ducks, of course. You're old enough to be

invested into the order now you're sixty. And Kim and Sophia will want to be there. Anita would too but I know she is off with one of her dance groups on a tour of Scotland. It's been booked for months. She has two new dresses, she said they needed their own suitcase, the skirts are so full. We are going to have such fun.'

I looked out of the window at the winter rain, which seemed to have been falling for days, if not weeks. I really needed to go out and get some milk, my tea consumption was rising to epic volumes now that I had retired. I had eaten my last KitKat yesterday too. Perhaps I needed to restock. And perhaps have some proper food instead of just snacking. Actually cook a meal. But then it always seemed too much of an effort, spending hours chopping vegetables and stirring and messing about in the kitchen just for me. And then it never looked like the illustration on the packet, so what was the point?

'So take a look at the details, I'm going to contact the others next, and force them to come. It's a shame Anita is away, but I know Kim will be up for it. She's a great laugh. Do you remember her? The maths teacher. Both of her kids are still trying to move back in with her, and she's talking about changing the locks yet again. What she really needs is a moat and drawbridge, but you can't really do that in Kidderminster, you'd never get planning permission. And Sophia – you haven't met her, have you? She lives on Rhodes with the handsomest man. She met him there. Wouldn't it be nice if you met someone in Mallorca? A gorgeous Spanish noble, or a backpacking billionaire?'

'I don't think I want to,' I said.

Juliette chuckled. 'Take my word for it, that's when it always happens. When you're not looking for someone. Look at me, I met Matthew in the queue for the ice cream van at the village fete. The old biddies around here will be livid when word gets around we are engaged, I can't wait to tell them. It's quite possible the parish councillors will explode with fury when Matthew books the church. And when the banns are read there will be newsletters and false teeth all over the place.'

I laughed. 'Troublemaker.'

'You know me. So you'll come?'

'Oooh, I don't know,' I teased, 'let me have a look at my diary.'

'That shouldn't take long,' Juliette scoffed.

No, she was right, it wouldn't. I had retired just before Christmas, my department head made me an offer no one would have refused, and I had somehow gone from being frantically busy with meetings and appointments to a desert wasteland of empty weeks.

Of course, at first it had been great, to wake up when I felt like it. Go out or stay in when it suited me. Not have to stress about deadlines or other people's inability to send coherent emails. But now, a few months in, I was beginning to feel I needed something more to fill my days. I'd spent decades, my whole working life, being sensible and disciplined. Suddenly, if I was honest, I was beginning to feel a bit rudderless. Yes, I was happy, but I was beginning to realise there's only so much satisfaction that can be gained from pleasing oneself all the time.

I went back to the conversation.

'I can cancel the trip to Cannes for the film festival if I have to, and the Buckingham Palace tea party...'

'You're kidding?'

'Of course I'm kidding,' I laughed. The excitement was beginning to grow as I took the news in properly. 'Congratulations! I wouldn't miss it for anything. Married!'

'Then you're definitely coming,' Juliette said. 'Good, because if she found out there was a spare place, my daughter would be angling to come, if nothing else so she could get a week away from the twins. Or worse than that, she might want the twins to

come too. Much as I love Melissa and her kids, and I do sympa-
thise with her problems with potty training, I don't think it would
be the same with them there. But then she was nearly forty when
the twins were born. Perhaps she doesn't have the energy I did at
twenty-two when I had her? I will send you over all the details
when I get them. Flights and that sort of thing. We could travel
together. And you'd better make sure your passport is up to date.
I'm going to start a WhatsApp group for us as soon as I hear from
the others. Right, I must go. I have a hundred phone calls to
make. Perhaps that's a slight exaggeration. Speak soon! I'm so
excited!'

With a last happy squeak, Juliette rang off and my house
suddenly seemed very quiet and peaceful again. Perhaps too
quiet.

I sat with my mouth open for a few moments, taking in the
news. So my stepsister was, after all these years, taking the plunge
into marriage again.

That was a surprise. Gary, her first husband, had been a disaster; handsome, charismatic, untrustworthy, unfaithful, and ulti-
mately unlikeable. Enough to put anyone off a second attempt.
He had left her with a daughter ten years after they had married
and gone off to find everlasting love with his secretary. And after
that fell apart, some other poor woman with more money than
sense. I'd lost track of him. Although I did occasionally see him
on Facebook, showing off about something.

It had reinforced my subconscious belief that marriage didn't
work, had probably never been a good idea and definitely wasn't
for me. I had been wise to avoid it.

So there I was at sixty, retired, reasonably healthy, just about
financially secure, and looking for the next chapter in my life. I
needed to find a new challenge. Or perhaps discover a new skill?
Maybe take up a hobby? I had no idea what that would be.

I'd become so immersed in work that I hadn't had time for hobbies. And I hadn't had a proper, getting-on-a-plane holiday for ages. I hadn't had a satisfactory relationship for years.

I'd enjoyed being retired at first, I'd even tidied the airing cupboard, and the drawer in my desk with all the cables and adaptors. Well, I had wrapped them into coils and shoved them all back in because everyone knows the minute you throw one away it's the one you need. But I had to admit the novelty of *not* going to work was beginning to wear off. I needed to do something different.

I suddenly had the awful feeling that something was happening to me. I was starting to behave and live and think like an old person. Eating the same meals all the time, wearing the same clothes each week. And in my head, I wasn't old at all. I was just the same me as I had always been.

Perhaps I would think about all this in Mallorca. I hugged myself with excitement. A real break from routine, with Juliette and her friends, in the sunshine. I hadn't been abroad for ages; not since the disastrous trip to Texas with Hal. If I was going to be looking around somewhere new, I'd rather it wasn't in one hundred degrees of heat with someone complaining about the humidity affecting his hair.

Perhaps this time I would be able to relax and enjoy myself. If Juliette was there, we were bound to have some fun.

I Googled the little town where we would be staying. There were pictures of cute cafés and restaurants. Wine bars with twinkling lights. Music and friendly locals smiling at the camera, who would show us where the best markets were. And I'd heard all about their last trip to Rhodes. Hopefully Juliette wouldn't get arrested this time.

* * *

My mother had married her third husband – Juliette's father – when I was twelve and Juliette was sixteen. So I went from being an only child to the kid who hung around her, getting in the way and being annoying. I'd been brilliant at that – Juliette had locked me in the garage at least twice when she couldn't put up with me any longer – but I couldn't imagine how that particular talent might be useful during my retirement.

Juliette had liked classical music, and I preferred T Rex and David Bowie. By the time Juliette went to university to study music, we had learned to at least tolerate each other. She was always the cool, talented one, with loads of friends in colourful clothes who lolled around in Juliette's room or smoked out of the window, talking about composers I'd never heard of.

I was the school kid with lank, mousy hair and spots, who never quite got to grips with fashion. The four-year age gap between us seemed to gradually widen into an unbridgeable crevasse. And she was on the other, more interesting side with boyfriends and tales of all-night parties and people growing pot on their windowsills.

But then as soon as she had got her degree, Juliette was pregnant and married to Gary and all her vivacity seemed to drain out of her. I, meanwhile, was off to university to study politics and economics, and unexpectedly I was the one with possibilities ahead of me.

By then, our parents' marriage was foundering – predictably, because my mother needed more excitement and male approval than Juliette's father – or, let's be honest, any man – was able to provide – and two years later they were divorced. But funnily enough, that was when Juliette and I became real friends.

Perhaps she had at last been able to see me as an adult, with a character and ideas and a life of my own, not just an annoying stepsister who borrowed her clothes without asking. Who had rifled through her make-up, spritzed myself with her Aqua Manda perfume and fused her heated rollers, hoping to transform myself into Farrah Fawcett.

* * *

When her fifteen-year-old daughter Melissa went on her first school trip to Florence, I'd taken Juliette away for a weekend in Paris as a treat. I'd been busy and quite successful by then and was rising through the ranks of the government department where I worked.

'It's all right for you, working in a building filled with men. I think I'm going to be on my own forever,' Juliette pouted as we shared a bottle of wine at a café with a spectacular view of the Eiffel Tower.

That day had been bright and warm, and the air was filled with the particular scent and excitement that was Paris in the spring. It hadn't seemed the day for sadness or pessimism.

I thought about some of the men I worked with. They all seemed rather pedestrian for someone as extrovert as Juliette, and most of them wore the same suits every day which predictably held the faint whiff of body odour.

'Trust me, the men I work with are not a deep dating pool. Jules, you are thirty-seven. Not one hundred and seven,' I'd said. 'You're bright, funny, clever, and good company. And you look terrific.'

She perked up a little. 'That's the cosmetic surgery, there's nothing like bridgework and a boob job to lift your spirits. I'm thinking of getting a face lift when I'm fifty. Anyway, I've not met anyone yet. No one halfway decent, anyway,' she'd replied. 'Are you still working on obscure papers for the government? Are you sure you haven't got any nice, single friends you could introduce me to?'

I'd thought about it. My own dating history was pretty unsatisfactory, and I'd never dated a co-worker. Alasdair from Health and Safety had asked me out once, he was reasonably attractive in a Clark Kent-meets-mad-scientist sort of way, but all he ever talked about was pie charts and he liked to do an annual analysis of his year using details he had logged in his diary. The largest slices of that particular pie seemed to be work and dental flossing. I suppose he did have quite good teeth.

Back then, I didn't seem to have the time or the will to commit to anyone. Perhaps it was seeing my mother's example? Perhaps realising how Juliette's life had changed once she married and had a child had put me off?

Once, long ago, there had been someone I'd loved, so I knew I was capable of love, I knew what that felt like, but not since then. The magic had never happened again.

I sighed. 'Not really. Most of the men I meet are off the market or desperately unattractive. Unless you are looking for a man with good dental hygiene. And look at me, I'm thirty-three and no significant other. There are worse things in life, you know. I can do what I like without asking permission or treading carefully around someone or listening to the details of their various allergies and ailments. And so can you. I don't have to worry about babysitters or playdates. I can afford to live a comfortable life doing a job I enjoy. And I'm hoping for a promotion soon. There's plenty of time for all the rest of it.'

'You always were the brainy one,' Juliette sighed. 'I just wish I had more to think about recently than my daughter's GCSEs. The only management I do these days is trying to find her PE kit on a Sunday evening. It's usually screwed up in a ball at the bottom of her bag with a rotting apple core.'

'So what happened to the last boyfriend? I thought you were quite keen on him.'

'Joe? I was till I found out he was still married.' She ticked off the names on her fingers as she spoke. 'Martin was selfish, Charlie was a player, Ben was tight-fisted. I could go on.'

I topped up her wine glass. 'You'll find someone. A man who is single, polite, generous, and fun. Who makes you laugh.'

'Yes, but when?'

Well, she did find him in Matthew, but she had to wait quite a long time. She'd been sixty-three. And I had been fifty-nine when she started talking about a retired lieutenant colonel she had met at the village fete, and I had still been resolutely single. And now she was getting married, and we were off to Mallorca to celebrate.

* * *

There's something marvellous about getting onto a plane in the rain and getting off in the sunshine. It's like a little additional bonus.

Palma airport was bright, light, and spotlessly clean with seemingly endless corridors and very interesting shops selling sparkly sunglasses and unusual sweets. There were people everywhere in huge numbers, trailing through to departures while we looked for baggage reclaim, which, judging by the length of the corridors ahead of us, was probably in Madrid.

We got through passport control, security and customs without incident and finally collected our luggage. All we had to do now was meet up with the other Old Ducks.

I knew quite a bit about them. Juliette was the instigator, and Kim and Anita, her university friends, were founder members. The three of them had drifted in and out of my life over the years. Kind, fun-loving women with their own problems and challenges. The friendship that had bound them together had deep-ened into something more. A support group, I suppose, a safety net when the world let them down. But contrary to expectations, the older they got, the more fun they seemed to have.

I had friends of my own, of course I did, but I could tell there was something special about the Old Ducks. They were positive, encouraging, and – remembering a Christmas party a few years ago when the three of them had got together at Juliette's house – very noisy. My own life had seemed very quiet and rather pedes-trian in comparison.

And then, not long ago, they had gone to Rhodes and met up with Sophia from Oxford, who had been recovering from some relationship disaster, and after a rocky start, she had joined them. Now I supposed I was indeed old enough to be an Old Duck. Did I have the energy? Was I interesting enough for them to accept me? It would be fun, I was sure of that, but would I fit in?

* * *

Kim had been visiting a friend in Bristol, and should have flown in an hour before us. Sophia would be arriving in a couple of days. She was delayed by a family wedding on Rhodes she needed to attend.

After a few minutes, Juliette – conspicuous in her yellow dress and gold Birkenstocks – reapplied her coral lipstick and scanned the crowds of people.

There were families, a gang of young men in Chelsea football shirts shoving each other and drinking lager at the bar, several hen parties in the usual pink sashes and learner plates hooting with laughter, and a crocodile of older couples who were the only ones who seemed to know what they were doing as they forged through towards the exits with grim expressions. I watched as they all filed onto a coach with *Redditch Gnome Appreciation Club* on the front and allowed myself a few minutes to wonder what they would be talking about. Suddenly Juliette gave a little yelp of excitement.

'There she is! I can see her!'

A woman of about our vintage came towards us, dragging a case behind her. Then she stopped as she dropped a bag of pick-and-mix, which scattered all over the floor.

The next few minutes were taken up with hugging and exclamations about how well everyone was looking. Meanwhile a resigned-looking young man rolled his eyes at us and hoovered up the dropped sweets with a sweeper cart.

I had first met Kim many years ago. She had liked cheesecloth shirts, patchouli oil, Dr Martens boots and maxi skirts. I remembered tales of their adventures at university, particularly when Kim had somehow managed to hoist the Dean's university gown up a flagpole, which had seemed absolutely thrilling to a teenager who was still neck deep in exams and revision. But that day I didn't immediately recognise her.

Now we were all in our sixties. Kim was comfortably shod and dressed for the sunshine in a voluminous blue dress, a scarf trailing around her neck and a chunky metal necklace.

'This can't be Denny?' she said. 'Golly, you're glamorous. You make me feel quite dowdy in comparison!'

I was dressed in jeans and a T-shirt, so I didn't feel particularly glamorous. Kim was already delving in a capacious handbag for her phone.

'Selfie!' she shouted, and the three of us clustered together, putting on big, static grins.

'No, wait!' Juliette said, and she unzipped her cabin bag and started rummaging around. 'Here, put these on.'

She pulled out three canvas bucket hats. Bright yellow and patterned with cartoon ducks.

'These are our Ducks-on-tour hats. I've got one for Sophia too. They must be worn at all times.'

'At least we will know where everyone is,' Kim said approvingly.

Laughing, we pulled them on, and Juliette fussed at them, pulling the brims up or down before she allowed us to take our selfie.

'Now then, there should be a travel rep here somewhere,' Juliette said. 'I hope so, anyway, otherwise we won't know where to go.'

Kim pointed to someone next to a help desk wearing a bright green dress and doing the 'walking about not really doing anything' stroll, presumably while she waited for people like us to find her.

'That's her, isn't it? Vista Villas?'

We grabbed our cases and trundled over to where the young blonde woman who had impeccably manicured nails and bright pink lipstick was standing, fidgeting, with a clipboard in her hand and an anxious expression on her face.

Juliette took charge. 'We've just arrived, the Juliette Davies party.'

The young blonde woman blinked a bit at our matching hats and then leafed through a few sheets on her clipboard and ticked something off. Her face relaxed into a lovely smile.

'Welcome to Mallorca! I'm Stacey, your Vista Villas rep. You've booked Villa Gloriosa, doesn't that sound lovely? And it is, it's new to us this year, I went to have a peek the other day. Just gorgeous. The groceries you ordered should be there, let me know if there's any problem. And you're next door to Villa Espléndida. There's going to be a party of four in there too, but

I'm sure they won't be any bother. Some old people... bird-watchers I think they are. We get a lot of those, especially at this time of year. They won't give you any trouble.'

We all smiled and nodded, and Stacey smiled and nodded back.

'So my travel agent told me apparently I am too old to be trusted with a hire car, so we have booked a transfer taxi. Where do we find that?' Juliette asked.

Stacey flicked through her clipboard again, a frown darkening her brow.

'In the car park, but I sometimes think Palma airport has a car park the size of France. Luckily it's not too busy today, as you can see.'

We looked out of the window, where dozens of coaches, cars and minibuses were lined up in orderly rows. Lines of passengers were standing hopefully, clutching their bags and grabbing their children as they wandered off. If that wasn't busy, I wouldn't like to have seen it when it was.

Stacey looked up at last with a bright smile. 'Out there and turn right. Or is it left? No, it's definitely right. It's only my second season here with Vista Villas and it's a bit confusing sometimes. You're booked with Carlos; he has a silver people carrier. This is his registration number. He should be standing by his car holding up a card with your name on it. I'm told he's very good, he'll look after you. Although I'd hardly tell you if he was a psychopath or an axe murderer just out of prison, would I?'

She laughed merrily and ticked something else off her list.

Kim and I frowned at each other.

'Come on then, girls,' Juliette said cheerfully, 'let's go and find Carlos the not-axe-murderer.'

Carlos, who was easily small enough for us to overpower if he had taken a nasty turn, helped us into his car with our luggage and we left the airport. We turned up lots of slip roads and joined busy highways at speed. There was a rosary and the picture of a fierce-looking woman we took to be Carlos's wife hanging from his rear-view mirror, which jangled as we hurtled around roundabouts.

'Look at those cactus plants! And there are mountains,' Kim said. 'I didn't know there would be mountains. I don't know why, I thought it would be flat.'

I pushed my hat to the back of my head and pressed my nose to the car window, admiring the scenery, which was fantastic. Already I was feeling we were going to enjoy ourselves.

'Those are the sort of mountains Sharpe would have fought in, aren't they? Do you remember Sean Bean fighting the French, or the Spanish? Or both at once, I can't remember. Hanging off a crag by his fingertips with a rifle in one hand.'

'Wasn't he wonderful,' Juliette sighed, 'and there would be a bandit, with baggy red trousers and fierce moustaches and a bandolero, laden down with bullets, hiding out in the mountains. And he would capture Sharpe and snarl at him through narrowed eyes. *Dondé es el gato?*'

'Oooh, that sounds thrilling,' Kim said, 'what does that mean?'

'Where is the cat,' Juliette admitted, 'it's the only Spanish I can remember, which after a ten-week course in the village hall is a bit useless.'

We all laughed, and Carlos took a wary glance at us in his rear-view mirror. I turned to look at my companions and felt a sudden burst of optimism. I think I had already laughed more that day than I had for ages. It was almost intoxicating.

* * *

Forty minutes later, we reached a roundabout which had been decorated with a huge metal sculpture of a plane, negotiated a few narrow streets and at last swung into a short driveway.

Carlos, who didn't like to do less than fifty miles an hour, perhaps because he was keen to get us to our destination and stop the incessant noise, not the least of which was Kim's laugh, skidded to a dusty halt on the gravel, startling a black and white cat out of its morning nap.

The villa was indeed glorious, very modern, with huge glass windows and polished stone floors. Despite the fact that we were all old enough to know better, we hurried around like children to investigate all the rooms, exclaiming at the size of the television, the views over the Mediterranean from the upstairs rooms, the lovely turquoise pool, the big bedrooms, and well-equipped bathrooms.

For the first time in ages, I felt that thrill of excitement that goes with having an adventure. Seeing something new with the anticipation of some good company and fun. Where no one who knew me as Ms Denise Lambert from the contracts division would appear and dump a pile of folders on my desk or raise their eyebrows if they saw me in a swimming costume. Not that I ever wore a swimming costume to work, I think if I had a couple of them would have fainted.

It didn't take long to sort out which bedrooms we would take, because they were each equally lovely. Except for the master suite, with a white four-poster bed and whirlpool bath, which Juliette nabbed. It seemed only fair, after all, she was the bride.

I was in one of the other rooms with a view of the sea, Kim had a room overlooking the back of the house, where there was a garden and the pool.

'I'm so relieved to have an en suite,' Kim said happily. 'I'm a bit funny about sharing a bathroom these days. At home, I have to jostle for space with Gemma's make-up and Simon's shaving stuff, which they leave there in case they need to crash at my place. It can get very depressing. They are both in their thirties, and I still seem to spend most of my time putting their clutter away.'

Later, watching Juliette darting around the huge kitchen, opening all the cupboard doors and drawers, pulling things out of the boxes of groceries on the worktop, it seemed as though the years had slipped away. I could still remember her as the vivacious, positive young woman she had been when we had been growing up together.

'Bottle opener, that's what I need to find. Please don't tell me there isn't one? Ah!'

Juliette held up a bottle opener triumphantly and then started peeling the foil off a bottle of red wine.

'It's eleven-thirty,' Kim said doubtfully.

Juliette gave her a look as she heaved the cork out of the bottle.

'Now look, Kim, during the week my body is a temple. At the weekends and on holiday it's a student union, with a sticky floor. With a punk band playing.'

'Fair enough. I'm going outside for a cig,' Kim said. 'I've got withdrawal symptoms.'

'I thought you'd given up?' Juliette yelled after her.

'I've cut down,' Kim shouted back, pulling the patio doors open.

A breath of warm air came into the room, bringing with it the scent of the sea and the sound of some small birds twittering in the bushes.

I abandoned my ideas of unpacking, logged my phone on to the internet and followed Kim out into the sunshine. It was a gorgeous, warm spring day, which after the dreary weeks of winter in England was absolutely marvellous. Perhaps it was possible to think more clearly when the weather was good. There's nothing like slightly damp shoes and a dripping raincoat to depress the spirits.

I checked the weather app on my phone, eight degrees and raining in Birmingham. Twenty-one degrees and sunny here. Marvellous. Sorry, Birmingham.

There were a few trees around the pool, which had been savagely pollarded at some point, but which were now sending out green shoots, the promise of new beginnings. It seemed symbolic. I needed a few green shoots in my life too. To open up my world, to think new thoughts, to take a few chances.

Kim lit a cigarette and took a deep, satisfied drag at it. She held out the packet towards me with an enquiring eye and I shook my head.

'Filthy habit, I know. And expensive. I remember when it was seventy pence for a pack. Ah, that's better. I will give up soon, just at the moment, well. It's no secret I'm a bit stressed. This holiday is absolutely what I need.'

'This is great, isn't it?' I said. 'So peaceful and the villa is lovely.'

Kim nodded. 'I think we should all go for a swim, get in the holiday mood. I hope I can still get my cossie on. I've been doing a lot of comfort eating, but I've realised cake is no comfort in the long run, is it? I'm still stressed and a bit fatter.'

I closed my eyes and lifted my face to the sun.

'I remember you when you were a kid,' Kim said at last, 'you used to be like a string bean. Skinny little legs, we were all so jealous of you.'

I raised my eyebrows. 'Were you? I was so jealous of you lot. You were all doing exciting things, going to university, having boyfriends, talking about going to discos.'

Kim laughed. 'We did have a good time all those years ago. But since then, we've all had our problems. Friendship is what counts in the end. Everyone bangs on about the importance of romantic love, but the affection and support of good friends is just as significant. I don't know what I would have done recently without the Old Ducks. Stewart did the dirty on me, left me for some trollop, and just as I was getting over all that, my kids keep trying to move back in with me. They say it's to look after me, which is a joke because the only kitchen gadget they know how to use is a microwave and they wouldn't think of cleaning it. I even got them their own flat share and that's worked for a while. But then two weeks ago Simon split up with his girlfriend again, for good this time, and worse than that, Gemma lost her job. I know what could happen, they'd revert to behaving like teenagers, a pile of shoes at the bottom of the stairs, nothing in the fridge except empty cartons, and they would spend all their cash on fancy phones and clubbing and then complain they can't afford their own place any more. Never mind, tell me all about yourself. I only get snippets from Jools.'

'I've just taken early retirement, never married, no kids.'

Suddenly it felt a bit pathetic to be able to sum up my life in one short sentence.

Kim nodded. 'So that's why you don't have any wrinkles. My therapist told me that wrinkles go where smiles have been, and I said to her, well, I don't remember ever being that happy.'

She stubbed out her cigarette in a bucket of sand by the door and dusted her hands together.

'Anyway, I'm back up to speed now. I'm going to go upstairs and unpack. Coming?'

'In a minute,' I said, 'there's no rush. I'm enjoying this.'

I sat down on one of the sunbeds, which were neatly lined up by the side of the pool. They were very comfortable, with thick yellow cushions and white fringing. How lovely to have that sort of thing in one's garden. In England there would have to be a continual to and fro of taking the cushions in when it rained, checking the weather forecast and putting them back out again.

I put my feet up, rested my head back and closed my eyes again. I took a few deep breaths. Out with that cold English air, and in with the warm Spanish sunshine. It felt very pleasant indeed.

I thought about Juliette and her daughter and her grand-daughters, Kim and her problems with her adult children, and for a moment I felt almost unsettled. I only had myself to think about. Which in a way was good, but possibly it wasn't. The worries, the emotional rollercoaster, the complicated plotting of parenthood, all of that had passed me by. Maybe after all I had missed something.

I don't think I had realised how frazzled I had been in the last few months. And I couldn't blame the pressures of work any more, just the difficulty in getting to grips with my new life, of *not* going to work any longer, *not* darting out of bed at six-thirty and battling with rush-hour traffic. I was having to create a new sort of pattern to each day, one which I wasn't always embracing very successfully if I was honest. In fact, on several occasions I had analysed my feelings and realised I was bored.

Instead, I'd filled my time with other things. Keeping on top of the laundry, painting the bathroom twice because the first colour I chose was too dark, making the effort to cook proper meals very occasionally, reading, more time being on my own.

I suppose this was what my mother had implied when she said that one day I would regret not marrying and having a family. This segment of my life when I didn't have a companion, grown-up children, at my age perhaps grandchildren. But as I had always said in answer to her criticism, I was not childless, I was child-free. And relationships were no guarantee of anything. If anyone knew that, then she did.

Of course not, she had said, if you want a guarantee, buy a toaster.

I heard the door to the villa next door open and the quiet sounds of other people on their patio, separated from ours by a medium-sized hedge and a white gate. Presumably for when one party rented both villas.

Perhaps these were the group of old people Stacey had mentioned. The birdwatchers.

'Nice pool,' a male voice said, 'we could have a dip later.'

'I need a drink first, me old mucker. Let's break out the lager. Has Vince got all the duty-free in from the car?'

'Think so.'

'I'll go and look.'

I wondered who they were and what duty-free they had bought. We should have bought some too, but we hadn't bothered. We had been too busy reading announcement boards and looking at the dinky little airport specials in the make-up departments.

I carried on doing my slow, controlled breathing.

Four-part breath, my yoga teacher had called it. Not that I had been for years, but it was one of the few things I remembered. I had quickly realised that Downward Dog and I would never be friends. I felt my mind relax. I should go in and unpack, but this was so pleasant, to be lying here in the sunshine without a care in the world. Knowing that in the villa there were other people I could talk to. Breathe in. Hold it. Breathe out. Hold it.

I was startled out of my restful trance by a male voice.

'Good God. Denny? Is that you?'

I gasped, opened my eyes and jerked round, looking around

to see who had spoken and nearly falling off the sunbed in the process.

I could see the head and shoulders of a man standing on the other side of the white gate; tall, close-cropped grey hair, a suggestion of designer stubble.

Who the...?

'Denny. It is you. I can't believe it!'

I stared at him for several seconds, my mind ferreting about to remember who he was. Not someone from work, there hadn't been anyone there half as attractive as this man. And I certainly didn't know any birdwatchers.

I swung my legs off the sunbed and sat up.

He laughed. The laugh was familiar, deep, and warm. It couldn't be?

'It's me, Denny. Bruno.'

I looked at him, my mouth open with shock.

Yes, I did know him. Of course I did. Bruno Browning. I hadn't seen him for nearly forty years. We had been to university together.

The memories came flooding back. He'd had an English father who had abandoned the family when Bruno was thirteen, and a Spanish mother who was hugely protective of her only son.

We'd taken trips together. We'd gone camping on the Gower one summer. He'd liked curry nights at the student union, he drank beer and occasionally whisky. He'd been the only one of us with a car, an old blue Morris Traveller called Janet. He'd broken down driving us to Stratford-upon-Avon one weekend and we had spent four hours on the side of the road waiting for someone to come and rescue us.

Bruno had rubbed Ambre Solaire into my back, trimmed my fringe when it was too long and I'd had a sprained wrist.

Bruno Browning had broken my heart.

2

I stood up, looking at him for a few moments, after all those years apart, just separated by the gate. Not knowing what to say. He returned my gaze in the same steady way he always had. Those blue-green eyes just as bright as they had always been.

He was tanned, his face had lost the smooth-skinned look of his youth and his hair was shorter and grey. But he was still broad shouldered and lithe. I remembered how he had wanted to bulk up with more muscles, but like me he had been too lazy to go to the gym all the time. I don't think people did back then, well, I certainly didn't. He played football occasionally in the park with the student team, but we had found our exercise in other ways.

'Bruno,' I said at last, my voice rather croaky, 'good heavens. What the hell... What a coincidence.'

I smoothed my hair down; it was inclined to spring into life at unexpected moments, and I was feeling very unsettled indeed.

I almost asked him foolish questions: what he was doing there, how was he? It was obvious he was on holiday, and he looked fine to me.

He grinned, the same dimple I remembered appearing in his

left cheek. How many times had I kissed that dimple? Pressed my finger into it. Told him it was ridiculous. Wasted on a man.

'What are you doing here?' he said at last.

'A hen holiday.'

'Yours?'

'God, no. My stepsister.' My mouth was dry.

Now I really needed a drink of some sort. Preferably not water.

'Julia?'

'You've got a good memory. Juliette. What are you doing here?'

He stuck his hands in his pockets.

'Stag holiday.'

'Yours?'

He laughed and shook his head. 'No. Johnny – my cousin's getting married again. He and the other chaps are keen bird-watchers. They're very keen to visit the S'Albufera Nature Parc.'

'Fascinating.'

'No, not really, but Doggie and Vince were up for it.'

I heard a burst of laughter from inside our villa and stood up. It made me feel better just to hear them. I had company, a support group.

'My friends are waiting. I'd better go and – you know.' I made vague gestures towards the open patio doors.

'Yes, of course.' He made a similar gesture, and we took a step away from each other.

'Lovely to see you again,' he said.

'And you. Are you still teaching?'

'Retired,' he said.

'Me too. I don't mean teaching because, after all, I was never a teacher. I mean I did think about it, but well...'

Now, instead of making a dash for it, I was babbling.

'It's good, isn't it? Being retired, I mean.'

I swallowed hard. 'Yes, terrific.'

He chuckled. 'When I was working, and I sloped off or messed up or sat at my desk doing nothing, I got into trouble. Now I can do that every day if I feel like it. I used to do some supply teaching at a local college very occasionally. Just to keep my hand in.'

'I see.'

We took another step away from each other.

I heard Juliette's voice calling me from inside.

'Denny, come on, forget about the wine, we've got champagne!'

'I must go,' I said. I gave a nervous laugh which became oddly shrill. 'Got to keep the bride happy.'

'Of course. Well, I'll see you,' Bruno said.

I went inside, tripping clumsily over the shallow step. My eyes taking time to adjust from the brightness of the sun outside.

Of all the people, in all the places, this was the very last thing I had expected. Bruno Browning was here. After all those years of not knowing if he was even alive or dead. And he was very much alive, he was next door. Looking just as attractive as he ever had.

I felt slightly sick and uncertain. An annoying little flurry of nerves in my stomach.

Juliette was standing at the granite worktop with a tray and three champagne flutes, wrestling with a champagne cork.

'I found this in the wine fridge in the utility room, wasn't that nice of them? We have flatbreads and ham. And some massive tomatoes. And some sort of cheese. That's *queso* in Spanish. I've been doing a course. Did I tell you? I don't think much of it has stuck, though... except, of course, where is the cat? I can't see that coming in very useful. I'll make us some snacks, shall I?'

'Lovely,' I said. I think I was still in shock; my thoughts were all jumbled up. Never mind four-part breathing, I was finding it hard to breathe at all.

Bruno Browning. After so many years of doubt and anger and disappointment. Wondering where he had been, what he had been doing. Why things had just ended between us. Had it been me, or him? Had he travelled as he'd said he wanted to? Had he married? I had so many questions racing around my head that for a few minutes I couldn't speak.

Juliette handed me a glass and we chinked the rims.

'Kim's having a shower, she won't be down for ages and I'm not waiting. Come on. Here's to us, here's to a great holiday.'

I downed half the glass in one, enjoying the feel of the cold, fizzy wine, and Juliette topped it up again.

'That's the spirit. Are you okay? You look a bit pale.'

Two glasses of champagne helped steady my nerves. Juliette and I produced some delicious snacks and, after a few minutes, Kim came downstairs in a bathrobe, a towel wrapped around her head, complaining we had started without her.

We sat on the leather barstools, drinking champagne and discussing what we were going to do with the rest of the day.

Juliette wanted to go for a walk by the harbour. Kim agreed, suggesting we find an early dinner.

She pulled out a piece of paper from a yellow folder with *Juliette's Hen Do*, some wedding bells, and a smiley face scrawled on the front in black marker.

'Look, I put everything in this spreadsheet. I pictured us at a café this evening, overlooking the sea, a carafe of wine and some delectable food. Tick in the box. I did some research, there's something called *Arros Brut* I read about in my guidebook, rice stew like paella but different.'

'I'd like a swim,' Juliette said.

'When we come back? I've only just washed my hair,' Kim said.

'Yes, when we come back,' I agreed rather too quickly.

There was always the possibility that our neighbours would have the same idea and I didn't think I was quite ready for that if I was honest. I needed time to get my feelings under control before I saw him again. And what was I feeling? Embarrassed or uneasy or flustered, or all three? Could I be cool with this situation? Pass it off as nothing important, maybe even laugh about it. He seemed quite relaxed at seeing me again. Maybe I could be too, or at least I could pretend. I didn't feel relaxed at all. I was used to my life being simple and uncomplicated. This was neither.

But I wasn't the important person here, Juliette was. It was supposed to be all about her. Not me and my inhibitions about meeting up with the one man who had really taken the time to know me. To love me. Or at least I thought he had.

I could just imagine his group and ours, separated by a hedge, listening to each other's splashing and conversations. The sort of racket the Old Ducks were capable of making for one thing. Would that be okay? Would they complain?

I could picture myself, rigid as an ironing board with tension in case one of them kicked a football over and wanted to come and get it back. No, they were birdwatchers, weren't they? Why would they be playing football?

'Oh, okay,' Juliette said, 'it would be a nice way to spend the afternoon.'

* * *

An hour later we left, walking along the pedestrianised route past the harbour, which was gleaming and beautiful in the sunshine. The Mediterranean was smooth and blue to our left. Boats of all sorts from streamlined gin palaces to glamorous yachts were moored there.

There were palm trees just coming into leaf, and cafés shaded from the sun with coloured awnings. There were happy-looking people strolling beside the harbour, eating ice cream, sitting on the wooden benches in the shade. There were places to hire mopeds and electric scooters, arrange boat trips, buy postcards, and the sort of beach toys all children want. Everywhere was spotless. No splodges of gum on the pavement, no graffiti, no rubbish in the hedges.

Every restaurant, each wine bar we passed looked enticing with their sharp white tablecloths, wire baskets of olive oil and vinegar on each table. The air was filled with the gorgeous fragrance of garlic, herbs, roasting meats, and seafood. It was hard to choose where to stop. Eventually we decided on a café overlooking the sea, in the shade of some huge blue parasols.

A waiter came forward with a carafe of water and handed out menus with a flourish.

After a lot of discussion, we shared an enormous metal pan of paella, and it was fantastic. Every spoonful was a delicious mix of garlic, herbs, seafood, sunshine and the occasional bit of shell. It was the sort of food that made us smile. And two bottles of Abadal wine helped too. We were there for ages, while the tables around us filled up and emptied.

There were a lot of cyclists for some reason, and occasionally they would stop, prop their bikes up and clomp about in strange-looking shoes, shouting congratulations to each other or sneering when someone turned up late.

'That meal was definitely a tick in the box. I'm full now, I think it would be a really bad idea to go for a swim when we get back, I'd sink like a stone. Perhaps we could just spend the evening in the garden, and chill out?' Juliette said.

I imagined the scene, which once would have been so simple and straightforward. Now there was the possibility that Bruno and his friends would have a similar idea. Would I be able to hear them on the other side of the hedge, all talking about man stuff, pick out that familiar deep voice?

How long was it since I had seen him anyway? Thirty-something years. Thirty-nine. We had been so close at one time, finishing each other's sentences, knowing how the other one felt in any situation, and now I didn't really know how to handle it. We might be like awkward strangers.

'If that's what you really want,' I said.

Juliette nodded and loosened the belt on her ruffled pink dress a notch.

'What the bride wants, the bride gets,' she said happily.

Kim went off to the rest rooms for the second time. As she left, Juliette rummaged in her bag, pulling out a small mirror and a cosmetic bag. It was no good, I would have to tell her.

I took a deep breath. 'You know when I was out in the garden earlier?'

'Yes,' she said, her mouth stretched as she reapplied her lipstick.

'Well, I spoke to one of the men in the next-door villa.'

'The birdwatchers? Was he dressed in tweed with binoculars round his neck? Was he snooping?' Juliette laughed and adopted a David Attenborough voice. 'Here we see a rare sighting of the lesser-spotted European Denny, lounging in the sunshine.'

'Not exactly,' I said.

'Was he nice?'

'Well—'

Juliette put away her mirror and clicked her bag closed. She looked at me and frowned.

'What's up?'

'Well, the thing is, I knew him.'

'The twitcher? That's weird. How did you know him?'

I was feeling distinctly giddy. Once I said something to her, once I explained, then everyone would know.

'He isn't a birdwatcher, his friends are. He used to teach languages, and now he's retired. He can speak Spanish, French and Italian. And probably some others now for all I know. He's here with some friends for a stag holiday. Not his, a cousin of his called Johnny.'

I realised I was gabbling, the words spilling out.

Juliette raised one eyebrow. 'And what's his blood group and inside leg measurement? You seem to know a lot about him on the strength of a five-minute chat.'

'No, as I said, I know him. I knew him years ago. We were at university together. He was a language student. We met in the hall of residence. He was on the top floor when I had a room on the second.'

I could remember it all so clearly. That uncomfortable single bed. The row of coffee mugs on the shelf above the sink. The carton of milk outside on the windowsill because we didn't have a fridge.

'Well, that's a coincidence. And were you friends?'

'Yes,' I said. I let my remaining breath out in a deep sigh. 'I suppose we were.'

Those endless summer days, on the beach, him chasing me into the waves, picking me up over his shoulder. Sitting huddled in a blanket on bonfire night, eating chips out of the paper, the tang of vinegar on my lips. Driving in his car, the wind against my fingers. Lying together on his single bed, his voice in my ear, while he spoke words of love to me in Italian, my insides turning over with desire for him.

'That's nice,' Juliette said, 'you could invite them over, perhaps we could have a barbie. Hen and stag do join forces. It might be a laugh.'

I didn't say anything to this. Juliette cocked her head to one side.

'Denny, when you say you knew him, did you mean you *knew* him? In the biblical sense?'

I looked away, trying to seem unbothered.

'We went out for a long time, so I suppose you could say that.'

'But you hardly went out with anyone, did you? Only that chap who dumped you. My God, it's not him, is it? Bryn... Bruno someone. It can't be!'

I nodded. 'It is. Bruno Browning.'

Juliette slapped her hands down on the table, making the glasses rattle.

'Flipping heck. Yes, I remember. You were like a wet hen for months. Wasn't he the one who went off to Italy – for his study year – and he never contacted you again? And by the time he presumably came back, you'd left university for the big city and that was the end of it? That Bruno?'

This wasn't the whole picture, not as I remembered it. There had been much more to it than that, but I'd never told anyone, not even her. I'd felt embarrassed, confused, angry, disappointed. Heartbroken.

I tried to sound untroubled, although I certainly didn't feel it.

'Yes, that Bruno. I can't tell you what a shock it was to see him again after all this time.'

'I bet. Right, when I see him I'll tear a strip off him, push him in the pool and hold him under until he apologises and explains himself, the rat,' Juliette said fiercely.

The prospect of this made me even more anxious. I knew she was quite capable of carrying out her threat.

'Please don't. It wasn't quite as simple as that. It would only make things worse, and he's probably forgotten the whole thing. It was a really long time ago. And I expect he's married, with a family. I don't want to rake up all that stuff again. There's no need to. There's no point.'

I felt increasingly panicky at this point. I knew from past experience what Juliette could be like when she got her teeth into something.

'I don't agree, he deserves to know what a—'

'Please, Juliette. It's only a few days, I'm sure I can cope with that without a major incident.'

I was beginning to wonder if I had done the right thing in telling her. Perhaps it would have been wiser to keep it all to myself. Would I have been able to carry out such a pretence? But it wouldn't have felt right. I knew that the Old Ducks called themselves a support network, perhaps just for once I was the one needing some support.

Juliette pulled a face and then she turned round in her seat.

'Well, we'll see. Where has Kim got to? I need the loo now, and she's been ages.'

We walked back to the villa through the warm evening. It might have been low season, but there were still plenty of people about. Families with sleepy toddlers in pushchairs, groups of friends, couples hand in hand, walking past the many restaurants, peering at the menus. New groups of cyclists in tight matching vests, sitting on the stone wall by the sea, comparing times and complaining about motorists.

We got back to the villa and Kim opened the patio doors.

'I'm sure there should be lights in that pool, I'll flick a few switches, shall I, and find out.'

'Perhaps we could have a swim after all?' Juliette said. 'It's such a gorgeous evening.'

'I'm going to,' Kim said, slipping off one of her flip-flops and feeling the water with her toes. 'It's lovely and warm. I suppose we'd better put our cossies on, we can't have the birdwatchers spotting us in the altogether. They might faint.'

'Well, one of them might,' Juliette said, arching one eyebrow at me.

I dug her in the ribs with my elbow.

'Behave!'

'Well, I'm going to get changed. It takes me a bit of time to adjust everything, so my chestal area is securely tethered. Last one in the pool is a rotten egg,' Kim said, going back into the house.

Juliette grabbed my hand. 'Come on then, Denny. Let's do it. You can't spend the entire holiday lurking indoors in case Bruno sees you. And anyway, you said he was quite friendly? It might be your chance to find out what happened all those years ago.'

'I know what happened, he went off for his study year in Italy and by the time he came back I'd graduated and moved to Guildford for my first job. And that was that. It doesn't matter.' I realised I was talking quite loudly and lowered my voice to a whisper. 'Remember we didn't have mobile phones or emails or the internet in those days. It wasn't so easy to keep track of people. Particularly if the other person made no effort. The younger generation wouldn't understand how we coped, and I suppose Bruno and I didn't cope. We just lost touch with each other.'

I gasped nervously as I heard the patio doors of the next-door villa open and then a couple of low male voices chatting. Something to do with birds, I thought. Juliette and I crouched down and edged closer to the hedge and peered through the thick branches. We could see a couple of men standing on the far side of the patio with beer glasses in their hands, both wearing trousers with several pockets down the legs. There was a faint drift of cigar smoke.

'Vince said he saw hoopoes the last time he was here. And a black-winged stilt.'

'*Himantopus himantopus*, if I'm not mistaken, Johnny. We might see that tomorrow, in Albufera. He says he saw a moustached warbler there. But that was the year he claimed to have seen Paul McCartney too, so I'll take it with a pinch of salt.'

There was some good-natured chuckling at this point.

I'd never known Bruno to have been the slightest bit interested in birdwatching. Perhaps he had changed. I certainly had. I wasn't the carefree, crazy girl he had known all those years ago.

The first voice continued. 'Anyway, I hope Bruno doesn't mind us dodging off, at least he has the car.'

My ears pricked up at the sound of Bruno's name.

Juliette looked at me, her eyes wide, and mouthed, *They've got a car.*

I dug her in the ribs and tried not to giggle.

'He says he's looking forward to visiting a few friends. I mean, he knows this island so well; he doesn't need us to babysit him, does he? And hasn't he got some family?'

'Can't remember,' said the first voice.

I raked through my memories, wondering what family this would be. I knew his feckless father hadn't been around and I seemed to remember his mother had been from Barcelona. A small, feisty, black-haired woman who, when she came to visit Bruno, looked at me suspiciously through narrowed eyes, sure that I was a threat to her son's moral compass. Which, of course, I probably had been, all things considered.

'And chasing after those kids, eh? Nightmare. Give me a flock of spoonbills any day.'

What kids? Bruno had children? Well, of course he had. Why shouldn't he?

I tried to imagine Bruno as a father. Picture him in a relationship with someone. It made him seem ever more removed from the man I had known all those years ago.

'Ah, well, I need a bit of a refill, and some of that casserole Bruno's knocked up. Smells good. I didn't know he was such a good cook.'

And Bruno had been famously undomesticated back then.

'Needs must, I suppose. We all have our strengths. He doesn't know one end of a pair of binoculars from the other.'

Juliette and I raised our eyebrows at each other.

Despite everything, I started to giggle, and Juliette snorted with laughter.

At that moment Kim came out to join us, in a bright red tankini, and she cannonballed into the water with a hyena laugh and a scream.

'Oh dear,' one of the men on the other side of the fence said, 'sounds like there are teenagers next door. They didn't warn us about that.'

'It's flipping brilliant, come on, you two,' Kim shouted, and sloshed an armful of water towards us.

3

We went and changed and by the time I got back, Kim and Juliette were both sitting in blow-up flamingos, sculling around in the water with their hands and bumping into each other. There was a lot of laughter and noise. I wondered if the birdwatchers next door would complain.

As the evening darkened, and the pool lights shone out more brightly, I lay on my back, floating in the water and looking up at the night sky. A couple of tiny bats swooped overhead. It was idyllic.

I wished I had done more of this sort of thing, travelled more widely, expanded my horizons. I'd had plenty of annual leave, I could have afforded it. Why hadn't I taken advantage of the possibilities? Why had I been so sure that the only one who could run my department efficiently was me? What a shame to have waited until now.

Being relationship-free, child-free, mortgage-free didn't mean that I hadn't ended up in a solitary confinement of my own making. Maybe I'd allowed the walls of doubt, stubbornness, and cynicism to build up over the years, so that no one could hurt me again. Where had that left me in the long run? I'd been safe but not secure. Confident in my ability but not always content. I hadn't needed all that sort of thing. Had I?

All this was rather unsettling, and I realised I'd never thought about it properly. Why hadn't I?

I did a few steady lengths of the pool, dodging the other two, who were trying to organise a race on their blow-up pool toys. I'd always been a good swimmer, and it was great exercise too. That could be something I could take up as a new hobby.

I imagined myself joining a gym with a pool, setting an alarm, and going there first thing every morning with a special bag and a towelling robe. Then I realised that knowing me, it was very unlikely. Perhaps I would take up wild swimming, joining a group of brisk, hearty older people, wading into freezing rivers and lakes. I'd have to get a wetsuit and some specialist footwear – the thought of treading in all that river mud was very off-putting. I would strike out through the weeds and enjoy the tranquillity, being closer to nature, and then drink hot tea out of a Thermos flask afterwards. I gave a deep sigh. That didn't sound like me either.

I was at heart lazy, and without the impetus of work and all that went with it, I was more likely to spend my free time curled up in a chair with coffee, a bar of whole-nut chocolate and some of those many books I had been meaning to read.

Was this enough? It didn't feel like it. I might live for another thirty years. Surely I could do better than that?

'So tomorrow,' Juliette said, sculling herself over towards me, puffing slightly with the effort, 'let's explore the town. There is supposed to be a really cute old church and some ruins some-where, and I know you always used to like that stuff. Remember when we went to Stonehenge, and you spent all your time trying to work out where the ley lines were? And you and my dad had a debate about how it was built. Which turned into an argument. And your mum pretended she had seen an adder, so we had to leave. And then we went to Glastonbury, and you were car sick.'

'You do remember the strangest things,' I said.

'I do. I have a mind just like a jumble sale these days. You know there might be something interesting in there, but it takes time to find it. Now tell me more about Bruno-next-door.'

'I think you know everything there is to hear. We dated, we lived together, he went off to Italy for a year and when he came back, I'd gone, and I never heard from him again. All the time he was away, he only sent two postcards. From Milan. And he was supposed to be in Naples. I sent a couple of letters to his address there, but he never replied.'

'How sad, and you were quite keen on him, weren't you?'

Keen on him? I'd been in love with him. I'd never found another relationship that gave me the same sort of happiness. That belief that he was the person I fitted with, who I could spend my whole life with, who would be a part of the good bits and the bad. Who felt the same way about me. And yet it hadn't happened. Despite everything we had shared, every magical moment, each laughter-filled evening, all the memories and things we had done, it hadn't lasted.

I shook my head, trying to be sensible.

'It was a long time ago. People change. And then I moved to London, I met Paul, and whatshisname with the beard. Lance. And then I was relocated to the Midlands where I met Hal. Bruno probably met someone else too.'

'Never mind, we will look after you.'

'I don't need looking after. I'm over it, all of it.'

'Your face says otherwise,' Juliette said.

I almost felt like telling her how I really felt. Confused, restless, and unsettled. But I didn't, I didn't want to admit anything out loud because that would make it true.

Instead, I spun her round on her inflatable flamingo, making her yelp.

'I think we are supposed to be looking after you, bride,' I said.

Juliette beamed. 'Bride, isn't that amazing? After all this time I'm getting married again. Now where's my drink?'

Juliette sculled herself over to the side of the pool and reached for her plastic beaker of wine. She gave a scream and a squeal, and the blow-up flamingo tipped over, depositing her into the water.

She came up, her hair over her face, spluttering, 'God, my highlights!'

Laughing, I helped to heave her back on board her unsteady craft. She carried on talking as though nothing had happened.

'And listen to me, I want all the Old Ducks to be my brides-maids. And I want to find something a bit different for you all to wear.'

Kim, who by then was sitting on the side of the pool with her feet in the water, cheered.

'We are hardly "maids", though, are we?' she said. 'Don't we have to call ourselves matrons of honour?'

Juliette laughed. 'Forget the honour bit, in view of what we all know about each other. Bride's attendants. Or just matrons?'

'Oooh, matron,' Kim drawled. 'We could wear nurses' outfits, that would be different.'

'A bit too different,' Juliette said. 'We are planning to get married in the local church, after all. I don't want to give any of Matthew's military friends the wrong idea. There are a couple of generals and a brigadier on the guest list. One of them has a pros-thetic leg, he likes to knock his pipe out on it. He's very sprightly, though, you'd never guess.'

'And what are you going to wear?' I asked.

Juliette closed her eyes and gave it some thought.

'Not sure yet. I'll need to find something outstanding. Something that will knock Matthew's socks off. Something sparkly, but not too obvious. I had a dress in mind, pale pink with beads. But it was a bit captain's dinner table, I don't want my bosom too centre stage, after all.' Juliette looked down at her chest rather proudly. 'Although it is looking rather splendid. Like a ship in full sail. The surgery did wonders.'

'A trouser suit with a marvellous hat?' Kim suggested.

'I spend a lot of money getting my varicose veins done, and Matthew likes my legs. I don't want to hide them.'

Juliette lifted one shapely leg in the air and fell off her flamingo again.

'Oh, for heaven's sake,' she spluttered as she came to the surface, 'what's the matter with this thing?'

It was dark by the time we went inside and getting chilly. We all changed out of our swimming things and into bathrobes. I for one was thinking about going to bed, but the Old Ducks were just getting started, it seemed.

'Cocktails before bed,' Juliette said, 'to help us sleep.'

'I won't have any trouble sleeping,' Kim said. 'I've hardly slept for the last month, I've been looking forward to this holiday so much. I re-packed my case at least four times.'

'Well, a toast to the bride then, before we turn in,' I said.

Kim did a bit of mixing and shook the cocktail shaker over her head for full effect, dancing and singing around the kitchen area in the style of Carmen Miranda: 'Aye aye aye aye aye aye like you veeeery much...' Which was a nice touch except she hadn't fastened the shaker properly and after a few seconds it exploded. She ended up showered with ice cubes and something blue and sticky. She screamed rather theatrically as some ice lodged the back of her bathrobe. Then, dripping, she rolled her eyes and went off for another shower while Juliette and I mopped the floor.

* * *

'I must say, it's wonderful to have you here,' Juliette said sometime later.

She looked at the cocktail Kim had concocted for us, which this time was green, smelled of mint and was decorated with a little umbrella, a glace cherry, and a slice of cucumber. 'What is this, by the way?'

'I've no idea,' Kim said, 'I just used some of the leftover stuff in the cupboard and a teeny bit of gin. There was nearly a full bottle of the green stuff. I think I'll call it a Mallorcan Memory.'

I took a cautious sip and choked a little. 'Mallorcan Mule would be more accurate,' I said, wiping my eyes.

'Listen up! After I had showered off all that blue goo upstairs, I was spying on the four chaps in the villa next door. They are all out on their patio drinking beer, I can just see them from my window.'

'Twitchers,' Juliette said, 'don't you remember?'

Kim looked puzzled. 'I didn't notice anybody twitching.'

'Birdwatchers, she means.'

'Oh, yes, of course. They don't look too bad, actually. None of them have binoculars around their necks, but it is dark. Two in Hawaiian shirts but then they are on holiday so I expect they are trying to blend in, one in long shorts, or they could be short longs, smoking a cigar. The fourth one is very tasty. Tall, nice shoulders.'

'I expect that's Bruno,' Juliette said, arching an eyebrow at me.

Kim frowned. 'How do you know?'

Juliette looked rather smug. 'Well, in a remarkable coincidence, which is worthy of an episode of *Miss Marple*, Denny knows him from way back when.'

Kim looked very interested.

'How,' she asked, 'and when?'

Juliette put her drink down. 'I really don't think I can drink this, it's absolutely disgusting, and I think I've had more than enough alcohol for one day. Denny was at university with him. He was her *boyfriend*. They were in *lurve*.'

All eyes turned to face me. Annoyingly, I could feel myself blushing.

'How marvellous! Tell us all about him,' Kim said. 'Did he dump you? Did you dump him? Was he a love rat? I bet he was, all men are rats of one sort or another in my opinion.'

Juliette bristled. 'Well, Matthew's certainly not a rat! He's more cuddly than that. Like a big – you know – vole or yes, a *sea-otter*. I like sea-otters. The way they balance their babies on their tummies in the water. It's so sweet.'

'Does Matthew do that with you in the bath?' Kim said, giggling.

Juliette pulled a face. 'Hardly, I'd probably drown him.'

'Bruno and I just lost touch,' I said, trying to sound unconcerned, 'nothing more to it than that. No ratty behaviour at all.'

'It's a sign,' Kim said, her eyes shining possibly with emotion, maybe from the Mallorcan Mule.

'A sign of what?' I said.

She shrugged. 'I don't know. It's just a sign. Let's go over there tomorrow and say hello. They could form the Old Drakes' Club.'

'You know, I'd rather you didn't,' I said, 'it's a bit awkward.'

'When did you last see him?' Juliette said.

I tried to remember but the Mallorcan Memory was clouding my brain.

'Nearly forty years ago.'

Kim waved one hand and the towel wrapped around her damp hair slipped off and over her eyes. 'Well, in that case it's just old friends meeting up again, isn't it? That's not awkward at all.'

'Not for you, maybe,' I said.

I tried to picture it, standing in a group with Bruno, failing to forget what we had done together, the way he had stood behind me and kissed my neck when I was cooking. That little stab of delight I had felt each time I saw him unexpectedly. The feel of his body, his skin, his breath mingling with mine. The way we had smiled at each other, our secrets in each other's eyes.

'Denny says he speaks lots of languages,' Juliette said, 'perhaps he can help us find the good places to go?'

'And the local markets,' Kim added, 'I want to see those. They always have fab stuff.'

'We haven't got a car, we can't go very far,' I reminded her.

'No, but *they do*,' Juliette said. 'I went and had a look outside earlier. They've got a people carrier. I expect birdwatchers need a lot of, you know, birdwatching stuff. Cameras and tripods. And picnic hampers with cheese and pickle sandwiches and lashings of ginger beer. And the *Observer's Book of Birds*.'

'Was Bruno into that?' Kim asked.

'Not when I knew him,' I said.

'Perhaps he's changed, now he's older. We all do. I never thought I'd get excited about warm vests and comfortable knickers, but the other day there was a three-for-two offer on in M&S, and I thought I might die of pleasure.'

'Sad sometimes, isn't it,' Juliette said, shaking her head, 'this ageing business.'

I held up a hand in protest. 'Ageing is a bonus, it proves we're still on the planet.'

Kim looked knowing. 'Yes, but which planet?'

Was ageing a bonus? Did I mind being sixty? I couldn't call myself middle-aged any more. I was past that. We all were. But suddenly it didn't feel as though I was sliding downhill into oblivion. There were still things out there to do, things to learn. Challenges to accept and deal with, and perhaps Bruno was one of them.

I slept surprisingly well that night, considering the alcohol, the travelling, and the news that Bruno Browning – instead of being lost for decades somewhere in the void – was only yards away.

The bed was wide and comfortable with beautiful smooth sheets and excellent pillows. I've often had trouble with pillows over the years. Too soft and they condense down into rocks in the middle of the night, too hard and in the morning my neck feels as though I've done three rounds with Hulk Hogan.

In the morning, the sun was shining though the curtains and I felt surprisingly positive. Leaving only a slightly pensive feeling and a headache, which I thoroughly deserved.

I showered and dressed, aware that someone else in the villa was also stirring. Downstairs I found Juliette in zebra-print pyjamas and dressing gown, feet up on one of the huge sofas, watching a Spanish children's programme on TV: a penguin, a cat and a bear interacting with various vegetables.

'Okay?' she said, not taking her eyes off the screen. 'There's a character on here which I think is half-pepper, half-shark. It's either very inventive or I've mixed up my cholesterol medication.'

I made a fresh pot of coffee and went to sit in one of the chairs opposite her.

'This place is just gorgeous, isn't it?' I said. 'I can't wait to get out and see the town.'

'Hmm. You might have to wait a while; I don't think Kim is anywhere near consciousness. She came into my room after you went to bed. She's still fixated on that rat of an ex-husband of hers. Okay, the internet dating didn't bring forth fruit, but Kim really should be a tiny bit less resentful, shouldn't she? After all, it's been years.'

'She needs something else to focus on,' I said, 'something new. A hobby or some interest.'

I was talking about Kim, but I was aware the same advice applied to me.

Juliette obviously agreed. 'True. And so do you. We Old Ducks are always saying we're never too old for anything.'

'Except perhaps skinny jeans, broderie anglaise and sitting on the pavement when we are waiting for a bus,' I said.

'Perhaps we should try sitting on the pavement at least?'

'But will we be able to get up again afterwards?'

Juliette chuckled. 'That might be a bit undignified. And it's not as though Kim would have Stewart back if he came begging on his hands and knees. She just wants him to be – I don't know – sorry for the way he treated her. And that's unrealistic. When one is twenty-something, all you need is a new dress, a fabulous pair of shoes and your mates to get over a break-up. At sixty-something, it's not quite the same.'

'But you have Matthew, and your daughter and the grandchildren, and Kim has her kids coming back like homing pigeons. Anita has Rick and their dancing group. Sophia has Theo.'

'And what about you?' Juliette said, turning to look at me. 'What do you have?'

I hesitated. I had my health, although I did need reading glasses and I had a hip that was inclined to twang a bit. I had some money, good friends, my home. That was enough, surely? Wasn't it?

I thought about it for a minute and realised that if I lived for another twenty or thirty years, it wasn't nearly enough. I needed something else. Fun, excitement, the challenges that make life worth living. That would keep my brain active and engaged with the world. And that wasn't just a relationship, or some adult children or decorating the bathroom. I needed to find myself again.

'I have eaten, slept, and dreamed about work for far too long.'

Juliette nodded. 'So now what? Now what are you going to eat? How will you sleep? What is there to dream about?'

'There must be something,' I said, feeling rather unsettled.

'There will be,' Juliette said wisely.

'I think my life so far can be summed up in one sentence; *well, I didn't see that coming.*'

'I hope you realise it's the same for all of us. But it's not where you start, it's where you finish. That's what I think. Why, do you have regrets about retiring?'

'Yes, I do. But I knew it would happen sometime. I think I'm starting to understand that from now on my life isn't just *not going to work*, there has to be more to it than that. Life is short, time is fast. There's no replay, no rewind, no pause button. Now I have the "what next" thing to deal with.'

'This is far too sombre a conversation to be having sober,' Juliette said, swinging her feet off the sofa. 'What's next is breakfast and there are some glorious Portuguese tarts in the fridge. I'll put some in the oven to warm up a bit, shall I, and then we can talk about more cheerful things.'

4

The little town, just a few steps away from our villa, was lovely.

We sorted out bags and sunglasses and all put on our bright yellow duck hats, giggling as we did so.

There were, as Juliette had promised, cobbled streets, with funny little stone arches that led enticingly between houses. Tiny dark delicatessens with strings of garlic and various cured meats hanging from hooks in the ceiling, and aromatic bakeries where flour dusted the pavement outside the door. Open squares with fountains and thoughtfully placed benches under the shade of trees. By the time we got there, some of the cafés were putting out tables and chairs, ready for the lunch trade. A man in blue overalls was sweeping up some dried leaves and dust, and he had stopped to lean on his broom and talk to a black cat that was sitting in his way. It was all so relaxed and pleasant, and nothing like being at home. We came to the end of a lane and there in front of us was the blue, shining Mediterranean again.

I stopped and sighed, my hands clasped together in front of me.

'How amazing; if I lived here, I would never get tired of that view. At the end of my road back home there is a corner shop and a skate park covered in graffiti.'

Far out to sea was a large ship, a tanker perhaps or a cruise ship. A reminder that for thousands of years this place had seen ships from other countries. The Phoenicians, the Romans, Crusaders, the Spanish. And now the newer invasion of tourists, of which we were a part.

'There's a market held in the square twice a week,' Kim said, consulting her guidebook. 'Fruit, vegetables, and crafts. We must find it.'

'We need to get a few more supplies in too,' I said, 'there must be a supermarket somewhere.'

'I'm not planning on doing much cooking, not with all these gorgeous little cafés on our doorstep,' Juliette said. 'Talking of which, let's have some *churros*. I've read about those on the internet.'

'What are they?' Kim said suspiciously. 'Cake? We had cake for breakfast.'

'Ah, but these are a national dish; deep-fried crispy cinnamon doughnuts. With ridges. You have them with hot chocolate or coffee.'

Kim frowned. 'They sound fattening. I've been on a diet for absolutely ages. Well, years, if I think about it. I've tried everything and I have gained and lost the same two stone so many times. And sometimes I wonder why. I would have been better off not bothering. All those disgusting drinks and supplements. I realise the sellers got just as fat as I did but in their case it was money. I tried the cabbage soup diet again recently; it worked in the seventies. Now my house smells like something died under the kitchen cabinets.'

'No, not at all fattening as an occasional treat. I read that the Mediterranean diet is one of the healthiest in the world,' Juliette

said reassuringly. 'Churros are a bit like profiteroles with attitude.
Dunked in chocolate sauce. We'll eat yours if you don't want any.'

'Like that's going to happen,' Kim said, checking the buttons
of her shirt hadn't popped open.

We wandered about for a while, admiring the little shops, and
buying a few souvenirs, and then Juliette saw a stall helpfully
called *Churros*, near the marina, which she decided was just
perfect.

We sat on either side of a long bench under the shade of the
trees, and Juliette managed to order for all of us, by pointing at
the menu and smiling brightly at the very pretty young woman
who was serving us.

The churros and coffee came a few minutes later on a huge
tray.

'My God, how many did you order?' I said.

'*Ten cuidado,*' the waitress said, 'be careful, *muy caliente*. Very
hot.' She blew on her fingertips to emphasise the point.

There were big bowls of creamy coffee, little dipping pots of
chocolate sauce and a plate of crispy churros, covered with
cinnamon sugar. They were absolutely delicious.

'Perhaps I'll have a salad for dinner to make up for this,' Kim
said.

'And perhaps you won't,' Juliette said. 'Gosh, these are good.
Why have I never had these before?'

'I tried them once, frozen from the supermarket. They were
minute, about half the size of these and rubbish. When in
Mallorca, do as the Mallorcans do,' I said, chewing happily.

'I think they are *mallorquís*, actually. Good morning, ladies,'
boomed a voice behind us. 'I think we are neighbours! Well, this
looks like a splendid idea. Would you mind terribly if we joined
you?'

And there, standing in the sunshine next to our bench, were

three rather spry grey-haired men and Bruno. The birdwatchers from the next-door villa. My heart did a little jolt at the sight of him. Just as it had all those years ago. Surely I was over that?

I swallowed my mouthful and took a sip of coffee, which was very hot and made me splutter, spraying milk foam down my chest.

'Please do,' Juliette said cheerfully, handing me a paper napkin without comment, 'we've been talking about you.'

The man who had been speaking beamed and held out a hand.

'Johnny Walker, by name and by nature,' he said. 'I do like your ducky hats, ladies. We should have done something like that. Enormous fun. Now this old reprobate is Vince,' he indicated a worried-looking man in a flowery shirt, who nodded and smiled, 'this is Doggie—'

'Douglas,' the other man said hastily. 'Doggie is just a nickname.'

He did have the hopeful rather sad eyes of a spaniel, so I could see why.

'And this is Bruno the Bear, my cousin, our tour guide and boon companion. We'd love to join you. Mind if we sit down?'

I took a breath and flicked a look at Bruno the Bear. I wasn't sure but I think he winked at me.

Juliette gave me a kick under the table.

'Of course not. We're having *churros*. They are really good. Make yourselves at home.'

'If I was at home, I wouldn't be eating those,' Doggie said wistfully. 'Lorna watches my cholesterol like a prison guard. I won't tell her when I get back. If she's even talking to me.'

'That's the spirit,' said Johnny cheerfully, 'and you're here now, the deed is done, so make the most of it. Can't change it. I think we'll have some too.'

He waved at the waitress and placed an order.

'This is my stag holiday, well, one of them,' he said when everything had been sorted out and Bruno had explained in fluent Spanish Doggie's need for decaffeinated coffee. I think he was hoping it would counteract some of the damage he intended to do with the churros. 'A sort of pre-stag holiday. Come September and I'll be hitched to lovely Polly.'

'What a coincidence, this is my hen holiday,' Juliette said with a brilliant smile.

'Not birdwatchers, are you?' Vince said hopefully, hunched over the table.

'You must be joking,' Kim muttered. 'I mean, no, we aren't.'

'That's a shame,' Vince said, polishing his spectacles on his napkin, 'there have been sightings of Marmora's warbler, apparently.'

'How absolutely marvellous,' Juliette said. 'So where is the wedding? Everything organised?'

'We're getting hitched in September, in some barn near Basingstoke. Second time round for both of us. I assume everything is organised. Polly is a very organised gal. I'm just writing the cheques and doing what I'm told.'

'You're going to make Polly very happy indeed,' I said, 'I can tell.'

Johnny beamed. 'I do my best. Happy wife, happy life, isn't that what they say?'

'Oh dear,' Doggie said, folding a paper napkin into a small square and looking rather agonised.

They plunged into a discussion about families at that point and I looked up to see Bruno watching me across the table.

'How are you enjoying it so far?' he said.

I felt my face began to burn.

'Oh, lovely. It's a gorgeous place, isn't it?'

Bruno leaned across and said something very quietly.

'You've got powdered sugar all over your face, by the way.'

I wiped my mouth energetically with my paper napkin and he grinned.

That smile, the sparkle in his eyes was suddenly so familiar to me that I had to look away, focus on the boats, the coffee, the other people strolling past us.

It had been such a long time since I had seen him, surely I shouldn't be feeling like this all over again. Wasn't I too old?

'So Johnny is your cousin,' I said. 'Are you the best man?'

Bruno sipped his coffee. 'No, that's going to be his brother Harry, he lives in New York, which is why he isn't here. He's at some conference. Johnny is going over there for his second stag holiday later in the year. I'm going to be an usher. Are you going to be a bridesmaid for your stepsister?'

'A matron, apparently. We all are. We are too old to be bridesmaids.'

'Nonsense, you haven't aged a day,' he said, grinning.

'You obviously need a reality check,' I said, 'and a visit to the opticians.'

'So what are your plans while you are here?'

Juliette and Johnny were laughing uproariously about something at the far end of the bench. Kim and Vince were talking about football, which was a surprise, as only that morning she had been saying how much she loathed it.

I scraped the foam off the inside of my coffee cup with a spoon.

'Kim has worked out a schedule apparently, well, at least some ideas about what we might do. Juliette isn't very easy to organise. And another friend is going to be joining us soon. She lives on Rhodes. She's been to a family wedding, that's why she's late.'

'So, lots of weddings still taking place then,' he said, dunking his churro into the chocolate dip.

'Seems that way. I thought they had gone out of fashion.'

'What do you think?'

I licked the milk foam off my lips. 'About what?'

'Weddings. I mean, do you like them?'

I couldn't think what to say for a moment.

'I suppose so,' I said at last. 'Weddings are the easy part. I think it's the marriage that's more difficult.'

He raised his eyebrows, which always had been thick and impressive.

'Is that the voice of experience speaking?'

I realised he was trying to find out the same thing I wanted to know.

'No,' I said, feeling my shoulders relax, 'I've never been married.'

He looked up, surprised. 'Really? Never? I would have thought someone as attractive as you... well, never mind.'

So, he still thought I was attractive. Interesting.

'I had offers, obviously. Loads of them. Several very handsome, strong, clever men wanted to marry me—' This was a lie. I'd only ever had one actual proposal in the last few years and both of us had been horribly drunk at the time. '—but it never felt right.' Well, that was true. 'What about you?'

He finished his coffee and put the cup down carefully.

'Oh, yes, once,' he said at last. Quite casually, as though it didn't matter.

Despite myself, I felt a ridiculous pang of something like outrage. Who? And why? And was that why he had never replied to my letters? Had he met some glorious Italian girl on his year out in Naples and forgotten all about me? Did he have several beautiful children somewhere, a large Italian family, who probably had a massive villa in Tuscany?

I could almost imagine the scene; precise rows of vines stretching down the Tuscan hills, bathed in a wonderful sunset, while Bruno sat at the head of the table under a pergola with his doting wife who looked like Monica Bellucci, while uncles, aunts and grandparents laughed and poured wine for each other. There would be a bell tolling somewhere down the valley, everything would be perfect and because Bruno spoke fluent Italian, he would understand the jokes and family stories and they would all idolise him. His two or three children would be running around in adorable smocked dresses and sailor suits... No, don't be daft, they would probably be in their thirties by now. Unless he had recently married some really young woman who wanted a baby and then, cleverly, had twins. Or triplets.

Had I imagined us marrying eventually, having a family together? I had been wrong. Out of sight, out of mind. He had moved on in a different direction. I had done something similar. It was thirty-nine years since we had seen each other. Thirty-nine? How did that happen? No relationship could cope with that degree of separation. And in the intervening years, everything seemed to have dropped. My boobs, my neck, even my expectations.

No, we were adults now, we should just acknowledge each other as old friends, nothing more than that. And we were only going to be in close proximity for a few days. We were both mature enough to deal with that.

But we had taken each other's clothes off. Many times. We had shared secrets and hopes. He knew just about everything about me, the sensitive place in the hollow of my throat, how I liked to be kissed and held.

I knew he was ticklish, that he didn't like pineapple, that he liked to be massaged with bergamot oil when his shoulders were tense.

I felt my insides give a little plunge of doubt. Well, he was probably mature enough. I wasn't sure I was.

'It was years ago. Wendy ran off with someone else two days before our first wedding anniversary,' Bruno said.

Ah. I hadn't seen that coming.

Abruptly the Tuscan valley and the family and the triplets vanished. And Wendy wasn't an Italian name, was it?

'Gosh, how awful. I'm sorry,' I said, my voice rather croaky.

'It's okay, as I said, it was a long time ago,' Bruno said.

'And you must come with us!' Johnny said loudly.

I looked up to see Juliette and Kim nodding.

'What's going on? I'm not going birdwatching,' I said.

'Vince says there's only a little bit of birdwatching in the morning. Then in the afternoon, they've booked to go on a boat trip and they want us to go too,' Kim said, 'Let's do it!'

Vince was sitting bolt upright with a pleased smile on his face.

'It would be enormous fun,' he said, 'and if you want to tag along for the birdwatching, you can come and hide in my hide if you like?'

Kim giggled and playfully threw a sachet of sugar at him across the table.

A boat trip, with Bruno on board. Did I like the idea? Yes, I did. Despite everything, I was opening my mind to the possibility of being more open about it all. Of doing unexpected things. It might be a chance for us to talk about something properly. Ordinary things. Our days at university, the people we had known, what he had been doing when he left for Italy. Why he didn't come back when he said he would.

I felt a sudden small burst of confidence. If I had been able to manage a whole government department, I could certainly do this.

Suddenly, a nun appeared beside our table, dressed in the usual black habit and wimple. She didn't speak but shook a collecting tin enthusiastically in our direction.

After a moment, we all started fumbling in pockets and purses for euros, and at last she gave a stiff smile and walked away.

'Collecting for the convent, I expect,' Johnny said, putting his wallet back in his pocket, twenty euros lighter, 'they live a very austere life. Polly went to a convent school, she said they were quite fierce, but good hearted.'

We spent the rest of the day sightseeing, after first shaking off Vince, who seemed to want to follow us around, talking to Kim about warblers. He was lured away by his companions and the prospect of a few beers in a bar that was showing the Mallorca football team playing Real Madrid. Obviously even Kim's attractions couldn't compete with that.

We hurried away into a dress shop and hid behind a rack of fridge magnets until we were sure he had gone, trailing disconsolately after his fellow stags.

'Well, someone's got an admirer,' I said, as we stepped out into the sunshine again.

'Well, actually I think he's rather nice,' Kim said, peering out from behind a rack of postcards.

'You're certainly breathing very heavily,' Juliette said, 'do tell us when you need gas and air.'

'I always did like tall men,' Kim said, digging her in the ribs. 'I didn't wear heels for years because Stewart was only a bit taller than me and he didn't like it. And now, of course, I can't. I think my feet have spread out, like elephant paws. I've got some beautiful shoes stacked in a cupboard; I can't get any of them on any more. It's probably the weight and the fact that I have lived in comfortable shoes for years.'

'Still, you and Bruno seemed to be having a nice chat,' Juliette said.

'Oh, nothing important,' I said. I pretended to investigate the postcards.

'Did you find out why he disappeared without trace all those years ago? I'll ask him if you like?'

'Don't you dare. The whole thing was a mess. He got married, he got divorced a year later. What he has been doing since then I don't know. And I'm not interested,' I said firmly.

'Liar, liar, pants on fire,' Juliette said.

She was right, actually. I was interested and I did care.

In the same way that Kim didn't seem able to finally stop wanting to know what was happening to Stewart, I had thought about Bruno a lot over the years.

I'd had an album of photographs of us together. Those were the days before smart phones could capture a life with the flick of a finger. Parties, celebrations, dates, birthdays, trips to the sea, the terrible little student house we had shared. I had looked at it many times, before drunkenly consigning it to the bin in a dramatic gesture about twenty years ago. And now he was back, unexpectedly, and here I was, dithering about, wondering how to deal with it in a grown-up way.

There was always the possibility that we had just enjoyed a typical student romance which fizzled out when life took us in different directions, and in the grand scheme of things it didn't matter.

But I couldn't shake off the feeling that our relationship had been important, for both of us, and I had once thought there was much more to us than that.

* * *

We took a stroll along the pedestrianised walkway beside the sea, away from the town this time. Past cafés and shops and enticing little wine bars. Beautiful white hotels and apartment blocks with swimming pools, and always to our right, the brilliant blue sea, sparkling in the sunshine.

Little concrete piers stretched out into the water. On one there were fishermen hunched over their complicated rods, on another a yoga class was sitting cross-legged in a circle, not really moving. Perhaps they were meditating, which must have been very pleasant with the sounds of the sea all around them.

I'd tried it once, years ago, and then given it up when work took over everything. Perhaps I would take that up again as a hobby; it didn't look very difficult and even I could sit down and relax. Perhaps it wasn't quite that simple.

'Doesn't this get flooded when it's high tide?' Juliette wondered.

Kim consulted her guidebook, flicking through the pages with a licked finger.

'There's a whole section here about that sort of thing, listen. The Med is almost landlocked, so it's like a big lake really, and the tidal range is only a few centimetres. Waves are a result of the wind and atmospheric pressure changes. So I'm guessing no. Do you want to know about the salinity? Or the net water influx from the Atlantic?'

'Not at the moment,' Juliette said, 'but thanks for the offer.'

Kim flicked over another page. 'I can tell you about over-fishing and bottom trawling if you like?'

'Sounds a bit uncomfortable,' Juliette said, 'poor old Mediterranean. I wouldn't want anyone trawling my bottom.'

The path narrowed and we walked in single file for a bit, pressing ourselves back against the sea wall when a crocodile of nuns appeared coming towards us. As they reached us, the nun at the front produced a collecting tin from under the folds of her robe and, with a very fierce expression, held it out towards us. Obediently we slipped a few more euros into it.

'They must be on a financial drive for something,' Kim said as we watched them walk away.

'That's twice in one morning,' Juliette said, 'still, it's as well to keep on their right side, isn't it?'

Then we resumed our stroll, avoiding the pine trees, some of which were obstructing the pavement, some were almost dipping into the sea. Occasionally the tree roots were pushing up through the pavement like underground monsters seeking the sunshine.

Juliette fell into step beside me.

'So how are you feeling about getting married again?' I asked.

She gave a little excited hunch of her shoulders. 'Great. I can't wait. It's going to be fine; I know it will. As long as my granddaughters don't throw a strop. Kya and Kiera want to be flower girls, but they can be very unpredictable. And I never say anything, but Melissa really does spoil them in my opinion. She's forever buying them presents for "being good". In my day kids got presents at Christmas and birthdays. Not for behaving in the supermarket or going into nursery without making a fuss. And don't talk to me about Easter eggs. I used to get one. Last year the twins got fifteen each. I suppose she waited for such a long time to be a mum; she doesn't like to say no to them.'

'I wouldn't know,' I said, 'I suppose things are different now. There is so much more of everything, and television encouraging them to want things.'

'Tell me about it,' Juliette said, 'and some of the toys are so ugly. In my day dolls looked like dolls. Now they look like gremlins with too much eye make-up. You'll have to come over and meet them again. I don't think you've seen them for a while. They are your – sort of – step-great-nieces, after all.'

'Gosh, that makes me feel ancient!'

'How do you think I feel, being a grandma? Matthew will make a smashing grandpa. He's endlessly patient when they come and visit, and he makes dens and plays tea parties in the garden with them.'

'How lovely. You've struck lucky with him,' I said.

'He's the lucky one. I keep telling him that. And you? Have you decided what you are going to do now you've retired?'

'No, not really, although I have been thinking about it. I suppose I would like to travel a bit more, learn something new. Otherwise I'm going to be slumped in a chair watching boxsets.'

'You need to meet some new people. I wish you lived closer, then I could introduce you to some. Although off the top of my head I can't think of any. The Brigadier is lovely and a dreadful flirt, but he has a very fierce wife called Bunny who would probably bite you if she felt threatened. But on the other hand, perhaps fate has dealt you a new hand. You know?'

Juliette rolled her eyes at me meaningfully.

'Meaning?'

'Bruno the Bear turning up after all these years. You were pretty hot for each other once, who is to say you couldn't rekindle the old fires?'

I sighed. 'I'm assuming there has been too much water under far too many bridges for both of us. I don't know anything about him any more, or what he does with his time.'

'Then ask him. I'm sure you would be okay asking any of the other three. Small talk; remember that? Just laugh at his jokes;

men like that. Right, I don't care what you say, I am going to ask the twitcher party over one evening when Sophia gets here. She is much better at the food side of things than I am, and we can have a few drinks, and a few laughs. And then you can find out.'

I felt slightly nervous. 'But—'

Juliette held up a commanding hand. 'This is my hen holiday. What the bride wants the bride gets, remember? It's sorted. One evening we will wait for them to come back from their bird-watching and divest themselves of their binoculars and water-proof trousers, and they can come over for an al fresco dinner on the patio. They only need to hop through that little gate. What's the worst that can happen?'

'You do know you should never say that? He might have changed. He might be set in his ways and crabby. We might have nothing in common now. He might not like the idea.'

Juliette tutted. 'If I know one thing about men it is that they like food and women paying them attention.'

'That's two things. And Bruno might not feel the same way about me any more. He might not want the same things I want. Actually, did any man ever know what women want?'

Juliette laughed. 'Well, Gok Wan had a good stab at it, all those makeover shows.'

'Okay, but without all the shapewear, those magic bodysuits under jeans just used to look so terribly hot. And so inconvenient in the loo.'

'You don't need shapewear, Denny. You just need to be your-self. That's the thing Matthew liked about me when we met. He'd spilled ice cream all over me, and I just roared with laughter. The next thing you know we were going to dinner at The Ivy, and I made him laugh some more. He said he hadn't had so much fun in ages. Did you and Bruno make each other laugh all those years ago?'

I stopped to look out over the sea, and the many boats moored there. In front of us was another concrete pier, there was a couple standing there, they looked my age, maybe a bit older. The woman was wearing a dull brown coat and flat boots, the man a blue windcheater zipped up to the neck with a canvas cap on his head. They didn't seem to be talking. Perhaps they had been together for decades and didn't need to talk much, maybe they had children who had grown and gone off into the world.

Suddenly the woman laughed and slapped him on the arm, and he looked down at her with a fond smile. Whatever they were, they were companions.

I had friends, I had Juliette, a few cousins dotted all around the world. I was not alone, and I wasn't lonely. But this wasn't how I had imagined myself, while I had been working so hard, dealing with complex financial spreadsheets and problems. I don't think I had given any thought at all to my future when I was old. Older.

But I was used to looking after myself, I was independent. I didn't need anyone to prop me up, support me through my sixties and seventies and who knew how much further. But now things had changed, I was getting a new perspective on life. It might be nice to have someone to laugh with. To talk to in the evenings about inconsequential things, like what colour to paint the bathroom. Where to go on holiday without having to pay a single supplement. I hadn't thought about that.

'Yes, we did,' I said at last, 'we made each other laugh all the time. Perhaps it was just because we were young and everything seemed hilarious, anything seemed within our grasp, because we had no real worries about the future. And now the future has caught up with me.'

I felt quite cold for a moment.

'There's nothing wrong with renewing an old friendship, no strings, no commitment,' Juliette said, 'a lot of things are still possible. Look at me. It's so easy to always say no, it's much more fun to say yes sometimes.'

Kim realised we had fallen behind and she was waiting for us further along the path, taking pictures with her mobile. Turning around with the sea behind her and grinning into the lens to take a selfie, her yellow duck hat pulled low against the sun.

'Is it lunch time yet?' Kim called as we got nearer. She looked down at her phone again. 'Well, I'm deleting that one. Who knew I could make the Mediterranean too small to fit in the picture?'

'I thought you weren't having anything else after those churros?' Juliette shouted back.

'That was ages ago, and I'm thirsty. We've walked miles.'

'Ice cream then?' I suggested. 'We passed some fantastic-looking ice cream stands on the way. We can sit on one of those benches in the shade and look out at the boats.'

'Excellent idea,' Kim said, beaming, 'and we can decide what we are going to wear for the wedding. I'm just saying, I look terrible in yellow. You can tell by this hat, can't you?'

'Yellow it is then,' Juliette said.

5

That evening we sat out on the patio again with some wine and cheese, enjoying the wonderful colours in the sky above us as the sun set. In the distance I could hear music, and occasionally the faint sound of people laughing. It was very pleasant.

'So tell us how Matthew proposed,' Kim said.

Juliette gave a pleased smile. 'It was very romantic.'

'Did he go down on one knee?' I asked.

'Not a chance, he had a knee replacement last year. If he had, I would have had to fetch his stick and haul him back up and it would probably have spoiled the moment. No, we were at his house, which is an old rectory, all Virginia creeper over the outside and dado rails on the inside. He has a gardener called Eric once a week, which is a relief because the last time I pruned anything I cut the thumb off my gardening glove. I frightened myself silly. Anyway, Matthew had just cooked me dinner. We were sitting in his dining room, which is massive with a chandelier, and we were at either end of this huge table like Lord and Lady Humphrey Biscuit-Barrel. There were candles on the table too, and flowers. And proper linen napkins with silver napkin rings.'

Kim sighed. 'That sounds so lovely. What it must be like to live so elegantly.'

'Oh, he doesn't live like that all the time. When I met him, he seemed to live in the kitchen, and the rest of the house was left to get dusty,' Juliette said.

'Even so, I bet he has a set of fish knives. And the proper glasses for wine, not just tumblers from Ikea. The kids either nicked all mine or broke them. What did he cook for you?'

'Sausage, egg and chips. Don't look like that, Kim, it's my favourite meal. He'd even put the ketchup in a little bowl, and there were three sorts of mustard too. And not in sachets. So thoughtful. But then he's like that. And then we had Viennetta for afters because he knows I like ice cream, and then cheese and biscuits. And perhaps we had a few glasses of wine.'

'And what wine pairs well with sausages?' I giggled.

'Anything and everything. And then Matthew said he couldn't see me properly because we were at opposite ends of the table, and it was a bit dark. Candles are lovely, of course, and very flattering to the more mature complexion, but I did feel as though I needed a torch to find the butter. And I said, well, come down this end, big boy, if you're brave enough. And then he looked sort of thoughtful and asked if I'd like a Cointreau, and I said does your dog dig holes? He has a border terrier called Maurice, who does dig holes, believe me. Anyway, when he brought my Cointreau to me, he said he'd been wondering something. And I said, oooh, what? How I keep my girlish figure when I eat so much? And he said no, he'd been wondering if I would marry him.'

We all sighed with pleasure at that point, and I think Kim dabbed her eyes with the end of her paper napkin.

I stood up and went to give Juliette a hug. 'How lovely.'

I'd met Matthew a few times and he was delightful, even if he wasn't the type for me. Still, Juliette was so happy and relaxed with him that I couldn't help feeling a little twinge of envy.

'And of course I said yes. And he got a little leather box out of his pocket, and he said, how absolutely marvellous, you might like to have this then. And it was a rocking great diamond, like a car headlight.'

'Well, where is it then?' Kim asked, peering across the patio.

'At the jewellers, being re-sized because it was a bit big.'

'That's so sweet,' I said, 'did you hesitate at all?'

'Not for a moment, in fact I burst into tears, I was so happy. And he got a bit emosh as well, and his moustache went a bit bristly. That's always a sign. I said we could have Maurice as the ring bearer, make a little cushion for his back. And Matthew said Maurice would throw a strop and probably eat it. And the rings too if I know that dog.'

'Aw, how adorable,' Kim sighed. 'So will you move in with him now?'

Juliette looked a bit arch. 'I practically moved in six months ago. I think we were seeing if it would be okay. We had to be a bit circumspect because Matthew's local fan club in the Parish Council might have been a bit outraged. But he has a glorious grand piano in the music room, a Bosendorfer—'

'Listen to her, music room! And what's a Bosendorfer? I've never heard of them,' Kim added.

'—and we spread the word that I was just rehearsing. And pianos like to be played. And Bosendorfer are really amazing. Matthew's first wife was a good pianist, but Matthew can't even master "Chopsticks".'

'And how old is he anyway?' Kim asked.

'Sixty-nine, nearly seventy. And before you ask, no, there are no particular problems in the bedroom department, thank you very much.'

'I wasn't going to ask,' I said, with faux outrage.

'Not much, you weren't! Anyway, there's nothing we can't solve with a bit of ingenuity anyway. Neither of us is as flexible as we once were, after all. Or as needy.'

'Outrageous,' I said, 'the Parish Council would excommunicate you both if they knew.'

'They probably would,' Juliette agreed with a satisfied smile. 'Enough about me, any news of Anita?'

'I was told her husband was obsessed with his compost heap?' I said.

Kim laughed. 'No, I am happy to say he is not any longer. After our last Ducks' holiday, the one in Rhodes, she went home and told him in no uncertain terms that they were going to do something new. Together. Eventually they discovered square dancing. Now they can do-si-do with the best of them. She sent me a picture, she even has some special dresses to wear, rather full, flowery skirts. She says they do get in the way a bit but all the women have them.'

'And what about you, Kim? Any more luck with the internet dating?' Juliette asked.

Kim puffed out her cheeks.

'I realise Matthew is a paragon of virtue and an example to all men everywhere, but I only seem to attract two types. Either younger ones who want to investigate my bank balance or my willingness for uncomplicated sex, or older ones who are looking for a nurse. You wouldn't believe the pictures some of them have sent me. No sooner do you say *hello, my name is Kim*, than they send back pictures of their anatomy. It's very off-putting indeed. Especially over breakfast.'

'I've heard about that,' Juliette said, nodding, 'I think it's called sexting. Do you ever reply?'

'Indeed I do not,' Kim huffed, 'anyway, my arms aren't long enough to get a decent picture. You think about it.'

We all pretended to hold out a mobile phone at arm's length, angling up and down and wondering why anyone would do that in the first place.

'Perhaps you should take a picture in a mirror?' Juliette suggested.

Kim shook her head. 'Stewart hung all the mirrors too high, so I can only see my head, and I can't exactly take rude pictures of myself in the Marks and Spencer's changing rooms, someone might come in. Anyway, why are we even discussing it? Sometimes if I think about it, I realise I quite like having the company of a man, you know, someone to do all the heavy lifting, and someone to snuggle up to. But if I'm honest, I'm not—'

There was a long silence and Kim picked at a hangnail.

'Not what?' Juliette asked.

'Not that bothered about the sex part. There, I've said it. I never found many men attractive. Particularly not men who wear cravats or grey shoes and lots of men our age seem to. I think sex for me became part of the marriage thing. Yes, I was furious when Stewart started screwing around, but that wasn't what hurt me the most. It was the rejection. Of me. As a companion.' Kim seemed to gain courage, having made her admission. 'And I'd be quite happy if a man had his own hobbies and I had mine. I wouldn't want him trailing around after me asking what I'm doing and criticising. And I'd never want us to wear matching jumpers, even at Christmas. If I could find a man to just keep me company occasionally, talk to, help me with things I can't manage, that would be enough.'

'That sounds like a taboo,' I said, 'to admit that we are still women, but some of us are not sexual beings.'

'I'm beginning to realise I'm not a sexual being,' Kim said. 'I mean, I like to chat and look after a man and feel appreciated. I'd like the companionship. But the mechanics of it all – well, I can quite happily do without it. Let's be honest, it's a bit uncomfortable sometimes, isn't it?'

'Perhaps you need HRT?' Juliette said. 'It did wonders for me.'

Kim sighed. 'But I like having the bed to myself. I'd like to have the bathroom to myself. Which is why this place is so perfect. I just occasionally like a bit of male company. Especially when the light on the landing needs a bulb replacing. It's awfully high up and I'm hopeless on ladders.'

We sat in silence for a few minutes, thinking about this. I hadn't been in a relationship for a couple of years, yes, there had been the opportunity for uncomplicated sex, but I hadn't wanted that. I suppose I too wanted the companionship, the silly familiarity that came with a loving relationship. At my age it seemed like wishing for the moon.

'Well, I like sex,' Juliette said after a while, 'I always did. But I can see what you mean about the bathroom thing. Why do men empty their razors all over the sink? It's like there has been a fall of soot. And they never seem to see it. Or perhaps it's a primitive man thing, marking their territory. This woman is mine, and I've left my whiskers all over the sink to prove it.'

'Men are from Mars, women are from Venus,' I said.

'At least all the loo seats on Venus are down,' Juliette snorted. 'Matthew is getting the idea; I can't expect him to change too quickly when he's lived on his own for so long.'

'And what about your kids, Kim? You say they are hinting they want to move back in yet again? I thought Juliette said you'd sorted them out a flat of their own?' I asked.

Kim pulled a face. 'I did and for the moment it's okay, but I can see it's all coming to nothing. I just hope they haven't stolen a spare key and are having a party in my absence. I've hidden my wine supplies in my wardrobe. I bet they find it.'

We heard the patio doors from the next-door villa slide open. Juliette raised an eyebrow.

'I bet that's Vince, out on the prowl like a hungry wolf looking for you.'

She gave a little howl and Kim tossed her head and refilled her wine glass.

'He seems quite nice, actually. He's growing on me.'

We all made rather immature oooh-ing noises and seconds later, Vince, because he was so tall, looked over the hedge that divided our gardens.

His round, cheerful face broke into a smile, the evening light glinting off his spectacles.

'Evening, ladies, have you had a good day? We went to the reserve and saw a Balearic warbler, and any number of marbled ducks. Quite astounding. We are off out again early tomorrow too; apparently someone saw a purple swamp hen recently. My day doesn't get much better than that.'

'Would you fellows like to join us for a drink?' Juliette called out.

His bushy eyebrows shot up with delight. 'That would be great. If you're sure we wouldn't be in the way? I'll go and round them up, shall I? Back in a tick.'

He disappeared from view.

'Stop it, you rotten thing,' I said, slapping her arm.

'It'll be a laugh, you wait and see,' Juliette said with a grin.

'Not if they are going to talk about birds all evening,' Kim said.

'You said you didn't mind a man having a hobby of his own, well, he's obviously got one. I'll go and find some snacks, shall I?

Come on, Denny, give me a hand. Kim, you stay there and smoulder at Vince when he comes back.'

'I'm not sure if I know how to do that any more. I'll give it a go,' Kim said, sucking in her cheeks, pouting her lips and angling one arm along the back of the chair.

'Perfect,' I said.

I followed Juliette into the kitchen, feeling unsettled at the prospect of seeing Bruno again. And at the same time, I was rather excited.

She handed me a big bag of pretzels and a ceramic bowl.

'Put those in there. I'm going to cut up some celery sticks to go with this hummus. And stop looking so worried. It will be fine. You can't skulk about trying to avoid Bruno. Just have a few laughs. Look, I'll put some glasses on a tray, shall I? And I'll open this bottle of—' she peered at the label, '—whatever it is. Mallorcan red.'

I did as I was told, Juliette had always been very persuasive, and I could hardly go and hide in my bedroom, although the thought did cross my mind. It was like being a teenager all over again; focused on some random boy. *What if I like him but he doesn't like me?*

By the time I went back out to the patio, Johnny, Vince, and Douglas were sitting around the table, and Johnny was telling a very loud and chortling story about their day. He also seemed to have a lot of birdwatching jokes to share with us.

Kim, who was sitting opposite him, bore the brunt of this.

'How does a bird with a broken wing land?'

She frowned. 'I've no idea, surely it couldn't even fly?'

'With its sparrow-chute! Did you hear the one about the bird-watcher who fed cannabis to sea birds? He wanted to leave no tern unstoned!'

Johnny laughed uproariously at his own humour, and nearly fell off his chair. Then he turned his attention to me.

'Ah, me, I do love a good laugh. So how are you ladies getting on?'

'We are having a great time,' I said, 'really enjoying the island, and the scenery. And the food, which is excellent.'

So where was Bruno, I wondered. Had he decided against joining us? I certainly wasn't going to ask. I didn't have to.

'Is Bruno not coming out too?' Juliette said, flashing her impressive bridgework at the others.

I kicked her under the table, and she kicked me back.

'Bruno has gone to visit someone, and then he was going to check on something. He'll be back in the morning,' Doggie said, helping himself to some celery and crunching happily.

I was disappointed, to be honest. It's one thing to consider avoiding someone, and quite another to realise that person might be avoiding me.

'I understand you were at university together?' Vince said.

'Yes, we were,' I said, taking a swig of my wine.

'Were you tweethearts?' Johnny interrupted. 'Ha-ha! That's a birding joke, do you see what I did there? Tweethearts.'

'It was a long time ago,' I said.

'Not that long, surely,' Vince said gallantly, with a shy look at Kim.

Kim looked down and straightened in her chair. And then she lowered her lashes and tried the pouting thing again.

'So when is the happy day?' Johnny asked. 'The wedding, I mean.'

Juliette smiled. 'June. Matthew is sorting it all out with the vicar. What about you?'

'Oh, we are just nipping to the registry office in September. I think it's the 4th, or it might be the 14th, none of that churchy

stuff anyway,' Johnny said. 'Sign on the dotted line, noose round
the neck, off we go.'

'Lucky Polly,' Juliette murmured.

It was a really pleasant evening once Johnny had calmed
down a bit. He was very rumbustious, and quite loud. Polly must
have been made of strong stuff, or perhaps she was a bit deaf.

I, meanwhile, was still struggling with my mixed feelings
about Bruno not being there. Relieved and yet dissatisfied.

The more I thought about it, the more I did want some sort of
explanation from him. Why had he never replied to my letters
back then? Why had he never tried to contact me? He knew my
home address; he could have done more than send a couple of
postcards. He could have rung my mother or any of our shared
friends. He could have called in. He could have tried.

Then the thought struck me, perhaps I could have made more
of an effort too.

I'd imagined myself secretly flying out to Naples at half term,
Bruno greeting me with a delighted smile and a hug. A week
spent catching up with each other's news. Being together. But I
hadn't. By then I had begun to wonder if I would be welcome,
perhaps he would have been irritated by my turning up. I'd made
all sorts of assumptions.

'You must all come over one evening, and have dinner with
us,' Juliette said during a lull in the conversation.

As one man, their eyes lit up.

'That would be enormous fun,' Johnny said, 'we chaps are a
bit rustic when it comes to the dark culinary arts.'

'We have a friend arriving tomorrow, Sophia. She's an excellent cook. And perhaps one evening when Bruno is around to
even up the numbers. Boy, girl, boy, girl,' Juliette added, 'we could
have a bit of a celebration.'

'Is Bruno visiting his children?' I said airily.

Doggie looked vague. 'I don't think so, I didn't think he had kids. Johnny. You'd know.'

Johnny poured the last of the wine into his glass and peered down the neck in case he was missing something. 'No kids, mate. Just going to see some chap from the local paper, I think.'

Juliette sent me a knowing look.

I realised I had been holding my breath, and I let out a long sigh as the angelic children in their smocked dresses vanished forever.

Johnny stood up. 'Now then, we should go back to our place and fetch a few more supplies to make the party go with a swing.'

The others muttered their agreement and went back to their villa over the hedge. Vince lingered for a few moments.

'Don't go away, will you? And when we come back I'll bring another couple of bottles of this excellent wine, shall I?' Vince said, looking at Kim. 'Before I go, I've just remembered one. Knock knock.'

'Who's there?' Kim asked obediently.

'Who.'

'Who who?'

'Mum, there's an owl at the door. Now don't go away, I'll be quicker than a peregrine falcon after his dinner,' Vince replied and tottered off, chuckling.

Instead of opening the gate, he made a spirited attempt to jump over the lowest part of it and tumbled onto the other side with a cry of alarm. Kim was halfway out of her chair, but Vince sprang up, cartoon-like, his spectacles dangling off one ear.

'I'm fine. Nothing to worry about. Just call me Roadrunner. Who is in fact related to the cuckoo family. *Geococcyx californanus.*'

'Where's an Acme hammer when you need one?' Juliette murmured into her wine glass.

Kim sat down again. 'I don't think I could ever have sex with him.'

Juliette and I gave another little synchronised wolf howl and Kim slapped my arm.

* * *

They came back about ten minutes later; Vince had changed into a red striped shirt and a purple cravat which surely knocked any possible romantic possibilities with Kim firmly on the head. He had also apparently broken one arm off his glasses in the fall and had secured it with a strip of pink sticking plaster.

They were laden down with wine, some giant bags of crisps and a ribbon-tied box of expensive truffles.

'These were supposed to be for Polly. But she won't know. I can always buy her some more,' Johnny said.

At eleven-thirty, with a headache threatening from too much red wine, I made my excuses and went to bed. I didn't think I could hear one more bird pun from them without screaming. Why did Kim find Vince so interesting in light of what she had said? They seemed to be getting on like a house on fire. Perhaps it was the wine?

Fortunately my room overlooked the front of the villa. It was peaceful and I had a lovely view of the Mediterranean, rather than the patio, where I had last seen Doggie trying to do bird impressions.

It was dark, with just a few lights from houses further along the coast and fishing boats out on the water, and when I opened my window the air was fresh and clear and scented with the sea. I rested my elbows on the windowsill and closed my eyes. This was such a lovely place, the Old Ducks were fun and great company, and the last of our party, Sophia, would be arriving the following day. I'd heard a lot about her over the last few weeks, how she had gone to Rhodes to get over an unsatisfactory love affair and fallen in love with the man who owned the rental house.

Did I envy Sophia and Juliette, both of them finding someone special late in life? Possibly I did.

It was the thing I realised I was going to miss the most having retired. Not the work as such, but the people I met. There was always someone having a birthday in our crowded office block, cake being passed around, and then Secret Santa presents at Christmas. Always someone asking how a holiday had gone, whether someone had recovered from the flu or how a new grandchild was getting on.

Away from all that, I could see it would be easy to be lonely, not just alone. Wasn't that the main problem with old age, being lonely? Having no one to talk to? I would have to do something about that.

Perhaps when I got home, I really would join a club or a group. I still had all my faculties, although I did tend to forget things if I hadn't written them down on my wall planner. Before the weeks had been filled with stuff, meetings, and conferences. Now there was a risk that unless I made a proper effort, there would be nothing and no one. It would take a whole new mindset on my part.

6

The following morning we put on our Old Ducks hats and went out especially early because Juliette had read about an idyllic little cove nearby and she wanted to get there before the crowds gathered.

It was a beautiful, warm start to the day, and the bell from the local church was chiming seven. Only a few small delivery vans were trundling around the narrow streets and even the cafés and restaurants were still closed.

'This is what I wanted to see,' Juliette said, 'somewhere peaceful and quiet. Just us and the sand and the sea. Isn't it lovely?'

We agreed it was. Even though it was low season, the main beach did tend to get quite busy in the afternoon, with families and their windbreaks and cool bags.

We reached the end of the sand and saw a faded sign tied on with string to a broken-down wire fence and beyond it a little private cove, just as Juliette had hoped for.

Área restringida, comuníquese con de Iglesia

'What does that mean?' Kim asked. 'Anyone got a phrase book?'

Of course, none of us did.

'Come on, Juliette, you've done Spanish,' I said.

'Well, *área* means area, I'm guessing. *Restringida* is probably something to do with the string fence, although it isn't all string, and it's broken down anyway. *Iglesia*. Does that mean English? Or does Julio Iglesias live here?'

'He's Spanish, so it makes sense, and that would be a bonus,' Kim said.

'And *comuníquese* probably means communicate. So it means if you want to know about the fence with the string, you have to ask Julio Iglesias.'

'That makes no sense at all,' I said, 'but you're the expert.'

'He wouldn't mind if we took a little walk, would he?' Kim said.

'Of course he wouldn't, he seems very friendly in his videos,' Juliette said, stepping over the remains of the fence.

It was absolutely beautiful, sheltered from the sea breezes and completely empty of people.

Juliette took off her sandals, lifted the hem of her maxi dress above the water and went for a paddle.

'It's so warm! It's fabulous. I want to go for a swim. I wish I'd brought my cossie,' she called to us.

We all did the same thing, and yes, unlike England, where the sea temperature in the spring could be an endurance test, here the water was clear and warm, almost like a footbath.

'I could do wild swimming if the water was like this,' I said.

Juliette went in a bit further, tucking the folds of her dress into her knickers.

Luckily Kim and I were wearing shorts, so we didn't have the same issues.

I was up to my knees in the water. My feet were scuffing up little swirls of white sand and there were strands of seaweed drifting in the water.

'How lovely to live somewhere like this,' Kim sighed. 'Everywhere is so clean.'

We splashed on for a few minutes, enjoying the tranquillity of the little cove, and then Juliette called across.

'We could swim, you know.'

'But we don't have any swimming costumes, or towels,' Kim said.

'Julio Iglesias wouldn't mind,' I added.

'Of course he wouldn't,' Juliette said, and pulled her dress off over her head. Underneath she was wearing bright blue underwear which could easily have passed for a bikini. I thought about it and had a look down my T-shirt top. A rather unremarkable beige bra and probably some black knickers. Oh, well.

I pulled off my T-shirt and shorts and laid them in a pile with Juliette's dress on the sand. After a few moments' indecision, Kim did the same thing.

Then Juliette realised her underwear was silk and probably wouldn't do well in the sea water, so she took it off and quickly ran back into the sea, her hands over her boobs.

'Come on, ladies, strip off, we don't get this chance very often!'

'But what if someone sees us?' Kim said. 'I haven't done this for decades.'

I hesitated for a moment, and then I remembered my decision to try new things. To be more adventurous. Ms Lambert in the contracts department would never have done such a thing. The new Denny would.

'Nor have I. There's no one around,' I said, struggling with my bra clip. 'Come on, let's do it.'

Kim took off her bra and waved it above her head, shouting,

'Yay, let those girls out for some air!'

Giggling, we put our clothes in a pile and weighed them down with Juliette's handbag.

Then we ran quickly into the water and hurled ourselves in.

'Now this is perfect,' Juliette called, the water lapping under her chin because she wasn't keen on getting her hair wet, 'don't you think?'

'Absolutely,' I agreed.

The sun was warm on my shoulders as I swam out and then back again. No waves to knock me off my feet, just smooth warm water.

It was marvellous. Not just the sea or the sunny morning. But the feeling of being with friends, of doing something unexpected. Of – what did people say – stepping out of my comfort zone. Well, I'd stepped out of my clothes too, which I realised were a sort of barrier to life in themselves. I didn't think I had it in me to become a nudist in my retirement, but for the first time I could see the appeal.

'Great idea, Jules,' Kim said, puffing a bit as she swam up to us, 'I haven't been skinny dipping since I was a kid.'

'Perhaps we should go to a nudist beach. The Europeans aren't nearly so squeamish about that sort of thing,' Juliette said.

'Hmm, I don't know. I've seen some pictures on the internet. It's not always the Brad Pitts of this world that take their kit off in public,' I said, 'and my figure wouldn't bear close inspection!'

Then Kim found a big strand of seaweed and threw it at me, making me yelp. I threw it back and we had a bit of an undignified and noisy fight.

We spent a very enjoyable twenty minutes swimming and splashing about and at one point Kim and I both fell over, coming up spitting out sand.

And then we turned back to the shore. Even with the salt-water and sand stinging my eyes, I could tell we weren't alone any more.

There were people dressed in black walking along the water's edge, and they had stopped to look at us. Well, we were making quite a racket.

I'd found a child's plastic bucket somewhere and I had it on my head.

Kim had been using a piece of driftwood as a sword, trying to knock it off.

Kim gasped. She stood up and then sank down under the water again, hiding the stick behind her back.

'Joseph, Mary and the wee donkey! It's those nuns again!' she hissed.

We were suddenly silent, watching them watching us. There were about five of them this time.

'What do we do?' Kim said, trying and failing to stand up as the sand shifted beneath her feet.

'Don't make any sudden moves,' Juliette said. She was slightly wild-eyed, and she had a chunk of the seaweed on top of her head.

'They're hardly commando-nuns,' I said.

'Talking of commando...' Juliette said, crossing her arms across her chest.

The minutes passed. We looked at them and they looked at us, seemingly in no particular hurry to leave. Then Juliette groaned.

'I've just remembered *iglesias* means church, it's nothing to do with snake-hipped Spanish crooners. We must be trespassing on church property. That's what that sign meant.'

'Do nuns need a private beach?' Kim asked.

'By the looks of their faces they do. And they are standing right by where we left our clothes,' I said.

I'd forgotten about the bucket on my head and at that moment it fell off, hitting me on the nose.

'How long do we have to stay in here? I'm getting a bit prune-like,' Kim said.

'I bet they can stay there longer than we can,' Juliette replied, 'they have a lot of patience, nuns.'

The stand-off continued for a few more minutes and then one of the nuns beckoned us towards her.

The three of us looked at each other, not sure what to do.

'We could escape along the beach,' Kim said.

'Yes, if you don't mind walking back to the villa with nothing on,' I said. 'Could we rush them and grab our clothes?'

'You can't rush nuns!' Juliette tutted. 'Anyway, they look rather fierce to me. One of them has got a foot on my bra. I'd have to tip her over with a judo throw.'

We all agreed this was not acceptable, so in the end we slunk out of the water towards them, trying to hide the fact that we weren't dressed for the occasion.

They were standing in a row by then, their hands folded under their robes in the accepted manner, until we reached them and one of them suddenly thrust a familiar collecting tin in our faces.

'Oh, not again,' Kim said, 'what are they saving up for, a private jet?'

Juliette hurried to pull her sundress over her head and then found some euros, which she stuffed into the tin.

We hurriedly dressed, which isn't easy without a towel to dry off on, pulled on our distinctive yellow duck hats and sidled away.

Looking back, we could see the nuns were still watching us.

'Well, Denny. You are definitely, officially confirmed as an Old Duck,' Juliette said.

I took a deep breath. 'Does this sort of thing always happen?'

'We've just been mugged by nuns,' Kim muttered, 'again! That hasn't happened before.'

Juliette fidgeted a bit with her damp dress, shaking sand out of the folds.

'Could have been worse, up the other end of the beach is a military base,' she said.

* * *

Just before two o'clock that afternoon, Sophia arrived. We had returned to the safety of the villa and changed into some dry clothes. We were sitting outside under the shade of a parasol, still giggling about the morning's escapade, and Juliette and Kim were in high spirits at the thought of seeing her again.

'You wouldn't believe how much she has changed in the time we have known her,' Juliette said. 'When we met her, she was very buttoned up, the first thing she did was complain about the noise we were making, which was ridiculous because we were just singing. The next thing you know, she was joining in, larking around. We like to think we gave her a new lease of life. And then she met Theo, who owned the houses we were staying in, he came over to complain about the noise too, so perhaps... anyway, ker-pow, the sparks flew. But really, who could blame her? He really is gorgeous.'

'So did she marry him?' I asked.

'No, I mean I wouldn't be surprised if she did, but she's a bit too independent for that. She bought a house there, moved in and rebuilt her life.'

'Good for her, it sounds wonderful.'

'Yes, that holiday was a big moment for all of us, I think,' Juliette said thoughtfully, 'it made us all see ourselves rather differently. And made us all think about what we were going to do next.

Anita realised she needed to work at things with Rick. I found out I was missing Matthew. Sophia stopped regretting her past relationship and moved on. Kim made changes too.'

'That's exactly how I've been feeling,' I said.

'I thought I had life sussed out,' Kim added, reaching for another grape from the luscious bunch in the bowl, 'but now I wonder. The thing I said yesterday about not really wanting sex again, I think it's true. And perhaps it just takes more than one try to prise the kids out of their bedrooms for good. I just have this awful feeling that when I get back they will be sitting on the doorstep with all their stuff, like a pair of waifs, asking for something to eat.'

'Perhaps you need to make it a bit less comfortable for them,' I said, 'occasionally say no?'

Kim shook her head. 'Yes, I know you're right. I need to show some tough love. But then I see an advert on the television for some poor kids, living on the streets, and being scared, and I just can't do it.'

'But they're not kids, they are in their thirties, aren't they?' I said.

'Tell them to move in with Stewart and his latest wife,' Juliette said.

Kim laughed and then started coughing as she almost inhaled a grape. 'I'd like to see them try.'

There was a sudden loud rap on the front door and Juliette leapt up, almost knocking her chair over.

'That's got to be Sophia!'

She hurried back into the house, and I heard her give a shout of excitement and a lot of babbling, welcoming sounds. Kim hurried in to join her and then they brought Sophia outside.

She was a tall, slim, attractive woman with silver hair who looked younger than her years. She must have been over sixty to be classed as an Old Duck, after all. She certainly didn't look it. Her smile was wide and happy. She came forward and took both my hands in hers.

'You must be Denny,' she said. 'I'm so pleased to meet you at last.'

'She's the newest Old Duck,' Juliette said, smiling.

'Welcome to the club!' Sophia said. 'Did Juliette tap you on the shoulder with a breadstick? That's what she did to me!'

'No, she didn't! I feel quite cheated! Nice to meet you at last, I've heard a lot about you.'

Sophia laughed, her eyes sparkling. 'All good, I hope!'

'Absolutely. Would you like some coffee? Or a drink?'

'I'd love some tea if you have it. I might be an ex-pat but I'm still a Brit at heart. I flew in late this morning and one of Theo's cousins met me at the airport and drove me here. She wouldn't stop either, said she had some business to do in Soller. He has cousins and relatives everywhere, it's very useful sometimes. Now tell me what you have all been up to.'

The others ushered Sophia to a chair on the patio and she sat back on one of the loungers with a happy sigh.

'This is your official Old-Ducks-on-tour hat,' Juliette said, handing one over.

Sophia put it on at a jaunty angle.

'Excellent! I shall be proud to wear it, Juliette. You'll certainly be able to pick us out in a crowd. Now how are the wedding preparations going? Kim, how are those children of yours? How's Anita? I'm sorry she's not here. Gosh, there is so much to catch up with!'

We sat out there for ages, getting up to speed with each other's news. It felt lovely to be included and part of the group. And it was official. I was an Old Duck; Juliette had said so, even if I hadn't been knighted with a breadstick. It was very different from the previous few weeks when I think I had occasionally struggled with my own company.

'And you will never guess! There are some chaps on a stag holiday next door,' Juliette said, 'and one of them, the handsome one, turned out to be Denny's boyfriend from university. Can you believe it? He is single and so is Denny. We are all hoping they will rekindle the flame under the influence of the Mallorcan sun and the Old Ducks, of course.'

'Oh, Juliette! Stop it!' Sophia said, laughing. 'You can't expect a result every time.'

Juliette looked offended. 'Indeed I do! We have a 100 per cent success record so far at matchmaking.'

'Why? How many times have you done it?' I asked.

'Once. But that doesn't mean anything,' she said. 'Now let me show Sophia where she is staying, it's the one with the blue wet room, I nabbed the only bath. I'm used to being up to my neck in hot water, as you all know!'

'That never-to-be-forgotten night at The Hot Potato. That policeman's face,' Kim added, '*go and feed your cats, Trelly yaya*! It was hilarious.'

'Not at the time it wasn't,' Juliette said ruefully, 'it was Theo's sister who got me out of trouble. How is she?'

'Hera? Glamorous as ever, I see her every few weeks at the family gatherings.' Sophia turned to me. 'As I said, Theo has a huge family. Uncles and aunts, nephews, nieces, there is always another one appearing from somewhere for me to get to know. It's completely unlike what I was used to. I've learned how to make so many Rhodian dishes. I must try a couple out on you while you are here. Pitaroudia – fried chickpea balls with mint, entrada, proper dolmades. Only the other day I had to make trays of melekouni for the wedding, which are soft honey and orange treats flavoured with cinnamon and nutmeg. So delicious. Do you remember Hera's son, Alexis? He was marrying such a lovely girl. Her father runs a restaurant down by the harbour. She's a legal secretary. I'll show you some pictures later.'

'You're hired!' Kim said. 'Can you start this evening?'

'Come on, let's get you and your bags upstairs,' Juliette said, 'and once you are settled in we want to hear all about their wedding.'

'And I want to hear all about what you have been getting up to since you got here,' Sophia said, putting her tea mug down.

We looked at each other and burst out laughing.

'We had a bit of an adventure this morning. We went skinny dipping and met some nuns,' I said.

Sophia shook her head and chuckled. 'Yes, that sounds like the Old Ducks. Never a dull moment. Right, I'll be back in a tick, and you can tell me all about it.'

'I'll just put these things in the dishwasher,' Kim said.

I watched them go indoors, chatting all the way, and again, thought just for a moment what I would be doing if I was still back home. Somehow I couldn't picture it. But I wasn't back home, I was here, with the opportunity for laughter and lively company. Never a dull moment. Well, that was true, even if it had been rather embarrassing at the time. How marvellous! I felt quite invigorated by it all.

I didn't need to be Ms Denise Lambert any more, I could be Denny again, someone who had bunked off school to see David Soul make an appearance at the local record shop, danced on tables in the student union, hitchhiked to London to see the Silver Jubilee celebrations, queued to see *Monty Python's Life of Brian* at the cinema, much to my mother's disgust.

I had spent a week in Paris during the long student summer holidays, seeing all the tourist hotspots, the man feeding sparrows on the steps of Sacré Coeur, the empty glories of Versailles.

A Sunday morning lying in bed while the sunshine and the sounds of the bells drifted in through the open window.

We had been to Venice too, staying at some cheap little *pensione*, spending our days getting hopelessly lost. We had been to Edinburgh for the Festival, and Holyrood House, where we had gazed at the blood stain on the floor where David Rizzio had been murdered. We had stayed at a strange bed and breakfast where there were three double beds in our room, a champagne cork blocking the hole where the door lock should have been, and ghostly footsteps had echoed overhead.

And Bruno had been there every time, smiling, his head propped up on one hand, telling me that he loved me, and I had believed him.

I swallowed down a new pain of regret because it suddenly seemed to me that since then I had been frozen for so many years, stuck in a routine where nothing ever really went wrong, but then nothing gave me those unexpected flashes of joy that make life worth living either.

I wondered what it was like for Sophia to adjust to having – what had she said? *Cousins and relatives everywhere. A huge family.* And like me she didn't have children of her own or many relations. So what was it like to suddenly be a part of something much bigger?

For a moment, I could almost imagine her, renovating her house in a practical boiler suit, her face splashed with paint. Or busy in a cute whitewashed kitchen, making meals, and cakes for the latest family gathering. People popping in, family gossip to catch up on. Perhaps the newest baby in the family to admire.

I rested my head back on the cushions and wondered how hard it would be to change my life, like she had, to do something different now that I was retired. It wasn't too late.

The prospect was suddenly rather exciting. The world, my

future, was out there, waiting.

* * *

'Well, are we going birdwatching with Johnny and his friends tomorrow?' Kim asked when they returned.

'Birdwatching, no, thank you, boat trip, yes, please,' Juliette said firmly. 'He says we can swim too if we want to. With swimming costumes this time, I think. Perhaps we could arrange to meet up with them down at the harbour tomorrow afternoon. I don't want to stand in the way of your little flirtation with Vince, but I have my limits. You'll just have to corner him on your own somewhere. Ask him if he heard the bitterns booming yesterday or was that just indigestion?'

'I don't know what you mean,' Kim said, her cheeks suddenly pink.

'Is this a modest blush on your cheeks, or just the menopause?' Sophia grinned.

'I think I'll open a bottle,' Juliette said happily. 'I wonder if there will be drinks on the boat?'

'One of us could nip through the hedge and tell them all to come over for dinner this evening and we can ask them. At about six-thirty. I'm not terribly good at late nights any more,' Kim said. 'I vote Denny goes.'

'Yes, I thought you might,' I said.

Juliette made shooing motions with her hand. 'Off you go then, no time like the present. It won't take you a minute. If Sophia doesn't feel like cooking, we can just order something from one of the restaurants. They all seem to do take-out.'

'Really?' I said.

'Absolutely. The bride insists,' Juliette said with a grin.

'You're playing that card a bit too much, I think!'

'Probably. Go on, hurry up.'

I went out onto the patio and stood next to their hedge, listening for some signs of life from within. Apart from the muffled chattering from my friends in the next-door villa, it was really quiet. I think I could even hear my own heart thudding away. I took a deep breath and told myself to calm down.

Their patio doors were closed but I could hear a television inside and some groans of disappointment. More football by the sounds of it. Perhaps I should go round to the front door?

Suddenly the door slid open and Bruno – dressed only in swimming trunks patterned with parrots and a towel slung around his neck – came out into the sunshine.

I gulped a bit with the shock of seeing him and then stared. Annoyingly I could feel myself blushing.

Look away. Look away.

He might have been too lazy as a student to work on his muscles but evidently all that had changed. He'd found the time somewhere. Not exactly Mr Universe and bulging biceps, but I've never found that a very attractive look anyway.

'Oh, hello,' he said, coming to stand opposite me, 'I was wondering what you lot have been up to. Have you had a good day? Done anything exciting?'

I had a brief flashback to the beach and the skinny dipping and the nuns, and then forced myself back to the job in hand.

'Great, thanks. I was—' I cleared my throat because I was afraid I was going to laugh. I looked for something else to focus on. The sky. That tree that looked like a stegosaurus. 'I was just coming to see you. I mean not just you, all of you.'

Bruno jerked his head back towards the villa.

'They had an early start and some birdwatching out on the marshes, and now they are watching football and drinking beer. I thought I'd come out for a swim. What are your lot doing?'

'Drinking wine. Sophia has arrived. I've been sent over to ask you two things.'

'Two things, that's interesting.'

'One, would you – I mean would you *all*, not just you – like to come over to ours this evening for dinner on the patio? And the birdwatching trip that Vince suggested for tomorrow, we don't much fancy that and we haven't got the right footwear or clothes to go tramping about in the marshes, but we do like the idea of the boat trip afterwards. So they have asked me to ask you—' I took a deep breath at that point as I was running out of air, '—if you would mind if we just came along for that? If it's possible. I mean, we'll pay for ourselves, of course.'

How had I forgotten how handsome he was, the humour in those eyes, that dimple in his cheek that flashed when he smiled?

I blundered on. 'I mean, we wouldn't expect you to pay for us, and of course it might be fully booked, I'm sure these things are very popular.'

Bruno reached across at that point and just for a moment gently put the tips of his fingers over my mouth.

I felt a bit giddy for a moment. How long had it been since he had touched me like that?

'Breathe, Denny. Yes to both. Of course we would love to have dinner with you. We were supposed to be having a night in, and Doggie was going to cook. I'm absolutely sure he hasn't a clue and the fridge is filled with beer and wine anyway. And of course you can join us for the boat trip. It's a private tour, but it's run by a friend of mine; it's only a few people, but Luis is very hospitable. The more the merrier. Now what time do you want us to come over? I'll go and tell the others.'

I took a deep breath and smiled back at him.

'Gosh, it's been a long time, hasn't it?' I said, the air collapsing out of my lungs like a balloon being let down.

He nodded. 'A very long time.'

We stood and looked at each other.

So many memories were flickering through my mind, places we had been, the way we had laughed, sworn never to part. Things I thought I had forgotten. I wondered if he remembered too. Surely he did? And how awful if he didn't.

I decided to broach the subject. 'So what happened, why did you...'

'Come on, Bruno, me old mucker, your beer's getting warm. I thought you were going for a quick swim?'

It was Johnny, shouting from inside their villa, and the moment when I had been about to ask Bruno why he never replied to my letters, where he went, passed.

'Come over about six-thirty?' I said, taking a step back.

'Ideal,' he said, and he pulled the towel from around his neck, 'well, we'll see you then. I'd better have my swim.'

'Yes,' I took another step back, still rather mesmerised by the sight of him, 'that would be great.'

I swivelled my gaze back to the stegosaurus-shaped tree. It was going to be okay. Mission accomplished and no embarrassing moments.

'We can bring some beer and some wine. Heaven knows we have enough,' Bruno said.

'Great,' I said and took another step back and, of course, fell into our pool.

I surfaced, spluttering and coughing, my hair in my eyes, my pale sundress ballooning out around me like a jellyfish.

I struck out for the side and hung on to the rail, gasping for breath. I felt a complete twit, especially when I heard Bruno laughing, and looked up to see he had come through the gate and was standing on the edge of our pool, holding out a hand to help me.

'Now that's the Denny I remember,' he chuckled, 'I never knew anyone as accident prone as you were.'

I ignored his hand and walked as best I could to the shallow end and dragged myself up the metal steps.

'I'm fine,' I said with as much dignity as I could muster, 'no harm done.'

I wiped the water out of my eyes and realised my fingers were stained with obviously *not* waterproof mascara. Rats. Why had I not thought about that?

'I must look a sight,' I added, wringing water out of my dress.

'It's not your best look,' Bruno agreed, 'but I've seen worse. The Branston Pickle-eating competition for one.'

Oh, God! I'd forgotten about that. Part of the student games during our freshers' week at university, all those years ago. A race to see who could finish off a bowl of pickle with a teaspoon. Me against a burly-looking chap with glasses who years later was to become a professor of astrophysics.

I'd had the bright idea of not using the spoon but instead trying to tip the lot into my mouth, not knowing the organisers had slackened it off with some water. It had gone everywhere. Over my face, hair, down my cleavage.

Bruno had thrown me a towel from the bar and helped wipe the worst of it off. Both of us laughing so much we could hardly stand. He had called me Pickle. I wondered if he remembered that. And after that day we had been inseparable.

'I'm going to get changed,' I said, pulling my wet dress away from my legs where it was clinging very unpleasantly. 'I might be a while.'

I giggled. I couldn't help it and then I started laughing. And, still chuckling, padded back into the villa.

'See you later... Pickle,' Bruno called.

7

Just after five o'clock, Sophia went out with Juliette to the little supermarket at the end of our lane to find some supplies for our evening meal while Kim and I set the table out on the patio and cleared up some of the debris which had started to spread over the villa. There was a box full of empty wine bottles, the bin was full and there were a surprising number of sweet wrappers under the cushions of the armchair where Kim usually sat.

They returned laden down with sturdy brown paper bags about an hour later and Sophia started her food preparation. We hung around watching.

'If someone wants to slice these potatoes into fries, not too big, and then soak them in water. Then they will be oven baked, and seasoned with oregano and dill, you'll love them. And I'm going to make some baked orzo, with chicken. It's one of Theo's favourites, but we don't have pasta often, and it doesn't take long. And then of course a big bowl of proper Greek salad – there's a lovely ceramic dish over there that would be perfect. And I have bought some beautiful *horiatiko psomi*, which is what the Greeks call village bread. So simple and delicious.'

We watched, admiring, as Sophia moved around the kitchen, and in no time there was a delicious fragrance of herbs and garlic and tomatoes. We sniffed the air appreciatively.

'You should be the size of a house, Sophia,' Kim said enviously.

'Ah, but it's all really healthy stuff. Greeks love fruit and vegetables and olive oil. And I've been very busy working on my renovations so I'm pretty active.'

'You seem so happy,' I said, as I sliced the loaf up into chunks and arranged it in a basket.

'I am,' Sophia said, 'I really am. It's very unexpected. Life has opened up for me again. I have time with Theo, and space for my own life, but he is there when I need him, and we are good friends.'

'See? That's what I was talking about,' Kim said, 'that sort of relationship. Are there any others like him?'

Sophia laughed. 'Maybe. I don't know. Perhaps I was just lucky.'

She assembled the orzo dish in no time, on top of the stove in a skillet, and soon it was bubbling away, a rich, steaming mixture of tomatoes, chicken, and tiny orzo pasta. Then she showed me how to make a real Greek salad, which was huge and scattered with paprika croutons.

By six-thirty everything was ready, and we took all the dishes and plates out to arrange them on the patio table. Kim switched on all the fairy lights which were strung along the pergola above it, and then the whole thing suddenly looked festive and inviting.

A few minutes later, the party from the next-door villa appeared with some spare chairs, holding more bottles of wine and beer than we could ever have hoped to get through.

Vince made a beeline for Kim and was very gallant, pulling out a chair for her.

'Anything we can do to help?' Johnny asked.

'No, not really,' Sophia said.

'Oh, good show. You have to ask, though, don't you?' Johnny beamed.

Doggie looked at the food rather suspiciously at first. 'I have to watch my cholesterol, you know. I'm on tablets. Oh dear. I'm going to get into such trouble.'

'No, you won't and trust me, none of this will harm you, or your cholesterol levels,' Sophia said reassuringly, 'the Greeks have high life expectancy thanks to their diet.'

Doggie shook his head. 'But Lorna...'

Bruno hovered uncertainly, waiting for the others to choose their seats, and then we found that we were sitting at the end of the table next to each other anyway.

'Thought you two could do with catching up,' Johnny said, and gave a booming laugh, 'we will try not to earwig too much.'

'Thanks for that,' Bruno said.

He sat down beside me, his knee touching mine for a moment.

I was sure I shouldn't find that exciting and slightly erotic at my age, but I did.

'Are you all having a good time?' he said.

'Yes, we certainly are. This is such a lovely place. I hear it's freezing cold and raining back home. We wouldn't be able to sit outside like this.'

He passed me the basket of bread and I took some. Further down the table, bowls and platters of food were being passed around with great eagerness. I thought Sophia might have over catered, but the way things were going, she hadn't.

All the food was delicious, fragrant with herbs and wonderful colours. Wine bottles were opened and passed around the table. There was chatter and laughter and apprecia-

tive ooohs and aaahs as we tasted the dishes Sophia had
provided.

'So tell me what you have been doing since we last met,' I said
at last.

Bruno tilted his head to one side, thinking.

'After I graduated, I taught for a while, in Spain and France. I
travelled a lot, Egypt, which was mind-blowing, the Canadian
mountains, absolutely beautiful, and Thailand – such an exciting
place. And did a road trip across America. That was an adventure,
it's a tremendous country. And then I went back to Italy, I made
some good friends there.'

Good friends, what did that mean? A girlfriend?

I pulled myself up with a start. I had no business being
jealous or possessive of him, certainly not his past, when we had
gone our separate ways so long ago.

'And then after my mother died, I moved to France, where I
got married.'

'Wendy.'

'That's right. She worked as an estate agent dealing with ex-
pats who wanted to move there. It didn't work out, too many
distractions, and the whole thing was a mistake. Well, you know
that already, we didn't make it to our first wedding anniversary.'

'What an absolute... what happened?'

'I was busy with teaching, and she went off on holiday with
her sister. She met up on the flight with a chap from Florida. He
had a boat, apparently, in the Caribbean. And one thing led to
another, and he asked if she would like to join him. Well, of
course she did, and a month later she went for good. And that
was the end of it.'

'So you didn't have any children?'

Bruno gave me a look. 'We hardly had time, if you think
about it.'

'No, I suppose not. Although—'

I stopped myself just in time, I wasn't going to enter into an embarrassing discussion about gestation periods.

'And you,' he said, 'what happened to you?'

I speared a chunk of chicken and chewed it thoughtfully.

My goodness, what a question. What did happen to me? I had filled the months and years with activity, but now, a lot of it seemed very uninteresting and unremarkable. In fact, I couldn't remember what the heck I had done.

I'd been good at my job. I'd been efficient and reliable. I'd bought a house, paid my bills, had the occasional relationship and holiday. I'd kept myself healthy, read critically acclaimed books and seen important films. What had I achieved with my life so far? Had I made any sort of difference to anybody?

'I went to work for a finance company in Guildford, and after that I moved to London. Working for the government most of the time. And then I was relocated to Birmingham.'

God, how dull it all sounded now. As though I had been bobbing about on the surface of life, treading water instead of striking out for the far bank. Exploring, challenging myself. I was almost embarrassed to tell him.

'You're not a spy, are you?' he laughed.

'I could tell you, but then I'd have to kill you with that pepper mill. No, nothing so exciting. Just spreadsheets and breakdowns of departmental finance planning. It sounds boring, doesn't it? But I enjoyed it at the time.'

'And no – what are they called these days – significant others?'

'There were some insignificant others, but no, not now.'

'That's a shame.'

My hackles rose a little. 'Why? Do you think I should have married and had a family and been a good wife to some minor government official?'

He held up his hands. 'Not at all, a cabinet minister at least.'

His eyes were twinkling at me, he was teasing me.

I felt a wave of nostalgia. For the days when I had been younger, more optimistic, when life had held so many possibilities, and everything seemed funny. So many roads not taken. Was there still time to start again? To do what I had wanted to do, take myself in a different direction?

What had been missing from my life anyway? Excitement. Challenge. Adventure. Joy. All the really important things. And suddenly I began to wonder if perhaps those things were still out there, waiting for me to grasp the opportunities.

At the other end of the table there was a burst of laughter. Juliette was holding court, in the way that she did. Making people laugh with her vivacity, her easy charm. Johnny was chuckling over something she had said. Kim was covering her mouth and spluttering with laughter.

'She's quite a character,' Bruno said, 'do you know the chap she is marrying?'

'Matthew? Yes, I have met him a few times. He's really nice. Very quiet, formal. Nothing like Juliette, but they seem devoted to each other.'

'They are lucky then,' he said, 'to have met the right person at the right time.'

'Very lucky,' I said, helping myself to more Greek salad.

'Not like us then.'

I stopped, not knowing what to say. The salad servers hovered over my plate.

Eventually I deposited the salad and poked about with my fork for some of the feta cheese and the paprika croutons. At last, one of us had mentioned the subject of our past.

'No,' I said carefully, 'not like us at all.'

'So one of has to ask,' he said quietly. 'What happened?'

He reached for the wine bottle and topped up our glasses. It had a bold red and orange label, the wine deep red, almost black in the evening light. I looked at his hand, tanned, strong. A hand that had held mine, touched me.

I lifted the glass to my lips and tasted it. A ripe, smooth taste full of promise.

I took a breath, trying to think of what to say.

'You think so too, don't you, Bruno,' Johnny shouted from the other end of the table.

We turned towards him; the moment of intimacy between us broken. Damn.

'What do I think?' Bruno called back.

'That rugby is a far more interesting game than football. All that falling over when anyone gets near them, pretending they are mortally wounded. Almost comical if they weren't paid so much.'

'Overpaid,' Kim said.

'And all that horrible spitting,' Juliette added.

'I can't argue with you,' Bruno agreed.

'I could never imagine eleven women wanting to wear the same outfit unless they were being forced to,' Juliette said, 'but then everyone knows I was never one for team sports.'

Kim laughed. 'I'm saying nothing!'

I put my glass down and stood up.

'Just need the loo,' I said, 'back in a minute.'

I went into the villa, my mind racing. Were we going to go there at last, dive into our past? To explore the time, the years we had missed. Did it really matter to him as it mattered to me?

I went up to my room and splashed some water onto my face. What could I say? You went off to Italy and I didn't hear from you again. It was all so long ago, Bruno. I got over it.

Had I got over it? Had I really erased those memories as easily as I had thrown away the photographs? I don't think I had. As I looked at my reflection in the bathroom mirror, it didn't feel like it.

I took a few deep breaths and went back downstairs. Outside I could hear the chatter, the laughter. I was a part of it, of course I was, and yet at that moment I felt strangely alone.

Bruno was standing in the doorway, silhouetted against the glow from the lights around the pergola. Waiting for me.

'So, are we going to talk?' he repeated.

He took hold of my wrist as I tried to pass him.

'What happened?' he repeated gently.

I looked up into his face. He seemed taller, or perhaps I had shrunk. Women did that, didn't they? As they aged. And apparently noses and ears kept growing. I would end up looking like a Norwegian troll by the time I was ninety.

The old Bruno was still there, older, greyer, his features more defined than they had been when he was twenty-one, but still the same man.

'I don't know,' I said, 'you tell me. I wrote, you never answered.'

'I wrote, you never answered,' he said.

'No, you didn't. You went to Italy, I never heard from you again apart from a couple of postcards.'

His hand on my wrist tightened a little.

'I was studying and travelling around. I went to Rome, to Florence, Milan. I visited other universities. You knew I would be coming back. I just never thought that when I did you would have gone. That you meant what you said.'

I pulled away from him.

'You thought you could just disappear for a year, and I would wait for you?'

He sighed. 'I suppose I did. If I thought at all. It was so long ago, Denny, we were so young, and I was an idiot. We were different people then.'

'And we are different people now.'

'I suppose so. But—'

I stepped past him towards the laughing group around the table.

'Look, this shouldn't be about us. I don't want there to be an atmosphere. This is Juliette's holiday, time for her to enjoy herself, to have some fun before she gets married.'

He let go of my wrist and stuck his hands in his pockets.

'And there's your problem, isn't it? You think that getting married, committing yourself, means that the fun ends. So you blamed me. I expect you still do.'

'You don't know anything about me any more,' I hissed, 'you don't know what I think or feel.'

'I'm right, though, aren't I? Your mother, your father, all those stepparents, your stepsister. The way things turned out for all of them. I remember you at university. Always with that little part of yourself held back in reserve. Never quite daring to completely relax into it. Into us. Never believing in yourself.'

'You're a psychiatrist now, are you?' I said.

I walked away from him, down the step onto the patio. In my absence, everyone had moved seats, shifted around so they could talk to different people. Kim, Sophia, and Juliette were together, Johnny, Vince and Doggie in a huddle at the other end of the table, still talking about football. It sounded quite heated.

I'll never understand that – how people can get so angry, so involved in a silly game. It's the publicity, I suppose, the money, the endless tabloid stories.

I retrieved my wine glass and sat down in an empty place, away from where Bruno had been sitting. I didn't want to give him the chance to continue our conversation, but part of what he had said stung. Had I really been so unwilling to fully commit myself to anything other than my career? People could let you down and disappoint you. Spreadsheets and rows of figures couldn't.

I knew he was right, and it was an uncomfortable feeling. I'd never accepted my part in what went wrong between us. It had been easier to blame him. I'd assumed too much.

He had taught me how to love him, but not how to stop. And alarmingly, I had the sudden awareness that the feelings I had buried for so long were still there.

My wine glass was full, and I knocked back half of it in one go. Dutch courage.

I wondered if Bruno could speak Dutch.

8

Bruno returned a few seconds later. I tried not to look at him, but I could sense him looking at me. I threw out a generic question to the table about birdwatching and Vince, of course, took up the challenge. He could have gone on *Mastermind*. He talked earnestly about the Albufera National Park, the expansion of the wetlands, the possible reintroduction of species. Including something called a red-knobbed coot.

This made Kim almost choke with laughter, and Vince slapped her on the back, rather confused as to what he had said that was quite so amusing. Then he continued talking. The problem with alien plants, feral cats, and the importance to the local economy of reed-based handicrafts.

I was trying to join in, but at this point I imagined a feral cat, sitting up on its haunches, weaving a basket, and zoned out.

Kim went off to the loo and Sophia came to sit next to me.

'Lovely villa, isn't it?' she said. 'I've been trying to have a decent shower installed in my house on Rhodes. It seems to be taking forever, even though Theo is helping me. It's a real treat to have a bathroom like the one here.'

'It's gorgeous, isn't it? I'm so glad I agreed to come.'

Sophia patted my hand. 'Me too. Juliette told me you were feeling a bit lost now you've retired.'

'Not lost exactly, just not sure what to do next.'

'I was like that when I went to Rhodes and met the Old Ducks. They showed me one doesn't have to be twenty-five to enjoy life. I took a leap of faith, opened my mind to the possibilities.'

'But you're so positive, so together.'

Sophia laughed. 'Trust me, I wasn't. I was in an unsatisfactory relationship which lost me a lot of my self-respect and some friends too. And then I realised I deserved better. So when the opportunity came, I gave it a go. After all, what was the worst that could happen?'

I frowned. 'People keep saying that, and in the past it always made me wonder about the worst that *could* happen.'

'For me, life began at sixty, up until that point it was all research. Unless one is actually dead, one's never too old to find another goal,' she laughed and gave a discreet nod at Johnny and Doggie who were still arguing about sport, 'unless you're a footballer with bad knees.'

I laughed and Juliette, sitting opposite me, swivelled her head.

'What are you two talking about?'

'Getting older, of course, isn't that what people our age always end up talking about?' Sophia said.

Juliette snorted. 'The younger generation have no idea what's coming their way. My daughter said once I was at a "ripe old age" and I said, that implies you young 'uns are hard and bitter. And then I said I'm proud of who I am today, it took a lot to get here.'

That made me think; was I proud of who I was? I had done everything I could for my career, but perhaps not done much just for my future. I was beginning to see the opportunities I had missed.

Kim returned and came to sit in Bruno's empty seat.

'God almighty. Do men *ever* talk about anything interesting?' she said. 'It's always the same, either sport, power tools or their various medical issues. I went out to dinner with a man once who spent the whole evening talking about his glaucoma. And I was trying to eat spaghetti and meatballs. Good job he wasn't talking about his prostate, I suppose.'

'Only a matter of time,' Juliette said with a grimace. 'Matthew was complaining about his knee the other day, he says it feels funny in damp weather since the replacement. And I said, well, Matthew, that's getting older, isn't it? Various bits of your body saying to you, "well, *actually*, no dear, not today".'

We all laughed at that.

'You're absolutely right,' Kim said. 'The other day I got up on a kitchen chair to try and find something on top of the dresser, and I got all woozy for a second. My doctor checked me over and said it was low blood pressure. Something called post-prandial hypotension which happens a couple of hours after eating. And I said doctor, with me there are *never* a couple of hours after eating. Except at night. And even then I have some biscuits by the side of the bed. I just don't sleep like I used to. Sometimes I wake up and read for a couple of hours. That's the worst bit, I think. Being alone with just Jilly Cooper and some Jaffa cakes for company.'

'Anita told me she and Rick usually sleep in separate bedrooms,' Juliette said.

We all turned to look at her and she shrugged.

'She said Rick had man-flu last Christmas and it was like sharing a bedroom with a bad-tempered warthog. One that scattered tissues all over the floor and groaned in his sleep. I mean he was genuinely unwell, but like most men he liked to let everyone know every detail. She said to him, Rick, when I want to know the colour of your sputum, I'll tell you. Anyway, she moved into the spare room and had the best night's sleep she'd had for years. She recommends it. She told me she doesn't miss the duvet hogging or the unusual noises. I'm sure you know what she means. She said give Rick a five-bean chilli and it comes back to haunt both of them.'

By this point the four of us were doubled over with laughter, and the chaps at the other end of the table looked to see what all the hilarity was about.

'Well, I don't think you gals are talking about Egyptian vultures, are you?' Johnny called over.

I held on to my aching ribs from all the laughter and took a deep breath.

Sophia wiped her eyes with her napkin. 'We are talking about a really fascinating subject.'

Doggie's face brightened. 'I'll tell you what I find fascinating, I was clearing out my gutters the other day and I found a TV remote in there, three golf balls and one trainer. A pair I could understand but one? Lorna says it's not hers. Well, it wouldn't be, I don't think she's ever owned any. I've been thinking of getting some of that mesh to stop things getting stuck. Lorna didn't seem very interested.'

'Really?' Juliette said, with a sympathetic tilt of her head. 'No, we were talking about men.'

'I thought so, how marvellous,' Johnny said cheerfully. 'Do tell, nothing bad, I hope?'

'Of course not,' I said, 'just the usual stuff. How men like all the things women don't. Football...'

'The beautiful game, they call it,' Bruno said. 'Personally I don't agree.'

He was sitting at the other end of the table, running his finger around his wine glass. And then he flashed me a look.

I stuttered a little and then carried on. '...power tools...'

Doggie held up a finger. 'Ah, but where would we be without them? Do you know, I got an orbital sander from Aldi only recently. In what Lorna calls the middle aisle of doom. Cheap as chips and terrifically powerful. I did the coffee table with it. There were some ring marks on it, from before Lorna introduced the coaster rule. I was in the workshop for hours. Lorna was surprisingly encouraging. In fact, she was so impressed that when I finished she suggested I sand down the chest of drawers we have on the landing. I said, that's going to take ages. And she said, well, Douglas, if it makes you happy... She even helped me take it downstairs.'

'...and gardening.'

'Excellent exercise,' Johnny said. 'Polly says she wants us to have dance lessons, like on *Strictly*. Those girls are like whippets, and they must be cold half the time with those outfits. I said as much to Polly. I said, well, that frock won't keep her kidneys warm, and Polly said she hadn't noticed. She was too busy watching some Spanish chap in tight trousers, I think.'

'Cars,' Vince said thoughtfully, 'men like talking about cars. At least I do. I could hang around the VW dealership for hours given half a chance. There's something magical about the smell of a new car. The first few times the engine starts up. The whiff of leather from the seats. It's like catnip to me. My ex-wife never understood it. She said she'd rather have her wisdom teeth out again than go and buy a car. And I said...'

'Routes,' Juliette interrupted, 'men like to explain the best route whenever they are planning to travel anywhere.'

'I don't think we do,' Johnny said with a puzzled frown.

'Okay then, if you were travelling from Cardiff to Cambridge?' I asked.

'Well, that's easy,' Doggie said, 'I always do the navigating. Lorna insists on driving. A449, M50, then join up with the M5...'

'Nonsense,' Vince said, 'if you wanted to get there before dark, take the M4, M25, M1.'

'No one goes on the M25 unless it's a matter of life and death,' Johnny butted in, 'better off dodging up to Oxford.'

'Oxford? Have you tried driving through Oxford lately?' I said. 'It would be quicker to crawl on your hands and knees.'

'I second that,' Sophia said, 'I used to live there.'

'Well, not actually *through* Oxford,' Johnny added, 'obviously. But you could dart off at Swindon and head to Cheltenham...'

Doggie yelped with laughter. 'Don't be ridiculous. No one ever *darts off* at Swindon, have you tried it recently? Have you ever tried doing Nettleton Bottom at the weekend?'

'Oooh, I say, steady there,' I spluttered into my napkin.

Doggie looked confused.

'Case proved, m'lud,' Juliette snorted.

They carried on arguing for several minutes, and I thought it was a jolly good job we didn't have any near neighbours. They would have had something to complain about when it came to noise levels.

'Can I pour anyone a drink?' Bruno said at last, as his companions started a heated discussion about one-way systems and roadworks.

'Don't you have a preference regarding driving?' Sophia asked.

Bruno laughed. 'As I live here on Mallorca, I seldom have to worry about the state of the M25.'

'You live here? I didn't know that,' I said.

'Come on, girls, let's break up this drivers-fest,' Juliette said firmly.

She made a great play of getting the others up and they went to the other end of the table where it looked as though Vince and Doggie were about to trade blows. Juliette sent me a very theatrical wink.

'You didn't ask. I've lived here for years,' Bruno replied, turning back to me, 'over on the east coast, near Porto Cristo, and I take the inland route, before you ask.'

'I wasn't going to, I haven't much idea of where we are, if I'm honest; we don't have a car.'

'That's a shame. Wouldn't you like to see something of this area?' he said.

'I'm sure we would. We could always hire a taxi. I saw at the tourist information centre there are plenty of buses too.'

'I don't mind taking you somewhere. As I told you, the chaps are all spending most of their time at the park. I could go with them, but I can't pretend to share their enthusiasm and they know it. I could take you all somewhere.'

'But you can't ditch your groom!' I said. Rather unconvincingly. The prospect of spending more time with him, talking to him, was very appealing.

'Look, I'm sorry if I seemed a bit patronising earlier. I didn't mean anything by it. I just didn't know what to say, and – you know me – as usual I said something daft,' he said.

'I'm sorry too, I'm not handling this very well,' I said.

I looked away from his gaze, feeling unsure of myself.

'Johnny, you know I'm not joining you tomorrow morning?' Bruno called up the length of the table.

'Course not, the tour bus is going to pick us up at the bike place at six. You make too much noise anyway,' Johnny called back, 'I swear there was a moustached warbler there the other day and then you opened that bottle of fizzy water and it disappeared.'

Bruno held out his hands. 'See?'

He had that smile, that warm, gentle smile that I remembered so well from the past.

'I don't know,' I said, sure that I was blushing now.

He reached under the table and touched my hand. I pulled away and leant forward, my elbows on the table, straightening up the wine glass, scrunching up my paper napkin and throwing it onto my plate.

I felt rather odd; perhaps it was the wine or the late hour. Or perhaps it was Bruno.

'Denny. Let's be friends,' he said, 'we were friends once.'

'We were, weren't we?' I said.

But we hadn't just been friends. After all, we had seen each other naked. Many times. We had been lovers, intimate. We had known things about each other that no one else had.

But I remembered it then, that friendship. It had been another layer to our relationship, which fitted in with the love and the lust and the silly disagreements. We had always liked each other. And perhaps it had been that wonderful friendship which I had missed as much as anything. The knowledge that there was someone who liked me back in the same way. Who could forgive my faults, accept my obsession about punctuality and deadlines. Knew that I didn't like goat's cheese or sweet and sour food.

I checked my watch. 'It's late, it's nearly one in the morning, I think I should go to bed.'

I stood up, a bit unsteady on my feet. I made a grab for the table and the crockery rattled. Brilliant, I was having a discussion

I had thought about for decades, and now I was in danger of crashing headfirst into a fruit platter.

'It's funny, you always were the first to leave the party,' he said. 'You used to get to a place where you needed to escape.'

'Did I? I don't remember that. I'm sure you're wrong.'

'Tomorrow,' Bruno said, 'I'll see you tomorrow.'

9

I went up to my room, stripped off, tripped over my shoes and fell into bed. The sheets were pleasantly cool under my back. I could hear a church bell in the distance tolling the hour.

I suddenly remembered Exeter, a weekend trip Bruno and I had taken together in February to celebrate my birthday. God, I had been happy.

We had stayed in a guesthouse in the centre of the city. Our room had been small and badly decorated, the place had old wooden staircases and unreliable plumbing, but there had been a wonderful view from our window to the cathedral. Outside there was a statue of some worthy cleric, seated on a plinth, usually with a pigeon on his head. There had been a splendid old black and white tea shop with toasted teacakes the size of bicycle wheels. We had been up inside the cathedral tower, the many steps making the muscles in my legs burn.

I'd banged my head on a beam somewhere along the way and Bruno had kissed it better in the dim, dusty light. When we had returned to our room that night, the heating was off and the sheets icy cold. We had leapt into bed yelping, and shivered, close together, warming each other's feet. And yet it had been romantic, the brown paintwork, the hideous carpets, the smell of past meals clinging to the curtains. I'd known then that I – unremarkable, clumsy, insecure – was loved and was in love. And that feeling had swelled me, buoyed me through the cold night, the rainy weekend, the weeks afterwards of lectures and examinations. Right through until the September day when Bruno had left for Italy, and we had argued. He had promised to write letters, to phone me if he had a chance, to come back at Christmas. And he had done none of those things. And slowly I think I had shrunk back. Stubborn and self-reliant. The one who found it impossible to trust, to commit, to expect anything. Could I really blame Bruno for all that? Didn't I have some responsibility? Had it affected him and his view of the world and relationships too?

* * *

The following morning, I woke after eight o'clock, which was a surprise as those days I usually didn't sleep very well. But then again, I had been awake a couple of times in the night, wondering how many calories I had consumed in the last few days, not to mention units of alcohol. Thinking about Bruno, wondering how to handle seeing him again in the morning.

Perhaps I would start to be cool about it instead of stammering and blushing like a teenager, take it one step at a time, not put too much importance on our conversations. Just be myself. But then who was I these days?

I'd stopped being the efficient, dependable financial expert in a smart suit and heels. Now I was a single, slightly confused woman about to enter my seventh decade. That sounded awful. Worse than being actually sixty.

Why were there so many negative or bland statements about older people?

She's young at heart. Good for her age. Doing well under the circumstances. Still giving life a go, bless her.

Why were older people not more respected when we knew so much about so many things?

How about, I really envy her, she's having fun. She's on to the next phase and knowing her, she'll nail it. I hope I'm like her when I'm sixty or seventy or whatever.

Older people, especially older women, had become disregarded. Safe to ignore from every aspect. Especially fashion. Where apparently one needs to be a teenager, look miserable and be a size zero.

I'd fallen asleep after this particular rant. And it was probably just as well.

So that morning I showered and dressed in some of my brightest clothes to show my enthusiasm for the day. Some red jeans, a blue embroidered top. I could take a leaf out of Juliette's book. Those days she was always colourful, eager, very hard to marginalise. No wonder Matthew had found her irresistible.

Downstairs I found Juliette on the sofa watching an episode of *Tintin* in Spanish. I made coffee and went to sit beside her. There were numerous accidents with rivers, crevasses, and avalanches while Tintin met the Dalai Lama. After ten minutes, I gave a sigh.

'Why are you watching this?' I said.

Juliette frowned. 'I'm not sure. Perhaps to improve my Spanish?'

'And has it worked?'

She gave it some thought while Captain Haddock was buried under another avalanche.

'I don't think so. So we are going out this morning? While the birdwatchers go twitching?'

'Boat trip I'm happy to do this afternoon. Marvelling over hoopoes all morning, I can't,' I said.

'So what were you and Bruno talking about last night? You seemed a bit intense.'

'Oh, nothing important,' I said, 'just idle chit-chat.'

'I don't believe you. I've seen him looking at you with that look in his eyes.'

'What look?' I said.

'Sort of perplexed mixed with a deep reservoir of yearning,' Juliette drawled.

I picked up a cushion and bopped her on the head with it. 'Very funny.'

Juliette threw it back, knocking the remains of my coffee into my lap.

'The least you can do – what *I* would do – is ask why he dumped you.'

'He says he didn't,' I said, mopping at my trousers with a tissue, 'and anyway it wasn't like that. I think I need to go and change. It looks as though I've had an accident.'

'Oh, for goodness… what is the matter with the pair of you?' Juliette said, turning the television off. 'I insist you make the time for a proper talk with Bruno and get all this nonsense straightened out.'

'I know you're right. I have been trying to make sense of it.'

'About time too. Now then what shall we have for breakfast?'

'What have we got?'

Juliette went to look in the fridge.

'White wine and salad. And some eggs, potatoes, and cheese. And some stale bread. Perhaps we need to wait for Sophia? She could rustle up a three-course meal from that.'

In the end, Juliette and I just sat outside on the patio with some more coffee and a box of assorted Spanish biscuits. Some were chocolate, others were cinnamon, all of them were covered in a lot of powdered sugar.

'I'm not sure about these,' I said, wiping my face with my sleeve, 'I'll try another one to be sure.'

'Me too,' Juliette said.

Three biscuits each later and the others still hadn't surfaced.

* * *

When it got to ten-thirty, Juliette went inside, intent on waking the others up. Moments later, Bruno came out into the sunshine, one hand shading his eyes.

'Hello,' he said, 'are you okay?'

'You mean am I hungover? No, just a bit of a headache. I don't think this coffee is helping.'

'The others have gone,' Bruno said, 'I took them to the pick-up point just before six o'clock. I don't think they appreciated the early start.'

'No, I bet they didn't,' I said.

'Denny—'

'Bruno—'

We both started speaking at the same time, and both of us stopped, uneasily.

Bruno came through the gate and sat down on the sunbed next to mine. I could feel every muscle in my body tensing. Perhaps he was right. Maybe I did tend to run away from situations like this.

I took a deep breath and forced myself to relax.

'I'm sorry,' he said at last, 'for last night. I didn't mean to be so – confrontational.'

'It's fine. No harm done.'

'It's just when I saw you again, here after all these years. It was a bit of a shock.'

'How do you think I felt?' I said, my voice a bit shaky.

'I don't know because you didn't seem that bothered.'

Didn't seem that bothered.

I thought back, to all the weeks and months after Bruno had left me, my careless words echoing in my head, and then gradually I had realised that he was never coming back. The sadness, confusion, despair. Then the anger. That after all we had been to each other, that he could just go. It proved that I was right; I could only depend on myself. Anything, anybody could just disappear at any time.

I straightened my shoulders and looked at the patio doors.

'The others will be up soon,' I said.

'Do they know? What happened to us?'

I shrugged. 'I don't know what happened to us, so why should they?'

'Denny. Please. I really want to talk to you. Seeing you again—'

I stood up and so did he.

'That might be a good idea,' I said. 'What shall we talk about?'

Although we change on the outside, perhaps inside us there is always the person we have been. The child who was confused, the teenager who resented everything, the efficient economics expert who still occasionally counted on her fingers.

'We'll find something,' Bruno said.

He gave me his lopsided smile and my heart turned over.

'Why don't we just go on a new, first date?' he said. 'I'll take you out for a drink, for a meal. We can get to know each other again.'

'Pretend nothing ever happened?' I said.

'I don't mean that. I just want to see how it goes. No pressure at all. Let's try,' he said, 'while we still have chances in life. If we take them, who knows what might happen.'

Yes. Before we were too old to take chances. Before one of us got ill or fell over in the supermarket, or any one of the many problems we might encounter.

'We only have one life,' he added, 'and in the middle of that is the word *if*.'

*   *   *

Back in our kitchen, Sophia was standing at the stove, prodding at something in a huge frying pan, and there was a glorious smell of hot butter and onions in the room.

'Spanish frittata,' she said, 'it seemed appropriate. I'm just waiting for the potatoes to soften.'

Kim came slowly down the stairs.

'I'm absolutely starving,' she said, removing her sunglasses, 'and I have a hangover that needs feeding.'

'Then this will set you up for the day,' Sophia said.

I started to unload the dishwasher and set the table. Kim had a long drink of water and then went to find some plates in the cupboard. Moving them one at a time so as not to make too much noise.

'This holiday is undoing all the good my cabbage soup diet did,' she said, sitting down with a groan, 'at least I think it did. When I get on the bathroom scales at home, I hang on to the towel rail and just gently let go. I even caught myself trying to wedge my fingernails into the tile grouting once. Anyway, these trousers are getting tight again. And they were the only pair that were comfortable.'

'No trousers are comfortable,' I said, 'not in my experience. And no two shops have the same sizing.'

'That's true,' Kim said, 'these jeans are a size 18, my other pair from the same shop, same brand, are a 14. Those are my favourites. Even though they are starting to wear out at the knees.'

Sophia raised her eyebrows. 'And do tell us, what is it exactly that you do on your knees all the time?'

'Well, I do a lot of...' Kim stopped. 'Honestly! You've changed! I do a lot of praying that my friend, who used to be so prim and proper, will stop being quite so rude!'

Sophia threw back her head and laughed.

Kim sighed, got up again and started helping to unload the wine glasses from the dishwasher. There seemed to be a great many of them.

'And I sometimes cut the labels out of my clothes, so as not to depress myself, except for a pair of trousers I got in Gap, which are a size 12. They were obviously mislabelled and one of the pockets was put in upside down, but I could cope with that when I got used to it. And I've noticed my bum has changed shape. How can that happen? It used to be quite reasonable when I was young, quite pert, actually, if I am allowed to use that word. Now it looks squashed, as though something has been flattening it for a long time.'

Juliette came downstairs at that point, a vision in a fuchsia sundress and turquoise sandals, and overheard the conversation.

'They have,' she said, 'you've been sitting on it.'

Kim looked thoughtful. 'I suppose you're right. Not that anyone is ever going to rummage through my clothing any more, looking at the sizes. Chance would be a fine thing. Stewart used to, though. When he saw I had bought a size 18 dress – because the 16 was a bit tight around the bust – he said no wonder you're not getting a promotion at work.'

'Damn cheek!' I said.

'And at the time he was having one of his flings, and she turned out to be bigger than I was. Especially in the arse department. Which could have blocked the Dartford tunnel.'

Juliette poured herself some coffee and made a dismissive noise. 'His loss, that's what I say.'

'Me too,' Kim said.

There was a sizzling sound as Sophia poured the eggs into the pan, and we all turned to sniff appreciatively.

'So have the chaps next door gone? For their exciting wetlands tour?' Sophia asked.

'All except Bruno,' I said, and felt my cheeks flush.

Juliette pointed at me. 'Blushing, blushing, Denny. Shall I go next door and tell him my friend fancies him?'

'No! Anyway, he wants...'

Juliette came to sit beside me and dug an elbow in my ribs.

'Wants what? A night of unbridled passion? The chance to feel your lips on his as he holds you in a tender embrace. The stars shimmering overhead in a dark, velvet sky?'

'Oooh, that sounds nice,' Kim said, 'did he say any of that? My clothes would fall off in a trice if anyone said that to me. Well, unless I was wearing magic knickers. I'd need help with those. Probably a crowbar.'

I threw her a look and sighed. 'No, he didn't say anything like that. He just wants to talk.'

'That's a new word for it,' Sophia chuckled.

'He does!'

I think I was puce with embarrassment by that point.

'Then talk to him,' Sophia said, 'what's the worst that could happen?'

'Stop saying that,' I said, 'we all know the worst that can happen in these situations. I mean how do I deal with a man who ghosted me over thirty years ago?'

Juliette snorted. 'One strike and you're out, that's my motto. I'd had my suspicions for years, but when I found out about what Gary had been doing for sure, I had his stuff out on the driveway before he came home from work. And I pushed a chest of drawers in front of the door so he couldn't get in. I only let him back in once to get his personal stuff, including a bottle of artificial pheromones he had bought from the internet and hidden in his sock drawer. Supposed to attract women.'

'Well, he would say it worked,' Kim said, 'if women are attracted to the smell of lying pig.'

'I would talk to Bruno,' Sophia said after a moment. 'What is it people on American talk shows are always on about? Closure.'

'Hmm, I thought I had that already,' I said. 'There's nothing like a man promising undying passion and then disappearing to give you closure. But then I'm beginning to see that it was my fault too. and it's making me feel rather foolish.'

'He might have been ill, in hospital with amnesia,' Kim said, gazing into the far distance, 'tended by French nuns in giant wimples who couldn't understand his feverish mumblings.'

'For the best part of forty years? I don't think that's likely,' I said. 'He was travelling all over the world and teaching.'

While I had put my dreams on hold and led a rather dull life, avoiding any possibility of commitment. Bruno was right; I did have issues. I needed to accept that.

'Well, I wasted five years of my life with someone who wouldn't commit. Leaving was the best thing I ever did,' Sophia said. 'I definitely wouldn't be happy. I wouldn't be here for a start if I had still been with Lucien.'

There it was again, that 'if' word.

If I talked to Bruno. If I found out what had happened. If I took a chance.

'He wants us to have a date. To take me out for a drink, or a meal,' I said.

I could feel my resolve strengthening. I did want to talk to him, I did want to find out 'what if' after all. I wanted us to be friends again.

'Now that's more like it,' Juliette said.

Sophia brought over the pan and placed it on some heatproof mats in the middle of the table.

'Ooof, that's heavy. While you are thinking, try this,' she said. 'I was supposed to be dumping it out onto a platter, but I haven't got the strength. It might end up on the floor.'

'I'd still eat it,' Kim said, taking a forkful from the pan, 'this is absolutely delicious.'

'So?' Juliette said when we had worked our way through most of our breakfast and were on to a second pot of coffee. 'Bruno the Bear?'

'He does look a bit like a bear, actually,' Kim said thoughtfully. She topped up her glass of orange juice and took a swig. 'Sort of big and thoughtful. And hairy. Is Bruno particularly hairy?'

'As I recall, a bit,' I said.

'I once went out with a chap who was like Chewbacca, from *Star Wars*. He even had huge, hairy feet,' Juliette said.

'Wouldn't that make him a Hobbit?' I asked.

Juliette lifted one eyebrow. 'There was nothing small about Alex, I can assure you. He was good fun, even quite thoughtful occasionally.'

'So why did you end it?' Kim asked in astonishment.

'The Hoover kept clogging up. And the shower drain. It was like living with an Old English sheepdog.'

We all pulled disgusted faces.

'I don't think bears are thoughtful except when they are trying to decide which hiker to eat first,' Kim said after a while.

'The slowest one,' I said.

'Are you supposed to run from bears or play dead?' Juliette asked. 'I've often wondered.'

I helped myself to some orange juice. 'It's supposed to be different with black bears and brown ones. But I can't remember which. Anyway, they can both probably run faster than I can and climb trees a lot better.'

'When you decide to hike the Appalachian trail we'll go together,' Kim said, 'I can't run three paces without falling over. You'd be quite safe.'

I reached over and patted her hand. 'Never going to happen,' I said, 'but thank you for the thought.'

'Now then, what are we going to do with the rest of the morning?' Juliette asked. 'What's on the spreadsheet, Kim?'

Kim rummaged in her yellow folder and unfolded the battered sheet of paper.

'Nothing in particular. We were supposed to be getting the bus to Alcudia, but it's a bit late now, we can always do that another day. Anyway, now we have the boat trip this afternoon, which is much more exciting, if the chaps next door aren't devoured by black vultures or red kites.'

'Oooh, some of that twitching is rubbing off on you. You're spending far too much time with Vince,' Sophia giggled.

Kim bridled a bit. 'I told you; I like him, actually. Despite the cravats. And he knows a lot about car maintenance. He rotates his car tyres every year. He's offered to rotate mine.'

'I bet he has,' Juliette snorted.

Sophia started stacking the empty plates. 'So are we going out at all this morning?'

We all looked at each other and shrugged.

Juliette spoke up. 'I'm quite happy slobbing about here until the chaps get back. It's a lovely morning. We could sit outside in the sun and read. Or just chat and have some more coffee. And tell Denny what she should do.'

'I don't need to be told, I just need to think,' I said, 'and people keep distracting me.'

We cleared up the kitchen and the others made some more coffee and went out onto the patio.

'This is the life,' Kim sighed happily, 'no one can get at me here. No one can pester me for anything. No one can ring me up asking for a lift home. Or ask me for money.'

'Lend us a fiver?' I said.

Kim rolled her eyes at me and took out her mobile.

'Talking about phones, can anyone advise me about taking selfies? I've tried so many times and every time I look like some weird, wild-haired terrier.'

'You have to hold the phone up high,' Juliette said, 'and find out which is your best side. And never stand on the edge of a group photograph. It adds pounds.'

'So *that's* where I've been going wrong,' Kim said. 'I must have spent my whole life metaphorically on the edge of a group photograph. I'll remember that when it comes to the wedding pictures.'

Much as I was enjoying myself, I needed ten minutes to think about the present, to think about Bruno.

I got up from my sun bed. 'I'll go to the shop at the end of the road and buy some more milk. Anyone need anything?'

A few minutes later, I left the villa and turned left towards the end of the road. I knew there was a small shop there which sold the basics and the owner spoke pretty good English.

There was the bluest of skies above me and I took in a deep breath of warm air, closing my eyes against the sun.

'Where are you off to?' said a voice.

I turned, my spirits lifting as I saw it was him.

'Hello, Bruno,' I said, 'I'm going to buy some milk. Have you been lurking, waiting for me?'

'Not at all, I never lurk. I'm just sorting out my car. It's taken them no time at all to fill it with mud and rubbish.' Bruno held up a black bin liner as evidence and dropped two empty water bottles and a sandwich wrapper into it as evidence. 'Johnny's car is like a skip, the side pockets are always filled with empty crisp packets and half-eaten chocolate bars, so I shouldn't be surprised he's the same here.'

I walked over and stood watching as he grabbed a discarded coffee cup from under the passenger seat.

'You always did like your car to be tidy,' I said, 'remember the incredible fuss you made about someone putting apple cores in the ashtray?'

'How could I forget? I still think it was you.'

I laughed. 'It certainly was not! Well, it might have been.'

'So are you free tomorrow evening? I thought we could go out for a meal, or just a drink if you wanted to?'

'No, I can't leave Juliette on her own,' I said, 'it's not good form to abandon the bride on her hen holiday.'

'Well, in that case, Johnny was talking about inviting you all over to our place tomorrow evening. He's brought a game with him called Time's Up. He thought it might be fun.'

'A board game? Is that a good idea? They always seem to end in an argument.'

Growing up, Juliette had been fiercely competitive when it came to that sort of thing. I remembered one Easter holiday when we had played Monopoly for hours at a time, and by the time she went back to university, we were barely speaking.

'What do you think?' he said.

I looked at him, his face different and yet so familiar. I

remembered how we had once been so close, inseparable. How all those years ago we had spent every moment together, holding hands, having fun, wanting each other with a passion so fierce. Too hot not to cool down, my mother had said.

And now, had that fire really died down, or was there something about all this that was rekindling it? Some last little spark of recognition, of regret, of 'what if'.

'Maybe,' I said at last, 'anyway, I'm off to buy some milk, can't stop.'

'I'll ask you again,' Bruno called after me.

I walked down the road, feeling distinctly positive about things. He wanted to take me out and he would ask me again. It really was like being a teenager.

Maybe there was a way to work through all this after all.

10

The birdwatchers returned at lunch time. We knew because we were out on our patio and could hear them over the hedge, noisily comparing notes and arguing. Perhaps hours of being really quiet had been too much of a strain on them. They had seen something very exciting apparently, and Doggie had taken dozens of pictures.

'I think it's the best thing we've seen in a long time,' Vince said, 'a sub-alpine warbler. Just sitting there. Red underparts, white moustaches, and everything.'

'Red underpants and moustaches? I wonder if it said *dondé es el gato*?' I murmured.

Juliette giggled.

'I'm not entirely convinced,' Johnny said, sounding a bit peeved.

'Well, if you had listened to me and Doggie and not gone off looking for wrynecks, even though you were told it was too early...'

'Show me that photo again, Doggie,' Johnny grumbled. There was a long silence and then, 'Oh, well.'

Juliette stood up and called through the gate.

'So? Had a good time?'

'Yes, absolutely,' Vince replied, looking over the hedge, 'early start but worth it. Now, are you ladies still on board for the boat trip? See what I did there? On board?'

I turned to raise a questioning eyebrow at Kim, who blushed and pouted.

'I'll be there, Vince,' she called.

'Excellent news. I think we all need a quick shower to get the mud off, and then I'll be right with you, don't forget we are having lunch on the boat,' he said, and hurried away into the villa.

'You Jezebel,' I said to Kim, who looked pleased. 'But apparently you are officially not as interesting as a sub-alpine warbler.'

'Not yet I'm not,' she said, 'no bird is going to get the better of me. Just give me time.'

'We had better get some warm clothes on. It can be breezy on boats,' Juliette said, collecting her coffee cup from the table. 'We need to be ready in twenty minutes. And don't forget your swimming things, and a towel.'

'Oh dear, do we have to? That might put him off a bit,' Kim said.

* * *

When we were all ready, we walked down to the harbour; it was a beautiful afternoon. The sun was warm in our faces, a slight breeze from the Mediterranean blowing inland. There were people everywhere, but because it was still low season, it wasn't too crowded. The only problem was still the skeins of cyclists which appeared suddenly and silently from time to time, pedalling furiously, their faces set with dust and determination.

'Vince told me some of them are professional teams, they

come here to do their winter training,' Kim said as we waited for the latest group to pass us. 'They like the steep roads and the hair-pin bends.'

We gazed after them.

'They must have legs like iron bars,' Juliette said, 'and a lot of stamina. Quite sexy really, I suppose.'

'Hmm,' I said thoughtfully, 'but nothing can make up for those padded gel trousers they wear. I'm sure those saddles must be incredibly uncomfortable, but even so.'

We passed a tourist information centre, with a wire rack filled with leaflets and books in several languages. Next door was a spotlessly clean public loo, which Kim was very keen to take advantage of.

'I told you, things have never been the same since I had the kids. Never miss an opportunity, that's what I say,' she said, sliding the door closed behind her.

Once everyone was comfortable and sunglasses and our yellow duck hats had been donned, we made our way to the quayside, where the boat was waiting for us. Gleaming white and trimmed with blue, it looked very exciting.

There was a shout behind us.

'Hold up, ladies!'

And there was Vince, puffing towards us, a huge camera bag slung over one shoulder and a water bottle decorated with birds in his other hand.

'Lovely day for it,' he said, 'the others are just coming. Those team hats you are wearing was a brilliant idea. I could see you miles away. I thought I would run ahead to make sure you had got here all right.'

'Vince, it's a ten-minute walk,' Kim said, 'we were hardly going to get lost. We're not daft, you know.'

'No, of course not,' he said, chastened, 'it's just my ex-wife could get lost in a supermarket, she had such a terrible sense of direction. She was always slipping off and disappearing. She went missing for hours sometimes, especially at the weekends. I used to worry about her.'

'Well, that's very thoughtful,' Kim said a little more kindly, 'but you don't need to worry about us. We all have geography O level, and Juliette probably has a Guide badge.'

His round face cleared, and he wiped a handkerchief over his sweating forehead.

'Of course. Now, can I help you with your bags?'

'You've got more to carry than we have by the looks of it,' I said. 'Ah, here come the others.'

Johnny, Doggie, and Bruno were strolling along the quayside towards us. Johnny and Doggie in many-pocketed shorts and Hawaiian shirts and Bruno in jeans and a black T-shirt. He really did look marvellously attractive. Had he always been that handsome? I suppose he had. Anyway, at that moment someone lowered the metal gangway, and I hurried on board, following Juliette, who wanted to know if there was a bar.

'Well, this is nice,' she said, settling herself in a seat next to the window. 'Tables and everything. I'm looking forward to this. Although I never was a very good sailor. I remember a trip I took with Charlie. He had a boat, and we were supposed to be going across the Bristol channel but there was a force-six gale blowing and we never got anywhere. Still, we positively surfed back to Penarth once he turned the boat around. I think I might be better on a cruise ship, actually.'

I watched as Bruno and his friends wandered around. Then Luis, the captain, who had the strong features, dark eyes, and proud nose of a true Spaniard, appeared, and clapped him on the back and wanted to be introduced to everyone.

After a good few minutes when Luis and Bruno chatted away

in Spanish, he disappeared back to his post, wishing us all a pleasant trip.

It was rather sexy, actually, listening to Bruno talking in a foreign language. I'd forgotten about that. I remembered a time when he had wooed me in Italian and Spanish and occasionally French. It had worked every time. Even though one evening he confessed that while I thought he had been murmuring words of love, he had been talking to me about his need to get his car serviced, and his concerns about the front passenger tyre.

Then the gangway was raised and with a sudden, slow revving of the engines, we were off.

As we moved out of the harbour, we could see more of the coast. White houses, villas perched up on the cliffs, apartment blocks and hotels, although none of the high-rise buildings I had expected. Perhaps there were more strict planning regulations here?

I could see a white bus, labouring slowly up the slope on the mountain above us, I guessed it was on its way to Cap Formentera, just as we were, but our way was surely much easier and just as pleasant. And we couldn't exactly plunge off the side of a hair-pin bend and crash into the rocks below.

There were other boats moored in straight lines, the occasional large gin palace, little dinghies, sleek sailing boats with their sails furled and covered in blue canvas.

It was mid-week, so there wasn't much activity on board those craft. Perhaps at the weekend people appeared to scrub decks and sluice out bilges or whatever it was sailing people did. Perhaps they were entrepreneurs from Palma with laughing, attractive families, who would set off into the sun with champagne and picnics in wicker baskets. No small child would throw a strop because there weren't any Pom Bear crisps, no teen daughter would sit with her hands busy on an iPhone, rolling her eyes at the sight of her father in shorts.

I looked out of the window, admiring the curve of the bay behind us. It really was such a beautiful part of the world, and I hadn't really expected that. I'd been assuming it would be bars and nightclubs, and bands of rowdy teenagers celebrating the end of their exams. It wasn't like that at all. It was perfect.

'So, what do you think?' Bruno said as he sat down next to me. 'Pretty, isn't it?'

'Glorious,' I said.

I think I had got used to the idea of talking to him again, but I wanted to be sensible about it. The last few days had shown me that it was very easy to let Bruno's charm work its magic on me.

I'd been having all sorts of ridiculous thoughts. I was almost able to remember the feeling of being with him. Being a couple. It had been exciting and at the same time I had felt protected. From what? What an odd word. Because I hadn't been safe with him at all. He had disappeared into his future that September evening, leaving me to our past, wondering why. And over the years I had believed I hadn't done anything wrong except trust him.

I hadn't meant what I said that day all those years ago, it came out wrong, I was upset, that was all.

'I love living here,' he continued. 'The other day, listening to the others talking about traffic and delays, it made me appreciate being here all the more.'

'Hmm,' I said, looking out of the window.

There was a sick, silly crazy feeling in my stomach that had nothing to do with the motion of the sea.

'It's only in the high season that it gets busy on the roads. And there are always a few accidents, people not used to driving a left-hand car on the right side of the road.'

I laughed. 'The wrong side of the road, you mean,' I said.

Bruno stretched his long legs out under the table and rested his arm along the back of my seat. It would have taken no effort for him to drop his hand onto my shoulder, for me to feel the warmth of his palm through my thin shirt. But he didn't.

Did I want that? Actually, don't be ridiculous, I did.

I stood up. 'Would you mind, could I get past? I think I'll have a stroll around the boat. See where the others have got to.'

He stood up and politely moved aside for me. I went to look at the painted porcelain tile murals on the inside of the cabin. A rocky, familiar coastline, a painting of a cathedral, probably Palma. Then I heard laughter from the upper deck, and climbed the white metal stairs to find Juliette, Sophia and Johnny sitting in the sunshine with glasses of champagne.

'There you are,' she said, 'I said to Johnny, one whiff of champagne and you would find us.'

'Well, here I am.'

Sophia pointed. 'There's a lovely young man over there behind the bar, handing out glasses, and a spectacularly pretty girl with some canapés wandering around. Kim and Vince are at the back of the boat, getting stuck in if I know them. Isn't this fun?'

'Excellent,' I said.

I went to take a glass of champagne, and sipped it, feeling rather glamorous and sophisticated.

'There's the military base,' Johnny said, peering through his binoculars. 'Someone told me Franco set it up in the Civil War. They say seaplanes take off from there, but we haven't seen any yet.'

'Well, you stay there and keep an eye out, let us know if you see anything interesting,' Juliette said, giving me a wink. I think we were both remembering the skinny-dipping episode. 'Denny and I are going to find some food in a minute. This sea air is giving me an appetite.'

She slipped out of her seat and ushered me away. We found a place, leaning over the boat's rail, watching the smooth blue sea slip past below us.

'Poor Polly,' she said, 'he really is rather exhausting, but perhaps he has a lovely nature?'

'Or perhaps he's good in bed?' I said.

Juliette thought about this for a few moments.

'No, I'm sorry, I can't see it.' Her eyebrows shot up. 'Oh, good grief, my eyes! I just saw it. Quickly, think of something else, for the love of God. Ah, there are the others, I'll just focus on them and how lucky I am to have such good friends. And try to unsee Johnny with no clothes on. Doesn't Sophia look lovely? She really has blossomed since we first met her.'

'She's really nice too,' I said, smiling, 'are you claiming all the credit?'

'Not at all, I just think the Old Ducks showed her there was more to life than waiting for her married boss to give her the time of day. And that even at our age things can get better, more interesting.'

'I'm beginning to think you might be right.'

Juliette turned to look at me. 'Of course I'm right. Life is what you make it. I spent far too many years idling along in neutral and so did you. I'm hoping you can see that. There are chances every day for something new if you are brave enough. And don't let past silliness weigh you down.'

She raised her eyebrows at me in a meaningful way.

'You mean Bruno?'

'Of course,' she said, 'the way that man looks at you. The way you look at him. It's a shame neither of you are bold enough to take the first step.'

'Don't be daft,' I said, and then unable to stop myself, 'what do you mean, anyway; how does he look at me?'

Juliette laughed. 'See? You are interested.'

We watched as the boat rounded a headland and the sea below us shimmered, clear and turquoise, like something from a tourist brochure.

'I don't want to risk messing everything up again,' I said. 'Yes, I still find him attractive, and yes, I like him too. Everything went wrong back then; I want to be sure the same thing won't happen again.'

'Faint heart never won handsome bloke,' Juliette murmured, finishing her champagne. 'Come on, let's get a refill. And see what Kim's up to. I have a feeling that Vince, despite his cravats and terrible puns, is winning her over.'

'Really?'

'You are dense sometimes. Look.'

At the back of the boat, Vince was sitting next to Kim and she was chatting away with him. Vince was sporting a rather battered old Panama hat with a hole in the front where the straw had creased and broken. As we watched, Kim reached out and removed his yellow paisley cravat with a flourish. And after a moment, Vince laughed and stuffed it in his pocket.

'See? They are connecting,' Juliette said, 'she's training him with her subtle female wiles. Poor bloke doesn't stand a chance. We left you downstairs with Bruno, in the hope you and he would start doing something similar, but of course, you chickened out. Typical.'

'I didn't chicken out!' I said, perhaps rather too loudly.

Kim looked over and waved. I waved back.

'I just needed time to think,' I repeated more quietly.

'There's always a reason with you, isn't there?' she said with a shrug.

'You're interfering,' I said crossly.

'Of course I am,' Juliette said happily, 'it's what I do best.'

'Well, stop it.'

'Have you considered that perhaps he's still interested in you?' Juliette murmured.

'Do you really think so?'

Juliette sighed in exasperation. 'Yes, I do, and if you weren't the slowest, most cautious soul on the planet, you'd see it too. I mean look at him, he's lovely. A man like him, on his own. Living out here in the sunshine. It seems a waste.'

I gave her a nudge. 'Oh, shut up!'

'Is that your best argument? You shut up, chicken.'

Bruno was coming up the stairs with Doggie and they were laughing about something, not a care in the world. Was it all coming back to him? Could he remember the things I did?

He stood at the side of the boat, resting his hands on the rail.

He was lovely, there was no denying it, and the more time went by, the more I could see that although he had changed over the years, so had I. He had expanded his horizons and I hadn't. But that was no reason to accept it.

11

Juliette and I collected some more champagne as the boat rounded the corner of the bay. Above us the cliffs were high and craggy with clumps of bushes and stunted trees dotted around, clinging to the thin soil. We could just see a beautiful building towering above us, glowing like a golden castle in the afternoon sunshine.

'What a view they must have,' I said, 'the people who live there. Can't we stay there next time?'

'Have you won the lottery?'

'No.'

'Then you probably can't. Kim's guidebook says that's where Rafa Nadal got married. Look, food!'

There was a table in the middle of the deck under a blue awning, and the staff were setting out platters of seafood surrounded by ice and lemon wedges.

We went to take a closer look. There were only a few other guests with us, and they were already wandering about with loaded plates.

'Isn't this fantastic?' Kim said as she tried a lobster bruschetta, 'it certainly beats life at home. I only seem to cook three things. Shepherd's pie, spaghetti Bolognese and roast chicken occasionally with oven chips if I'm pushing the boat out.'

'Actually, I've been trying some new recipes recently,' Juliette said, 'things that don't involve mince. Or chicken. Or pasta.'

'What does that leave then?' Kim said, the last of the bruschetta halfway to her mouth.

'Duck,' I said.

Suddenly half a baguette hit Kim squarely on the back of her head, knocking her yellow hat and her sunglasses off. She turned to see Vince grinning cheerfully at her.

I shrugged and looked apologetic. 'I told you to duck.'

'Aren't you a bit old for a food fight?' Kim shouted at him. 'And you'd better not have broken my sunglasses. They are genuine Ray-Bans. They were nine euros in a shop by the harbour.'

Vince and Doggie pushed at each other like a pair of naughty schoolboys and chuckled.

'Perhaps taking off that cravat was a bad idea?' I said. 'It's unleashed his inner child.'

'I'll give him bad idea,' Kim muttered, but she was smiling. 'Just you wait.'

'Oh, come on, he's just like a boy in the playground, trying to get your attention,' I said, laughing, 'just ignore him.'

'Don't you remember? Ignoring them makes them try harder,' Juliette said. 'When I was at university, Gary stuck a wad of chewing gum in my hair at a disco. What with that and the hairspray, it hardened into a rock. We had a massive row.'

'And you still married him, so it worked,' I said.

Juliette harrumphed for a bit.

Gradually the boat slowed, and we passed over clear blue and green water, turning so the crew could drop the anchor.

On shore we could see a small café, surrounded by racks of

racing bikes. There were a lot of gel trousers and Lycra outfits on display and even from where we were we could hear their odd cycling shoes clattering on the stone slabs of the dock.

'Those shoes clip on to the pedals,' Sophia said thoughtfully, 'I bet that's dangerous when they fall over. I mean, you couldn't leap for safety, could you? At the very least you'd get a broken ankle or a crack on the knee.'

'Now look, Bruno is coming over. Talk to him, the bride commands it,' Juliette said, with an imperious air, waving a lobster claw at me.

'Oh, sod the bride.'

'Well, that's nice.'

Juliette drifted off to find more food and sat down at a seat overlooking the beach café. Almost immediately Johnny appeared, a large Scotch in his hand.

'I say, I think I just saw some red kites over the sea,' he boomed.

'We used to love those when I was little,' Juliette replied innocently, putting her hands around her throat, 'but the strings used to get tangled up. One time my cousin nearly garrotted me.'

Johnny looked troubled, his brow creasing up in confusion. 'Not that sort – ah, you're making a joke. Hahaha!'

A flock of small birds, startled by the noise, took flight, wheeling above us.

'Polly is a lovely lady, but she does suffer from hearing loss,' Bruno muttered in my ear. 'Perhaps that's the secret of their success?'

'He seems really nice, actually,' I said firmly, ignoring what I had already wondered, 'and I think you're being unkind.'

'No, just truthful,' Bruno said mildly. 'Have you tried those prawns? They are very good. I know you like them. I could get you some if you like?'

How intimate we had once been. Finishing each other's sentences. Laughing at the same jokes. A deep recognition of the other person, as though we had been made for each other.

We had been such a close couple that we had been regarded by our friends as unbreakable. None of the others ever flirted with either of us. We were just Bruno and Denny, which eventually had been shortened into 'Benny', a sort of generic name for both of us. I'd forgotten about that. And then, things had changed.

I shouldn't have said what I had, I thought, remembering a day long ago when everything had been right and then suddenly wrong. I shouldn't have said that.

Suddenly, the gentle rocking of the boat, the warm sunshine on my shoulders reminded me of a day when Bruno and I had taken a boat out on the lake in the park near the university. We had paused in the middle, when rowing became too much of an effort and I was complaining of a blister.

Bruno had hauled up a bottle of white wine from the cold water, where he had tied it before we set off, and we had shared it, thrilled with each other. And then somehow in the time when we had been kissing each other, lying together in the bottom of the boat on some damp canvas, I had lost my oar over the side and it had floated away, out of reach. Even that had seemed funny to us, marooned in the middle of the lake while the afternoon darkened into a warm evening. We had tried to scull with just one oar without success, just turning in circles, getting nowhere. Laughing hysterically. Eventually the lad from the boat house had come to rescue us, bad tempered and grim mouthed. I suppose we had just been the latest in a long line of students who had been foolish and wasted his time, delayed his return home, probably to an irritated girlfriend or a clucking mother.

The potency of that memory was almost visceral. There was a

terrible symbolism there, as though Bruno had been the oar that had floated away, leaving me stranded in the middle of dark water as the mosquitos nipped at my legs. But I had been the one who dropped it, hadn't I?

Bruno was standing a few steps away with Doggie, who was talking about cholesterol and wondering whether his wife would approve of the food he was eating, not to mention the amount of alcohol he was getting through.

'I really should phone her and tell her where I am,' he said, 'but I just can't pluck up the courage. She'll be furious.'

'Furious about what?' I asked, shamelessly earwigging.

Doggie looked embarrassed. 'Oh, nothing, really.' And then he took a deep breath. 'Look, you see, Johnny and I have known each other for ages, since we were boy scouts together. He was always more successful than I was, he was patrol leader. We were in Great Tit Patrol, which caused a lot of hilarity as you can imagine. And then he got better exam results than I did, I got into middle management, where I've stayed ever since, and he ended up a director. But we've always been great mates, you know? But Lorna didn't like him and when this holiday came up, she said I couldn't possibly go. That she needed me at home because she was thinking of taking the curtains down in the spare room and redecorating, which was news to me because once the curtains go up with Lorna, they stay up.

'And I said, can't we leave it for a week or so? It wouldn't hurt. And then she complained I never did anything with her; that I wasn't interested in whether we should choose Fantasy Green or Powdered Leaf for the walls. And I said I did but... anyway, she was going to stay with her sister for a couple of days in Maidenhead, Yvonne had just had a hip replacement, and while Lorna was away... well, I was sitting in the kitchen, and it was raining, so I couldn't even get out into the garden. Lorna had left me a list of things to do before she got back. I'd just had my cereal, and every-thing just seemed so dull and dreary. So I just packed a bag, found my passport, and left. I didn't even rinse my dish and put it in the dishwasher, that's how mad I was.'

He stopped, looking out over the sea with haunted eyes. 'I expect it's still there. On the kitchen table. With a few Bran Flakes in the bottom. I mean, why can't I have Crunchy Nut Cornflakes just occasionally?'

'I'm sure she will be okay, when you explain?' I said.

Doggie shook his head. 'No, she won't. I didn't even leave a note. And normally we do that, leave little notes for each other. She tells me to empty the recycling boxes and I tell her where I'm going and when I'll be back. She's got that *find my friends* app on her phone, so she usually knows where I am anyway. But I've turned it off. She won't have a clue. But I bet she will guess. I just wanted a bit of fun for a change. Some colour. Some laughs. And Johnny said he'd make things right with her when we got back. Say he's kidnapped me or something. She'll never swallow that. Perhaps I should ring her?'

Doggie passed one hand over his eyes and sighed.

Bruno clapped him on the shoulder. 'Look, you're here now. Just enjoy yourself for once.'

'I know you're right. It's just that the longer we are apart, the more I realise I'm enjoying myself. And that makes me feel terri-ble. We've been married for twenty-eight years. Once I'd retired, I couldn't even go to Sainsbury's on my own. But all the same, in a way I do miss her. I wonder what she's doing.'

He shuffled off back to the bar and twisted the cap off a bottle of lager, downing it with some enthusiasm as he fiddled with his phone. Perhaps he was ringing his terrifying wife to confess where he was.

I went to sit down on the other side of the boat and stared out to sea. There was an island there, with perhaps a few houses. The curve of the bay held others, sleek and modern with huge glass windows to make the most of the incomparable view. I wondered who lived there. How they spent their days, lazing in the sunshine, perhaps with staff to deal with the day-to-day problems of preparing food and cleaning leaves out of the pool.

Sophia came to sit next to me.

'So how are you, Denny?'

'Oh, fine, well... yes, absolutely fine.'

'I bet you're not,' she said with a small laugh. 'I know how I was when Lucien came back into my life unexpectedly. It was like a stone had landed on my chest, pressing all the happiness out of me. I can still remember it.'

'But you had Theo.'

'Yes, I did. I had Theo. And he made everything better somehow. Just by being there.'

'You don't think you just went from one relationship to another?'

She shook her head and her silver hair shone in the sunlight.

'It wasn't like that. I had changed. I could see how I had been behaving badly and pretending it was somehow different for me. I didn't need Lucien, I didn't actually need Theo, although he was of course a massive bonus; I didn't need anyone. I just needed to rethink my life and believe in myself. Stop waiting for someone else to tell me what to do. And Theo was a part of that, not the whole of it.'

'Perhaps that's what I need.'

'Every time Bruno comes near you, I can almost feel the waves of panic,' she said, 'which makes me think you care more than you are admitting.'

I sighed. 'I'm sixty, Sophia. Aren't I too old for all this sort of thing?'

She laughed. 'What sort of thing? Love? Friendship? No one is ever too old for that, don't you think? I certainly wasn't.'

'I don't know what I think. I certainly don't know what he thinks. And please don't tell me to ask him. Going through his rejection a second time, messing it up again would be awful. Yes, he was everything to me, once. But I've learned to live without him in my life.'

That much was true, but then I wondered, what would it be like to just take the opportunity and let him back in?

Sophia tilted her head to one side. 'Then perhaps you need to learn to live with him again. And have you even considered that he might want you back in his life?'

'We are only here for ten days; they are here for a week. I live in England; he lives over here. I'm not as young as I was, not as slim, not as resilient. And how could I overcome all those years of forgetting?'

Sophia patted my hand. 'You'll find a way if you want to. When you really love someone, age, distance, weight, they are just numbers.'

Was she right? Did I want to?

I imagined standing up and walking across the boat deck to where Bruno stood, a champagne glass in one hand, the other on the metal rail. I imagined putting my arms around him, kissing him, as Doggie spluttered with embarrassment by his side. Of course I wouldn't do that.

But if I did, I knew exactly how he would feel. His warm back under my hands, the light drift of his aftershave, perhaps. The rub of his stubble on my face. The scent of his skin.

I felt quite giddy for a moment. Perhaps I'd had enough champagne, maybe I needed a drink of water.

* * *

Juliette, always the exhibitionist, was the first to jump off the back of the boat. She had changed into a leopard-print tankini and an unflattering rubber swimming cap to protect her hair and came up out of the water screaming.

'It's a shock when you first get in, but lovely when you get used to it,' she puffed as she swam around for a few minutes. 'Come on, everyone in.'

Everyone went and changed in the spaces allocated in the lower deck and we came back to find Vince, Bruno and Johnny already in the water, shouting and splashing. It's a lot easier for men, of course, they can wear swimming trunks under their shorts. While we had to struggle into tight garments, tucking in flab and wondering if the whole garment had shrunk since we last put it on.

Doggie had cheered up and, chunky and resplendent in Union Jack trunks, was creeping unwillingly down the metal steps, with a great deal of oooh-ing as the water level crept up his legs. Johnny put a stop to this by grabbing his ankle and pulling him in. He gave a theatrical scream and came up to the surface blowing like a whale, his comb-over flopping over one eye.

'Not too bad really,' he said unconvincingly. 'Come on, ladies, take the plunge!'

Sophia went in next and for a few minutes they sculled around in the water, while Johnny yelped and splashed everyone. I wondered if it was hard for someone so noisy to go birdwatching where stealth and patience were required. Perhaps he was just letting off steam?

'Not going in?' Bruno called up. He was in the sea, hanging on to the sides of the metal steps and looking up at me. His wet hair was slicked back from his face, and at that moment he didn't seem a day older than when we had been at university.

'In a minute,' I said.

I had a towel wrapped around my shoulders and I was suddenly reluctant to drop it. He had known me in my early twenties when I had been fit and in reasonable shape. But time had changed all that. I had saggy bits, some extra weight around my middle, nothing was as firm as it had once been. I used to be a 34C. Now, without the support of a proper bra, I was probably a 36 Long.

He pulled himself up the steps, I could smell the scent from the clear seawater on him as he passed me.

'It's really quite warm,' he said.

'It doesn't look it,' I said, still hesitating.

'Only one way to find out,' he said with a grin.

'Don't you dare!'

In one smooth motion, he had whipped the towel off my shoulders and pushed me in.

My first thought was how undignified my fall must have looked. The second was that everyone had been lying. After hours under a hot sun, the water was freezing, the shock of it like a slap in the face. I surfaced, screaming.

'You rotten lot!'

'Too late now,' Johnny hollered, 'you're in now.'

He swam away doing a stiff crawl stroke, while Doggie, true to his nickname, did an ungainly doggy paddle.

Sophia and the others were sculling around, shouting at Juliette because she couldn't hear properly with her swimming cap on.

I lay back and relaxed into the water. I was a good swimmer, and actually, now I was getting used to it, it was quite refreshing. I turned round to look for Bruno, but then I realised he was still on the boat, taking pictures of us on his phone. Flipping cheek! I swam away so he couldn't see me.

The peace was blissful. Perhaps it wasn't as cold as I had

thought. The sky above me was blue and cloudless, an occasional sea bird gliding lazily up into the thermals of warm air. And a thought came to me. I might not be as trim as I had been, I might be older and greyer, but I felt suddenly alive.

I was aware of myself, and of the world. I needed to stop thinking about not being at work and start enjoying myself in the here and now. And I could. Because I was having fun. The brightness of the day and the positive energy of my friends who were splashing and shrieking at each other were both things that brought me the joy I had been looking for.

I didn't have family problems like Kim. I didn't have health issues or too many financial issues, although occasionally I worried about the future. I did have good friends and possibilities, opportunities that only I could take.

Perhaps I hadn't figured out everything as I had assumed I had. Maybe a lot of the things I had regretted, or been irritated by, didn't actually matter any more.

I opened my eyes and saw Bruno had followed me around the boat and was standing above me, leaning his arms on the rail. He waved at me. I kicked my feet in the water and splashed him and he moved back a little and grinned.

12

The following day was one of the market days in the little town and Juliette and Kim were very excited at the prospect. We were determined not to have another late morning and miss it. Juliette set an alarm on her phone and at eight-thirty banged on everyone's bedroom door, shouting, 'Bring out your dead!'

We walked through the narrow streets, hearing the faint sounds of music, to a beautiful old church framed by palm trees, and a large market square in front of it where tables under canvas were being set up.

There were dozens of stalls already doing a brisk trade, people wandering around with baskets laden with fruit and vegetables. Racks of towels and bedlinen, cotton throws and cushion covers. Tablecloths, shirts, and unusually frilly dresses which caught Juliette's eye almost immediately. She never could resist a ruffle. We left her trying things on and continued, marvelling at the beauty of the flower stalls, and wondering whether, if we bought some of the lovely local pottery, it would survive the journey home.

All of the surrounding cafés were open to take advantage of

the crowds, the tables and chairs set out invitingly under the shade of parasols and awnings. After a while we stopped for more coffee and some apricot *cocas*, which were small, very delicious sponge cakes. Around us people browsed the goods on display, men stood guarding shopping bags and smoking, children ran in and out under the canvas shades, it was all very enjoyable.

'Do you know Doggie hasn't told his wife he's here?' I said after a while. 'She told him he couldn't come, and he wanted to, so in the end he just left without telling her.'

'Why couldn't he come?' Juliette asked, confused. 'Is he wanted by Interpol?'

'Lorna wanted to decorate the spare room,' I said, 'he was talking about it yesterday on the boat.'

'Poor old Doggie,' Kim said, 'I heard that too. Vince says Lorna is scary. He went to drop in on them one day and she wouldn't let him in. She said Doggie was out, but Vince saw his car on the driveway, so he wasn't sure it was true.'

'Good heavens. If I told Matthew he couldn't go to all his regimental dinners, he would think I'd lost my mind,' Juliette said, 'anyway, I'm sure he must be exaggerating.'

'I'm going to buy some of that fantastic-looking lamb,' Sophia said, 'and make us some Souvlaki this evening. I can marinade it all afternoon when we get back, olive oil, lemon juice and herbs. We can eat it with pita bread and salad. Johnny says they are planning a games evening later on, and they want us to join in.'

'Perfect,' Juliette said, 'I can't wait.'

'Me too,' I said.

'I thought you said you might go out with Bruno this evening?' Kim said. 'For a second first date?'

'It's an excellent idea,' Juliette said firmly. 'If you won't go now, I insist you go after the birdwatchers go home. After all, Bruno won't be far away. As long as you tell us all the saucy details afterwards.'

After we finished our coffee, we carried on browsing around the market, Sophia buying some lamb and a bag full of fruit and vegetables, Juliette haggling over some colourful cotton throws.

Kim and I went to sit on a nearby bench in the shade. The sun was high overhead then, and the day was heating up. She was rather fidgety and nervous.

'I've got a confession, a secret,' she said at last, 'and I'm hopeless at keeping secrets. I really want to tell someone about it. And I know if I tell Juliette, it would be like telling Reuters.'

'Go on,' I said, intrigued.

'Vince has asked me if I'd like to meet up when we get home,' she said at last.

I looked at her in astonishment.

'Really? I thought his cravats had put you off?' I said.

'He's promised to stop wearing them,' Kim said, blushing, 'after I told him I didn't think they suited him. What do you think?'

'I don't like cravats either,' I said.

Kim shook her head. 'No, I didn't mean *that*. I meant what should I do about meeting up with him? Should I say yes? He only lives thirty miles away from me.'

'Give it a try,' I said, 'if you like him.'

Kim ducked her head and fiddled with her watch.

'I do rather. I didn't at first but the more I get to know him, the more I like him. I mean, he isn't particularly exciting or handsome, but he's very kind. And so thoughtful. He offered me his jumper on the boat when it was getting a bit chilly. And he always pours my wine first. And that sort of thing means a lot. Don't you think?'

'Yes, I suppose it does. Well, this is a bit of a turn-up for the books. Perhaps Juliette's matchmaking skills really do work.'

Kim turned towards me, her face earnest. 'Oh, golly, I'm not thinking of anything more than meeting up and having a drink. Not dating or anything. Just a bit of a chat. Although he did kiss me.'

'*What*? When? You kept that quiet!'

Kim blushed. 'We were downstairs on the boat. I'd gone to find one of the changing rooms to get dressed after we'd been swimming, and he was coming up the steps. And we sort of shuffled around each other for a bit and both started laughing. And he said after you and I said no, after you and he just – well. Pecked me on the lips. It was really lovely. He's been divorced for years. His wife went off with their builder. He was installing an en suite. With a power shower. And Vince wondered why it was taking so long. The builder said ten days and he was there for nearly a month. And in the end, Vince only got to use that shower once, which was a shame because he said it was really good too. And then he moved out because the builder came back to do some grouting.'

'That's a new name for it,' I said.

Kim gave a little laugh. 'Vince went to live with his mother, who was quite infirm, so in a way it worked out. And after she died a couple of years later, and he was divorced, he inherited her house and he stayed on. He used to be a biology teacher at the polytechnic. Well, it's called a university now. So he's quite clever.'

I thought of Vince. Tall, thinning hair, rather thick glasses but a kind face all the same. He must have been over sixty-five if he was retired. How old was Kim? Perhaps early sixties. Funny how life turned out sometimes.

Kim was looking at me, waiting for my response.

I nodded enthusiastically. 'Go for it. Find out if you really get on.'

Kim snorted. 'Listen to the oracle. What about you doing the same thing? And I'm going to. Just to see. Though what Simon and Gemma would say I don't know.'

'They'll get over it, I'm sure, if they see you are happy.'

'Well, perhaps we are getting a bit ahead of ourselves. It's only a drink,' Kim said, but her eyes were shining in a way they hadn't before. 'I feel better now I've told you. But don't tell the others? Not just yet?'

'I won't. Oh look, they are back.'

We watched as the familiar figures of the nuns walked around the square, chatting to the stallholders and rattling their collection tins.

'They are very determined, you have to admire that,' I said.

* * *

After about an hour, we decided we had bought everything we wanted to buy, and I don't think we could have carried much more. As we were leaving the square, we saw Vince, Doggie and Johnny coming towards us, and they looked rather glum.

Vince rushed forwards towards Kim.

'Let me help you with those bags.'

They did a bit of good-natured arguing about whether Kim needed help or not, and eventually Vince took the heaviest ones, and they started walking back together towards the villa with Sophia, who said she needed to start marinading the lamb for the evening meal.

Juliette frowned at Johnny.

'What's going on?'

'How do you mean?' Johnny said evasively.

'Why is Doggie skulking behind that tree, for a start?' I said.

The others looked around. Doggie was indeed trying to hide, rather unsuccessfully as the tree was only a small one and the brim of his baseball cap was sticking out one side, and his red shorts to the other.

'I'm not hiding,' he called, 'I'm just avoiding someone.'

'Who?' Kim said. 'We are the only people you know here.'

'At the moment,' Johnny said with a sigh. He removed his sun hat and wiped his brow with a handkerchief. 'I'm afraid it seems Doggie has been rumbled.'

'Who by? Have the police put out an alert?' Juliette said, with a snort of laughter. 'Interpol really are after him?'

'Worse than that,' Doggie said from behind his tree.

The penny dropped. 'Not Lorna?' I asked.

Doggie peered out and nodded. 'When I turned my phone on the other day, she saw where I was because of the app. And there were a lot of messages from her, asking what I was playing at. And then apparently when I didn't reply, she phoned Polly, pretending there had been a family emergency, and Polly told her exactly where we were.'

'In her defence, Polly didn't know all the facts,' Johnny said. 'I mean, none of us knew you came without telling her until you got here. You didn't even leave her a note.'

'She would have stopped me,' Doggie said, 'and now I'm really in for trouble when I get back.'

'Why? Surely not. And what on earth for? You will only have been away for a week.'

'I don't really know,' Doggie said, looking haunted, 'but whatever happens, it won't be good.'

We discussed the situation for a few minutes, and then made our way back to the villa, where Sophia was already hard at work in the kitchen squeezing lemon juice into a bowl and mixing it with oil and herbs.

We dumped our shopping on to the sofa and Juliette kicked off her shoes.

'Can I do anything to help?' I said.

'I'm nearly done, this only takes a few minutes,' Sophia said.

Juliette came over to see what we were doing. 'Let's have a swim to cool down. I'm going up to get changed. I'm sure it can't be as bad as Doggie says. And Lorna wouldn't be that ridiculous, would she?'

'What's happened now?' Sophia said.

We explained the situation to her.

'I don't understand why she would want to stop him coming in the first place,' she said.

'Apparently she's alienated most of his friends over the years, she gets very angry if she feels he is enjoying himself without her,' Kim explained.

'Narcissism,' Juliette called down from halfway up the stairs, 'that's what it sounds like to me. I was reading about it only recently. Gary used to make passes at my girlfriends and insult their husbands. It's usually a husband, controlling his wife. But women like Lorna can do it too. It's a sign of insecurity.'

We thought about this for a while and then Kim opened a bottle of wine, and we sat out on the patio, wondering what we could do to help. If anything. There was no noise from the villa next door. Perhaps Doggie was hiding upstairs?

'Poor Doggie,' I said at last, 'he wouldn't hurt a fly. And he's such a nice person too. But that would explain why he kept on about enjoying the moment, not thinking about going home.'

'Still, he should have left a note,' Kim said, 'otherwise Lorna might have thought he'd had an accident or something.'

'I feel quite sad for him,' I said, 'putting up with that for years. Perhaps he just didn't have the nerve to tell her.'

We sat in silence for a while and then Juliette came outside in another new tankini – polka dots this time – and got into the pool. She looked at us, our glum faces, and swept an armful of water over us.

'Come on, you lot, come in. The water's really warm.'

* * *

As the afternoon rolled on, we had an enjoyable swim, drank some more wine, and then set the table outside on the patio and enjoyed the delicious Souvlaki Sophia had made for us. There was another huge bowl of salad, some fresh and fluffy pita breads and a bowl of hot sauce which apparently Theo liked to have with them.

'You open up the pita bread, and stuff it with some lamb, some of that tomato and onion salad and some tzatziki,' Sophia said, 'and then just get stuck in.'

'This is delicious,' I said after one mouthful. 'When I get back, I'm going to try cooking some more interesting things. I haven't really bothered for ages.'

'So you and Theo,' Juliette said after a while. 'Are you going to marry him?'

'I might. I'm just happy the way things are. I don't need to change anything.'

'I'd like to get married again,' Kim said, 'despite the things I said the other day. I used to like being married. I just didn't like who I was married to.'

'Perhaps you will,' I said.

Kim shot me a warning look.

'Anyway, what about this games evening we are invited to next door?' I said, changing the subject.

'I thought you didn't want to go? You were going on and on about the Monopoly we played when we were kids. How much you hated it,' Juliette said, fishing about in the salad bowl for some leftover cherry tomatoes.

'Perhaps they are all hiding next door, with the curtains closed and the lights off?' Kim said.

Juliette flapped a hand. 'Oh, please. We are all a bit old for that, aren't we? Although I did that a lot in the early days after Gary and I separated. There was always someone banging on my door. Once it was the debt collectors who came to repossess my car because Gary had stopped the payments.'

Kim's eyes widened. 'What did you do?'

'I sweet talked them into giving me more time and then I sold Gary's collection of vintage Dinky toys and old boyhood comics. He was quite a hoarder, actually, although he was always very keen for me to get rid of my stuff. When he found out, he was furious. Most of them were in boxes in the attic, and he thought I didn't know about them. But there was nothing he could do because he hadn't declared them during our divorce, on the financial statements, as an asset. They were worth hundreds. I loved that car.'

'Well, I think we are finished here, don't you? Let's clear up and someone can go and knock on their door to see if they still want us round there,' Juliette said, 'perhaps Kim this time. Seeing how Vince has such a crush on her.'

'He hasn't!' Kim said, rather flushed.

The others laughed. 'Of course he has!' I said. 'He's been trailing around after you since we got here.'

'Well, I can't help that,' Kim said, 'but I'll go. I'm not bothered.'

Kim went through the gate between the gardens and knocked on the patio doors while the rest of us cleared up. After a few minutes, she came back.

'They actually do have all the curtains closed, and they are watching football on the television with the sound turned down. I think Doggie is drinking whisky. He looks a bit slumped.'

'Come on, girls,' Juliette said, 'let's go and cheer them up.'

13

We picked up a couple of bottles of wine and some salted almonds which Kim said Vince really liked and made our way through the gate to the next-door villa. It was, indeed, eerily quiet over there and the curtains were closed.

Inside it was dark, the room lit only by the light from the silent television screen. I would have thought watching football without any commentary was worse than with one, but what would I know.

Vince and Johnny were watching the screen intently, Bruno was reading on an iPad, and Doggie was, as Kim had said, slumped over, still clutching a tumbler of what we assumed was whisky.

He straightened up as we came in, and everyone blinked as Juliette pushed the curtains open, letting the early evening light stream into the room.

'What on earth are you doing?' she said. 'Why aren't you outside in the sunshine? This place smells like a distillery.'

'I'm worrying, and I'm lying low,' Doggie said.

'We are watching football,' Vince added.

'I'm waiting for everyone to come to their senses,' Bruno said.

'Come on, we have drinks and snacks, and we were promised a game of some sort,' I said. 'Much against my better judgement, I'm going to join in.'

'Fair enough,' Johnny said, 'it's nil-nil anyway and only five minutes to go.'

'Hardly worth watching then. They got their kit dirty for nothing,' I said.

'Yes, but they don't *know* it's going to be nil-nil when they start, do they?' Vince said earnestly.

'It's okay, Vince, nothing you can say will convince me it's a game worth watching.'

'I'll bet you my car keys you'd watch if England got to the World Cup final again,' he said.

I raised my eyebrows and gave him a look. 'When that happens, just bring it round and leave it on the drive.'

Vince rolled his eyes and nudged Doggie. 'Come on, Dog. Shape up a bit. Ladies present.'

We decided to go outside where there was more space, and they made a half-hearted attempt to clear up the table which was covered with glasses, beer bottles and an ashtray with cigar stumps in it. Then Johnny brought the game out and set the board up.

'Girls versus boys, I think. You have to draw and act and describe, depending on where you land,' he said. 'Polly and I play this a lot with her nephews. They love it when I draw. I had to draw *Pawn Shop* once, and I don't think anyone's ever forgotten it.'

Juliette drew the first card. 'How the hell am I expected to draw that? Can I change it for a different one?'

Johnny chuckled. 'Not a chance, you've got sixty seconds, starting now!'

Juliette did a few half-hearted pencil strokes and we tried vainly to decipher what she was drawing.

'Box. Square box. Tea leaves. Spoon. Dragon. Dragon scales. Hedgehog. Mouse.'

'It was a tortoise,' Juliette said at last when the timer ran out, 'isn't it obvious? Look at the arrows. The word was tortoiseshell. My godmother had a tortoiseshell tea caddy.'

'Well, we didn't know that,' I said. 'Come on, Johnny, your turn.'

We watched Johnny draw a kilted Scotsman and then a paddock with a fence all around it.

'Jimmy Crankie... field... Kenneth McKellar in a field... Billy Connolly at the races... farm... fences... grass...'

'You're hopeless, you lot. Scotland Yard, obviously,' Johnny said at last.

My turn.

I did quite well with New Moon, and then the game picked up speed with a lot of yelling and exasperation.

Then we got on to the speaking part, and Vince had to describe *guided missile*, which he did with a lot of sweeping about with one arm out in front of him accompanied by explosion noises.

We were all rather enjoying it, and there was a lot of laughter and shouting, just as though some kids were playing. The wine seemed to be going down quite well too.

Both teams eventually got on to the third section which was acting, when no speaking was allowed, and it fell to Doggie to act something.

He insisted he needed an extra few seconds to prepare and went out into the house where he stuffed a rucksack under his shirt and taped a white paper plate on top of his head before returning. His teammates were in hysterics.

'What on earth... fat... very fat person... shooting a bow and arrow... *The Archers*... Tony Archer... is he big?'

'He's eating now...'

'Come on, Doggie, give us a clue... eating bald man... bald archer...'

We Old Ducks, whether it was the wine or the sight of Doggie pretending to climb a tree and eat a chicken leg at the same time, were roaring with laughter.

'Time's up,' Sophia shouted, wiping the tears of hilarity from her face.

Then suddenly everyone stopped except for Doggie, who was facing the other way, still trying gamely to keep his rucksack in place, pretend to climb one of the palm trees in their garden and shoot a bow and arrow.

'Isn't it obvious,' he panted.

'It's obvious to me you've lost your mind,' someone said.

We turned to see a small, furious-looking woman standing clutching a holdall with her raincoat over one arm, having just walked around to the back of the villa. Someone must have left the gate unlocked.

She dumped her bag on the ground, and smoothed her brown dress, which was woolly and must have been rather hot.

'Oh,' Doggie squeaked, rather breathlessly, 'hello, Lorna.'

* * *

Everyone was suddenly very quiet, except for the sound of Doggie's heaving breaths, and Kim's nervous giggle.

'Lorna. What a nice surprise. We weren't expecting you. Would you like a glass of wine?' Johnny said, trying to sound welcoming.

'I'm afraid Doggie's not here,' Vince said, 'like he wasn't there that day I called in at your house.'

Lorna fixed him with a glare. 'Don't be ridiculous. I've been travelling all day. First I had to persuade Jillian to take me to the airport, so heaven knows when I will hear the end of that, and then on a horrible plane to Palma, then a taxi here with a man who stank of garlic, to find out what the hell is going on. It's taken me hours.'

'Well, your choice, no one asked you to come,' Kim murmured.

'Who are these – *people*,' Lorna said, fixing her with a frosty glare. 'I thought this was John's stag do. Not some sort of bacchanalian party.'

'Gosh, that's a big word,' Kim snorted.

Juliette giggled and dug her in the ribs and Kim put a hand over her mouth.

'Why are there women here? Who are they? I blame you, John. You always were a bad influence. All that nonsense about birdwatching. They don't look like birds to me, more like old boilers.'

'Blooming cheek,' Juliette said, finishing her wine and topping up her glass.

'There's no need for this,' Doggie said, 'it's just a game we are playing. A bit of fun.'

'A bit of fun? I was never more disappointed in you,' Lorna said, drawing herself up to her full height, which wasn't much, 'and you should be thoroughly ashamed of yourself.'

'Oh, he must have felt worse than this at some point,' Johnny said reasonably, 'after all, he didn't get his Queen's Scouting Award, did he? Or his chemistry O level. He was the only one in the class to fail, he had to do a re-sit.'

'John, would you be quiet,' Lorna snapped, 'you're giving me a headache. And Douglas, take that ridiculous plate off your head. You look half-witted.'

Doggie obediently pulled at the tape attaching the paper plate to the top of his head, but it had caught up in his comb-over and he looked despairingly at us.

Kim stood up and went to help, pulling gently at the tape.

'You really shouldn't have used Duct Tape,' she said. 'I hope I'm not hurting you?'

'No, not at all, you're very kind,' Doggie whispered.

'Take your hands off my husband. Who is this woman? I know what I *think* she is. Someone who needs to lose a few pounds or buy a bigger top.'

Kim looked down to see the buttons on her shirt had popped open; something they did quite often.

'Oh dear,' she said, 'they're always doing that.'

'Yes, I expect they are,' Lorna said waspishly, with a look.

Vince bristled and sprang into the arena to defend Kim, walking over to stand beside her chair.

'Here, I say, there's no need for that. No need for rudeness. This lady is a very good friend of mine.'

Kim gave him a pleased smile.

Lorna ignored them both. 'Douglas, I want to talk to you. I want to find out why you are here and who these people are. Polly said John texted something about kidnapping my husband, and I wasn't sure if she was joking or not. I did think about ringing the police, but what use would they be? John was always one to lead you into trouble, but this time he has outdone himself.'

'Hashtag very proud,' Johnny mumbled into his wine glass.

The rucksack fell out from under Doggie's sweater onto the ground with a clunk.

'I hope that's not your camera,' Bruno said.

'No, just a book,' Doggie gulped, 'and a water bottle.'

He took a step towards it and stumbled on a loose shoelace. Sophia went to pick the bag up for him and he clutched it to his chest like a security blanket.

'Douglas, I think you're drunk,' Lorna said.

'To be honest, Lorna, I think we all are in the *breathalyser* sense of the word,' Johnny replied, 'but not in the falling over, dropping our trousers, getting arrested kind of way.'

'You can leave that bit of it to me,' Juliette said proudly. 'I've had my collar felt.'

Lorna gave a gasp of horror. 'A bunch of grown men, behaving like this. Sneaking out, messing around with some random women, drinking...'

'Having fun, actually,' Doggie said heatedly, much to everyone's surprise, 'more fun than I've had in years. I told you I wanted to come along, and you wouldn't even discuss it. You just invented some story about wanting to paint the spare room. When we both know it was only done last year when your sister came to stay. Mushroom Dream, I believe, or more accurately beige, and light proof curtains from Dunelm. Which only reinforced my view that your sister really is an old bat. So, you see, I do take notice.'

'Go Doggie,' Vince muttered admiringly.

'You're talking nonsense,' Lorna said, 'you're obviously upset. Now then, it's too late to find a hotel, where am I sleeping?'

Bruno pulled out his mobile phone. 'I have a friend in the town nearby, with a B&B, I can ring him. I'm sure he will be able to accommodate you.'

'Right. So it seems I'm not welcome to stay here? Not after nearly thirty years of marriage? That's charming. Well. Come on, Douglas, let's get your things together.'

'No,' Doggie said very firmly. We all gasped and looked at

him. He swallowed noisily and carried on. 'We have a trip to the reserve booked for tomorrow morning, there are hoopoes there.'

'I don't know what's got into you. Hoopoes,' Lorna scoffed, 'as though that matters.'

'But I've been wanting to see them for years,' Doggie said, casting a nervous glance over at his friends.

'Lots of nice, fat caterpillars for them this year, apparently,' Johnny said, 'yum yum.'

'Did you know they are called hoopoes because of their call? Poo-poo-poo. Poo-poo-poo,' Vince added helpfully, giving a lilting trill.

'What?' Lorna said.

Vince obliged. 'Poo-poo—'

I quietly interrupted him. 'She heard you, Vince, she's just giving you a chance to say something different.'

'Poo-poo-poo,' Vince repeated slowly.

'Don't be disgusting,' Lorna said, her nostrils flaring.

Kim turned her face into Vince's arm and snorted with laughter. I noticed he moved his hand and squeezed her shoulder.

'And we haven't got a car and we won't be around either tomorrow because we are taking the bus into Pollença,' I added, 'it's Palm Sunday.'

Lorna turned to Bruno. 'You seem to be the only one here with any common sense, so you'd better drive me to this B&B you mentioned.'

'I couldn't possibly,' Bruno said, 'I've been drinking wine too, but I will call you a taxi. Another friend of mine has a firm in the town, he's only a few minutes away.'

'Well, I think that's more than enough for one day. I feel very stressed. I'll be back in the morning, Douglas. And I hope you will have sobered up by then and be ready to explain yourself,'

Lorna said with a last glare. Then she turned on her heel and stalked out, leaving Bruno to pick up her bag and hurry after her.

Kim blew a raspberry at her retreating back.

* * *

'Ooo, er,' Kim said after a moment, 'she's very cross, isn't she?'

Doggie sighed. 'Usually.'

'But why,' I asked, 'why didn't she want you to come? Surely she trusts you after all the years you've been together. You're only spending a few days here with some friends and birdwatching, after all.'

'But she caught me drinking and laughing,' Doggie added.

'And what's wrong with that?' I asked.

'Lorna only has a small sherry on a Sunday. And then she needs a nap after lunch while I do the washing up. I mean, we have a dishwasher, but Lorna insists I wash everything first because she doesn't trust it.'

'How sad,' Sophia said, 'but well done for standing up to her.'

'Yes, I did, didn't I?' Doggie said, sounding rather surprised.

'You did, me old mucker,' Johnny said, 'that's a turn-up for the books.'

'She'll be in a mood with me tomorrow, though. She'll say I embarrassed her.'

'I think she embarrassed herself,' I said, 'which is far worse to deal with.'

'I suppose I'd better pack the game away now,' Doggie said sadly, 'she's rather wrecked the mood.'

I felt so sorry for him, he looked so despondent. How awful to be in that sort of relationship where everything was criticised, and fun wasn't allowed. Life with Bruno wouldn't be like that, I was sure of it. What had he said, Egypt, Thailand, a road trip around America. Life was to be lived, not just tolerated.

'Doesn't mean we can't still have a nice evening,' Juliette said. 'I think we should get a few snacks, and another bottle of wine, and just chill.'

'By the way, who were you supposed to be,' Sophia asked, 'before Lorna arrived?'

Doggie smoothed the top of his head. 'Friar Tuck. I thought I was quite good, actually; I don't know why you didn't guess it.'

14

We were rather excited about using public transport because none of us often did at home.

'There's one bus a week in my village,' Juliette said, 'which is really not much use to anyone. And the council are talking about getting rid of that because they say hardly anyone uses it. It's ridiculous.'

'Well, according to the information sheet from the tourist information office, the buses here are regular, and the guidebook says they run on time, even on a Sunday,' Kim said, 'which is quite a novelty, I think you'll agree. If it's true.'

We were at the bus station in the middle of town fifteen minutes early, our yellow hats very conspicuous. The place was fairly cheerless, with a couple of concrete bus stands and a full car park on the other side of the road. However, three minutes before the bus to Pollença was due to arrive, several people appeared and joined us. And exactly three minutes later the bus drove up.

'Well, this is promising,' I said, 'and it's clean and air conditioned too.'

We found seats and the bus swung out onto the dual carriageway. We travelled past small villages, industrial estates and through tree-lined gorges, Juliette clutching her bus timetable firmly in one hand as though she didn't trust the driver to know where he was going.

'I haven't been on a bus for years,' she said, 'do you remember the school bus? How awful it was with those vile prickly seats? I was usually trying to do some homework I had forgotten. When I started at the grammar school, I once did some art homework with a pencil and two crayons, which was so bad that the teacher sent a letter home, complaining about my attitude.'

'What did your mother say?'

'She just laughed and used the edge of it to light a cigarette. And then she chucked it away. A few years later and your mother would have given me an ear bashing. She loved telling me off.'

'You were a bit of a pain,' I said, 'you have to admit.'

'And you were a pain too, sneaking around, going through my stuff. Stealing my make-up.'

'I didn't steal it, I borrowed it,' I said. 'I always wanted to be like you. You seemed so grown up, so confident. And when you went off to university, the house was so quiet, it was awful. I couldn't wait for the holidays when you came home.'

'Aw, my little sister. How sweet,' Juliette said, putting her arm around my shoulder and hugging me. 'Then you were the one having all the fun, working in London. While I was stuck in the suburbs with a wailing baby. Still, it all worked out in the end, didn't it? It's not where you start, it's where you finish. And we are far from finished. Agree?'

'Absolutely. Although, looking at us, we must seem like a typical bunch of crazy old ladies, having a nice day out. Especially with these duck hats on,' I said.

'They are a badge of honour,' Juliette said firmly, 'at least we aren't hiding out in the nature reserve like Doggie, terrified of his wife finding him.'

For a moment I imagined Lorna, with a grim expression, picking her way through the marshes in her beige raincoat and stout shoes, calling for her husband and frightening all the hoopoes.

'There might be more to Doggie than meets the eye,' I said. 'After all, he did stand up to her, and I think that surprised him.'

Juliette tapped me on the arm. 'Talking about there being more to things than meets the eye, what's happening with Kim and Vince? Did I imagine it, or is there a certain something going on between those two?'

'I have taken a vow of silence,' I said.

'That'll be a first. Go on, tell me.'

'Not a chance,' I said, 'ask Kim.'

Juliette leaned forward to tap Kim on the shoulder. 'Kim, tell me everything. What's going on with Vince?'

Even from behind, I could tell Kim was blushing.

'We're just friends,' she said, hanging on to the metal pole next to her seat as we swung round a corner.

'If you think you're getting away with that, you are mistaken. The first thing we are going to do is find somewhere for coffee and you must tell us. The Old Ducks don't have such a thing as a vow of silence.'

* * *

We got off the bus and made our way through the pretty, narrow streets, which were mostly pedestrianised, so no problems with traffic interrupting our slow amble towards the town square. There were flowers everywhere. In tubs, window boxes and baskets. A lot of people around, families and groups of teens in ripped jeans and bright colours. So not all dressed in black then, perhaps it was the sunshine that made people feel like dressing more colourfully?

Then in front of us were the famous Calvari steps, leading up towards an ancient pilgrimage chapel.

'Three hundred and sixty-five steps, ladies, one for each day of the year if you fancy the trip?' Sophia said.

'Not with my knee,' Kim said, 'it's playing up a bit today. I thought we were getting coffee?'

We made our way up towards another ancient church which had a pleasant open square in front of it. In honour of it being Palm Sunday, there was a woman sitting outside the church with a trestle table, selling intricate palm crosses in damp plastic bags. There were also market stalls selling jewellery and pottery, and underneath the canopy of white parasols, some cafés were doing a brisk trade. We found an empty table, which was decorated with a pot of red flowers, settled ourselves and ordered coffee and cake, because that's what we did. Juliette pointed to something on the menu and ordered in her best Spanish.

'*Cuatro tortells, por favor.*' Four of something.

'The coffee here is the absolute best,' I said, taking an appreciative sip, 'I wish I could make it like this at home.'

'And look at these cakes!' Kim said, her eyes wide as the waitress returned with a tray.

They looked like ring doughnuts, split and filled with cream.

'This is definitely not one of my five a day,' I said.

'We were born to be real, not perfect,' Juliette said, taking a bite. The cream squidged out and plastered onto the end of her nose.

'I'm far from that,' Kim said.

'We all are. Which reminds me. We need to know about Vince,' Sophia said.

Kim wagged her head from side to side. 'Okay, I like him. He's funny and good company.'

This wasn't nearly enough for her. 'And?'

'And he's asked if we could meet up once we get home. You know, for a drink or something.'

'Start with the drink and work up to the something,' I said.

Kim giggled. 'I'm too old for that, I think we all are.'

'Nonsense, speak for yourself! You're not old, you're a classic,' Juliette said.

'Like a Ford Zephyr,' I added.

'I mean, look at me, getting married in a few months to Matthew who is the nicest man. Anyway, old people are always fifteen years older than we are.'

'But will you say that when you're eighty?' Kim said.

'Yes, because then old people will be ninety-five.'

'But what if we can't do the things we used to?'

I stirred some sugar into my coffee. 'Remember when we were kids, and punishments were going to bed early, not going to someone's party, not going to the zoo? Those have become my goals now. If we don't want to do something, we don't have to. If we do, then we can.'

'I felt all tingly when he kissed me that day on the boat,' Kim said shyly.

'That was your common sense leaving your body, I expect,' Juliette said.

I tapped her on the arm in reproof. 'If you like Vince, take a chance. Go out with him and find out if there's something there.'

'Which brings us neatly back to Bruno,' Juliette said silkily. 'I think we have all seen and heard enough of this nonsense. Let's vote on it. Old Ducks, Denny is dithering. She's wasting time when she should be enjoying herself. She's very good at giving Kim the advice she won't take herself. I vote that by the power vested in me as honorary chair of this society, she should practise what she preaches. All those in favour?'

Everyone put up their hands, including Kim, who was so enthusiastic that her chair tipped backwards, and she barged into a passing waitress. Unfortunately the young woman was balancing a tray of coffee cups on her shoulder and the whole lot went flying. There was a moment's horrified silence and then we all sprang into action, scurrying to pick up pieces of broken china.

Kim offered to pay for the damage and was given a hard look from the owner and the waitress went off, still dripping, to get a replacement order.

We settled back down, Kim pulling her duck hat down over her eyes to hide her embarrassment.

I sighed. 'I'll take my own advice if Kim will.'

I held out a little finger towards Kim and we solemnly shook fingers.

Sophia shook her head. 'How old are you?'

'Still at least fifteen years younger than old people, remember?' Juliette said cheerfully. 'Now, when we have finished, I have seen some beautiful twinkly ornaments, like hair pins, on that stall over there. I think they might be just the thing to wear at my wedding.'

After that we wandered towards the nearby church, where there was a bagpipe and tabor band, leading all the people who had been to the Palm Sunday service, outside and up the Calvari steps. They were all waving palms, some of them five feet long and intricately plaited. When they had gone, we wandered into the church, which was beautiful, decorated with imagery, many candles and amazing stained glass, which threw colour over the walls as the sun shone through.

Then we went back to the market and Juliette bought one of the hair pins she had seen, which was decorated with intricate Moorish patterns in blue and green, Kim bought a lace tablecloth and some enamelled bowls made from coconut shells, and I thought about Bruno.

They were right, of course. Everyone saw things differently from their own perspective. Juliette and Sophia had found love in later life, Anita had repaired the distance between herself and her husband by both of them making an effort. Kim had found someone she was attracted to, despite her years of bitterness and self-doubt. Maybe I shouldn't be the one to turn my back on whatever life had to offer me?

My life could have been so different if I had been braver and had trusted myself. I couldn't let the rest of my life slide past mired in remorse.

All of a sudden, I felt very happy. What had Juliette said that evening? Faint heart never won handsome bloke. And Bruno was handsome. And more than that, he was still the same man I had loved all those years ago. Seeing him still caused my heart to race a little.

I remembered my mother on our shopping expeditions when I was grown up and spending my own money. What had she said? If you go home without that dress or those shoes or whatever, will you regret it? But then she had been an Olympic-standard shopper.

Still, if I did nothing about Bruno, would I regret it?

I started to look through some postcards. Beautiful sunsets and views. The bright blue Mediterranean, framed with pine trees. And there were some funny ones too, meaningful quotes and sayings. I picked one out and stared at it.

Fear is temporary, regret is forever.

I bought it and tucked it away in my handbag.
It was a sign.

* * *

We wandered around the streets, enjoying the sunshine and the relaxed, friendly feel of the place. We had ice cream in little cardboard cups which was sweet and delicious, all of us picking flavours we wouldn't normally have chosen. I had walnut cream, because it sounded so odd, and it was fantastic. The others chose lemon ripple, white chocolate, plum and cinnamon and no one was disappointed.

Then we found a glorious garden, the leaves in the trees unfurling, bright and green in the sunshine, and we sat on a bench to rest our aching feet.

'What a fantastic place,' Sophia said, 'I'm so glad we came.'

We all nodded in agreement.

'I wonder how Doggie is?' Juliette said. 'Do you think he's okay?'

'I hope so, he was quite brave last night, but I expect the alcohol has worn off by now,' I said.

'Come on, let's take a look in that art gallery before we go,' Kim said, standing up, 'we ought to get some culture before we get the bus home. It's free to get in. And more importantly, they might have a loo.'

Inside there was a huge hall, filled with drawings and ink sketches by someone who was apparently a well-respected artist. Several intense-looking people were wandering around with catalogues and pens, ticking things off, and there were rows of empty chairs set out in an enclosed courtyard. Either no one had come, or we had missed all the excitement.

There were also tables with glasses of wine and the battered remains of some canapés. We guessed the artist had been giving people a talk. A charming young man with a wide, white smile offered us wine, but Kim had spotted the cloakrooms and was in no mood to be slowed down. And even we weren't cheeky enough to accept wine for an art exhibition we hadn't been invited to.

After that we felt obliged to look around the art on display.

Amongst all the offerings, there was a drawing of one shoe. A charcoal sketch of the same shoe from a different angle, and a huge white canvas with three black marks in the middle which was drawing a lot of attention. It was €75,000.

Next to me, Juliette sighed. 'There are a lot of things in this world I don't understand, and most of them are in here,' she said. 'I'm not clever enough for this. I'm such a pleb. Let's go and get the bus home and find out what the chaps are doing.'

* * *

Back at our villa, we dumped our shopping and opened the doors to the patio, letting in the late afternoon sunshine.

Next door there was only silence and the gate between our gardens was shut.

The four of us went out and crouched like kids behaving like spies behind the hedge, listening for signs of life.

'Perhaps Lorna has shot them all, and they are lying on the floor in a heap?' Kim whispered. 'We will have to phone the police, and they will cordon it all off as a crime scene and take us in for questioning.'

'I wouldn't mind that,' Juliette muttered, 'I've seen a couple of

Spanish policemen, I wouldn't mind them taking down my particulars.'

We thought about this for a moment.

'Anyway, Lorna wouldn't have been able to bring a gun on the plane,' I hissed back, 'you can't bring any weapons or even a water bottle through security. And she only had hand luggage.'

'Kitchen knives then?' Juliette suggested.

'Don't be daft, how could she overpower that lot? She's only tiny, and she's shorter than I am,' Kim replied.

'Perhaps she immobilised them with one of her Medusa stares?' Sophia suggested.

Kim snorted with laughter. 'Maybe we should only look at her reflection in mirrors from now on?'

I straightened up. 'She must be very unhappy; it must be exhausting being that angry all the time. It's much easier being cheerful, even if you're just pretending.'

There were still no signs of life from the next-door villa, and eventually I went through the gate to peer through the open curtains. There was definitely no one inside, no bodies on the floor, no signs of a struggle. I went back to find the others sitting in the shade with some glasses of iced water.

Kim looked up from her guidebook, and the tattered piece of paper which had been Juliette's hen holiday itinerary.

'I went and looked round the side of the house, and the people carrier is gone. They must be out somewhere. Let's go to Alcudia tomorrow, we were supposed to go the other day and we didn't. We can go on the bus again.'

We all agreed this was a good idea, and Sophia looked out the bus timetables.

'There are modern bits and a medieval walled town,' Juliette said. 'Personally I'm avoiding nightclubs, after the trouble I got into in Rhodes.'

'Very wise, and Hera wouldn't be there to save you this time,' Sophia said.

'Shall we go out to eat this evening? Sophia seems to have been doing all the cooking,' I said. 'I'd like to try that restaurant with the yellow canopies. It's obviously very popular and we've never managed to get a table.'

After a break when everyone freshened up and changed, we walked down the lane to the sea front. The lunchtime trade was over, and the evening was still quiet and not too busy. Above us the lights in the restaurant canopies were beginning to glow in the dusk.

We found a table at the place I had suggested, and a very pleasant waiter came to bring us water. We ordered bread, olives, and the most delicious aioli to get us started.

'It's mostly seafood. But I'm going to have a salad. Which, after all the things I have eaten today, might be a good idea,' Kim said.

'And chips,' Juliette added, 'we don't want to go too mad to start with.'

'There something here called Blind Vegetarian Octopus pizza. What the heck is that?' Kim wondered.

We looked at our menus, rather puzzled.

'Seems a bit mean, cooking a blind octopus,' Kim said.

'No, they are different sorts, you twit,' Juliette said, 'a pre-baked, in other words blind-baked pizza, with either octopus or vegetables on top.'

'Oh, well, anyway, I'm not having that,' Kim said, 'I can't get the image of that poor octopus out of my mind now. Oh look,

Arros Brut, I can get a small one of those. That was what I wanted when we first got here.'

'What's that?' I asked.

'Dirty rice.'

'Dirty?' Juliette said loudly with a laugh. 'How dirty are you thinking?'

The waiter appeared by our table and blinked a bit rapidly. Then recovered his composure.

'Beautiful ladies, how wonderful you are here. What would make you happy this evening?'

We all giggled rather childishly at that point.

'Some bigger trousers,' Kim muttered, pulling at her waistband.

'We will start off with some white wine. And then what would you recommend?' Juliette said, flashing him her brightest smile.

The waiter pulled a thoughtful face. 'We have lobster. I can bring you some to check they are the ones you want?'

'That means he gets them out of the tank, and then we look at them and the elastic bands on their claws, and send them to their doom,' Kim said, leaning forward to whisper, 'I don't think I want to do that. And actually, how can you tell a really good lobster from a half-hearted one? It's not like they come with CVs and references.'

'What about tapas?' I said. 'We can order a load of different things and share them.'

'Wonderful. Wonderful,' the waiter beamed. He pointed at the menu with his pen. 'I will bring you your wine and I will return.'

There were so many different tapas dishes to choose from that it took quite a while for us to decide. *Patatas bravas*, fish and crab croquettes, steamed clams with saffron and pomegranate, calamari with romesco sauce, and all sorts of bruschetta.

By the time we had decided, we had almost finished our first bottle of wine.

The waiter returned and stood with his iPad, waiting patiently while we continued bickering.

'Balls,' Juliette said, and he flinched, 'rice balls, I mean. I love them.'

'We are going to have far too much food at this rate,' Sophia said.

'And no wine left,' I said, holding up the empty bottle.

We ordered another and our patient waiter went off to find it for us.

We had such a lovely meal that evening, and everything we eventually ordered was delicious. Kim was even brave enough to try octopus and declared she liked it after all.

I sat back in my chair and twirled the last of my wine in my glass, while the others discussed whether to have a dessert or not. Eventually we decided we were really too full for anything else and would have coffee at home.

'Although there is that ice cream place on the way back to the villa,' Kim said, 'we could have that instead?'

'Great idea,' Juliette agreed, 'and I think our waiter deserves something after all our messing about. What's a good tip?'

'In a fight, hit first and hit hard,' I said, 'that's a good tip.'

I looked around at everyone laughing and wished it could be possible to bottle the feeling I had inside me. I was sitting with good friends in a beautiful little town. There was a view of the sea, the memory of a delicious meal, and perhaps a wider view of my future than I had considered when I came here.

I would not allow myself to sit at home, just reading and

eating chocolate as I had imagined. I might even be bold enough to go on holiday on my own. Nothing about this experience had been difficult, after all. How exciting! And there was still the rest of the holiday to enjoy, then Juliette's wedding. And of course Bruno, who was never far from my thoughts.

What had that postcard said? Fear is temporary, regret is forever.

15

Next day, the mid-morning bus to Alcudia was just as prompt and pleasant an experience as the last one had been. I wondered why public transport wasn't like this where I lived.

The trip was about half an hour, and took us from the outskirts of the town, past several holiday resorts and water sports centres and the usual pelotons of cyclists. The sea to our left was shimmering in the sunshine, there were even a few paddle boarders out there, who seemed to be falling off a great deal. Behind us was the wide view of the bay, white houses, with the mountains in the background. It was absolutely gorgeous.

At last we reached our stop outside the walls of the old town and exchanged the aggressive air conditioning inside the bus for a pleasantly warm day outside.

The old stone walls of the fortress reared up in front of us, the gates and fortifications gone now to allow attractive views of stone-paved streets and the canopies of little shops along the way. There were strings of coloured bunting above us, strewn across the alleyways, stone troughs of bright flowers. It was delightful.

We wasted no time getting into the heart of the old town and doing what we did best, which was find a café.

'I know Sophia is always saying the Mediterranean diet is so healthy,' Kim said as she tucked into a slice of strawberry-garnished cake, 'but I'm sure I've put on pounds since we came here, despite all the walking we have done. I wish I'd remembered my fitness tracker. I bet we've done miles since we came here.'

'Moderation in all things,' Sophia laughed.

'I'll moderate myself when I'm back home,' Kim said. She put her fork down and looked a bit glum. 'The thought of that makes me a bit sad. I've loved being here with all of you. The prospect of going back and picking up where I left off is a bit depressing.'

'We still have a few days left to enjoy,' I said.

Kim looked mournful. 'Yes, but the chaps next door are going to leave soon. It's been fun having them around, hasn't it? And yes, before you ask, I will miss Vince.'

'Can we be bridesmaids?' I asked.

Kim made a half-hearted attempt to kick me under the table, making all the cups rattle.

'We don't need to be all lovey-dovey, it's just made a change to have someone pleasant to talk to. And he is tall. And he says he's done loads of DIY when he moved into his mother's house, and everything was falling apart. Painting and wallpapering. And fixing the fence when it blew down. Perhaps he could take a look at my porch?'

'I'm sure he would love to. There's nothing more attractive than a man with a tool in his hand,' Juliette said, making us all laugh.

* * *

Then we set off to walk around the walled town. There was a maze of little streets, all with something interesting to find along the way. Tourist shops and food stands. Two black cats curled up asleep in a big flowerpot. Bakeries and boutiques. Juliette ventured into one, attracted as always by bright colours and glitz. But in the end she decided that the flowing pink and orange striped dress she tried on was perhaps a bit much, even for her.

'I bet you'll regret not buying it,' I said.

She sighed. 'Probably, but I already stand out like a sore thumb in church. I don't need to deliberately provoke the parish councillors. They are sour enough as it is. I wore a fake fur once when the heating in the church had broken down, and I swear they miaowed at me. Anyway, I've stopped trying to make everyone like me, now I just focus on being the most annoying person they know. It's much more fun. I know I am too much for some people, but then they aren't my people.'

There was a walk around the top of the wall which we considered trying. I went to have a look while the others waited below for my verdict. Hundreds of feet through the centuries had left deep clefts in the steps, and although there was a very sturdy new barrier which wouldn't have been there in the thirteenth century, I decided it was too risky. I took a photograph of the others, standing in the street below me, and went down again.

'Probably just as well, I broke a bone in my foot stepping off the kerb once,' Kim said, 'so going up there would be dicing with death.'

'I once did my back in just switching on the kettle,' Juliette added, 'isn't this getting older business ridiculous? You can hurt yourself sleeping wrong, or yawning, or eating too fast. And underneath it all I'm still the kid that could do handstands against the kitchen door.'

'My cats have the right idea,' Sophia said. 'Castor and Pollux do nothing that doesn't suit them. They laze around in the sun, eating the food I provide, sleeping in the most comfortable places. It's true, when you are a kid you want to be a teenager, when you're a teenager you want to be an adult. When you're an adult you want to be a cat.'

* * *

We wandered around on the shady side of the streets as the heat of the afternoon was increasing.

'It must be boiling here in the summer,' Juliette said, fanning her face with her guidebook.

'And much busier. We could have gone to see the Roman remains, but for some reason they are closed,' I said.

'Perhaps it's because Easter is coming up. Anyway, they have been there for centuries, perhaps we will get in to see them next time,' Kim said.

Sophia raised her eyebrows. 'Next time? What are you planning?'

'Nothing,' Kim said, trying to look innocent, 'but we do need to plan the Old Ducks' next trip, don't we?'

As we walked back towards our bus stop, we discussed this. Santorini, perhaps, or Crete. Mykonos or Kos. There were so many exciting options. It was obvious we would have to do some research, and it was lovely to feel that I was part of the discussions. I was one of them.

When the bus came it was nearly full, with a lot of school-aged children already on board.

We stood in the aisle, hanging on to the straps, but within minutes, without any sort of discussion, several of them stood up and offered us their seats. We were so amazed we could hardly speak, except to give them a smile and *gracias*.

'I don't think we would see that happen where I live,' Kim murmured from the seat behind me, 'the school bus is generally one to avoid at all costs. Someone let a firework off in one the other day. It was all over the local papers. His parents said he was exercising his right to protest.'

'What about?'

'They don't do chips in the school canteen any longer.'

Being old, or at least older, had its benefits. Not the least of which was we didn't have to go to school.

A man in the seat next to mine stood up and pressed the buzzer for the next stop. After a few seconds, I saw that he had left a newspaper behind on the seat. There was something about the front page that caught my eye. A photograph. And, as I looked, it became more and more familiar.

I reached across to pick the paper up and looked properly. And then I gave a horrified gasp.

'What's the matter?' Juliette said.

I couldn't seem to get the words out. I just handed over the paper, pointing.

She gave a yell. 'Oh, my good God. What the...? I've been *pixelated*!'

Sophia and Kim looked over from the seat behind us.

'What is it?'

I shook the paper at her. 'Can anyone translate from Spanish? What on earth have they said?'

* * *

Back at the villa, the people carrier was back in its place by the side of the building and when we opened the patio doors, we could hear the men, talking quietly in the garden.

The four of us looked at each other and we hesitated for a moment.

'They probably won't have seen it,' Sophia said reassuringly.

'But they might,' Kim said.

'Oh, good heavens,' I said, 'we didn't know, did we?'

'We certainly didn't know one of those nuns had a phone with a camera. I thought they were supposed to live a simple life, far away from all the distractions of the modern world?' Juliette said.

'Not that simple. And not that far. What shall we do?' Kim said, grabbing hold of my arm.

'Nothing, we'll just act normally,' I said, 'and if necessary, brazen it out.'

Kim opened the gate between our gardens to say hello, and Johnny waved us all in.

'Have you had a good day?' she asked.

Vince stood up and doffed his battered Panama hat in our direction.

'Interesting,' Bruno said, looking up.

There was a moment's silence and then Johnny and Vince burst out laughing.

'What on earth have you gals been up to?' Johnny said.

'Nothing,' Kim said defensively. 'Why, what have you seen?'

'Perhaps I shouldn't say,' Johnny said, 'but you certainly caused a splash, didn't you? All over the paper.'

'Damn it, you saw it,' I said. 'Can someone tell us what it says? My Spanish isn't up to it.'

Bruno pulled his copy of the newspaper out from behind him and began reading. It was obvious from his voice he was having trouble not laughing.

'Serious breach of public decency on convent beach. Three unnamed women (see photo) were seen on the private beach belonging to St Catalina's. Five sisters from the convent saw the women and apprehended them. Residents and holiday makers are reminded that there are naturist beaches available on other parts of the island. This part of the coast is strictly off limits unless by prior appointment with the Mother Superior. Well, I am surprised at you.'

'We didn't know,' Kim said.

'And the fence was broken down already, we didn't do that,' I said.

'We thought it belonged to Julio Iglesias,' Juliette wailed. 'Oh, no, not again! Sophia, can you ring Hera? Can she come and help, like she did last time?'

I took another look at the photograph. Yes, there I was with a bucket on top of my head. Kim with her driftwood stick, Juliette leaping up out of the water, her impressive bosom pixelated out for the sake of those of a nervous disposition. They had also put discreet black lines across our eyes, but anyone who knew us would have recognised us.

'Are the police after us?' Kim asked. 'Do you think they are going to arrest us? Oh, God, what will my kids say?'

Bruno took another look at the photo.

'I shouldn't think so, unless you do it again.'

'No chance of that,' I said, 'although it was lovely at the time. I feel terrible, we didn't know it belonged to the convent.'

'It says that some saint came ashore here in the fifteenth century, and it's regarded as a historic site,' Bruno said, 'not a nudist beach.'

Kim buried her face in her hands and groaned.

Juliette took the newspaper and had another look. And then she looked a bit more cheerful.

'Not bad, actually, for someone my age.'

'Oh, Jules,' Kim wailed, 'you are awful.'

'No harm done really,' she said, 'it's not as though we lit a bonfire or had a rave. If the police come looking for us, we'll just say we are celebrating Easter. Getting back to nature, and the glories of the natural world.'

'Glories is about right,' Johnny chuckled into his wine glass.

'So let's forget all about it until they come banging on the front door. What happened with Lorna and Doggie?' I asked. 'Is he here?'

'Yes, I'm here,' Doggie said, stepping out from the house with a beer bottle in his hand.

There was something different about him, perhaps it was a new confidence, or perhaps he was putting on a brave face.

'We've been to Alcudia,' Kim said, catching Vince's eye and looking away, still rather embarrassed.

'How nice to see you safely back. Was it worth the trip?'

Kim beamed. 'Oh, yes. We had a lovely day. Splendid cake. And there are Roman ruins too, but we didn't see them.'

'Perhaps next time,' Vince said, pulling out a chair for her. She twinkled up at him.

'So what have you all been doing?' Juliette asked.

'Nothing as exciting as you, obviously. Bruno has a friend who owns a vineyard, and we went there for a wine tasting. Lovely stuff. Highly recommended,' Johnny said. 'Would you like to try some? Take your minds off your new notoriety?'

We decided we would and brought some of our chairs over from the next-door patio.

We spent a few minutes discussing the wine and agreeing how fruity/aromatic and red it tasted, and then Juliette was the first one to crack and ask the question that was on all our minds.

'So where's Lorna? What happened?'

All eyes swivelled to Doggie, who was sitting on one of the

sunbeds with his beer, a floppy canvas sunhat over his balding head. He looked up.

'Lorna? She was here this morning. Apparently the B&B where she is staying is unsatisfactory because they don't have instant coffee. Or Yorkshire tea bags. Or proper sausages, and to be honest, I can't remember Lorna ever wanting a sausage.'

'No, I can believe that,' Juliette said under her breath.

I nudged her with an elbow. 'So what did you say?'

'I told her she should have brought some tea bags with her,' Doggie said, 'and I gave her three of mine. She wasn't in the least bit grateful. But then what's new?'

'So what happens now?' I said. 'You're going home tomorrow, I'm guessing she will go with you, and you can sort things out?'

Doggie took a swig of his beer and shrugged.

'Perhaps I have other plans,' he said.

'Oooh, hello, international man of mystery,' Kim said. 'What plans?'

'I'd rather not say,' Doggie said.

'Go on, you can tell us,' Juliette said, 'we won't tell her.'

'Oh, I'm going to tell her,' Doggie said, and he looked a tiny bit pleased with himself.

What did this mean, I wondered. After all their years together, was Doggie going to leave his wife? It seemed rather a sad end to this holiday.

'I think it's an excellent plan,' Johnny boomed, 'and by the way, ladies, I hope you are all free to come along to my wedding in September? I'll just tell Polly. She'll be okay with it. She's very flexible.'

I thought of Polly crying over her table plans and wondered if this was true.

'That's very kind,' I said, 'are you sure?'

'Absolutely. We are having a hog roast, there's plenty of hog to go round. All Polly needs to do is order a few more buns.'

'I think there's probably more to it than that,' Kim said. 'I mean, what if we were vegetarians?'

'No one has asked me that before, I don't think I know any vegetarians. You could always just have the bun?' Johnny said after a moment's puzzlement.

'I don't think it works like that, Johnny,' Bruno said.

'No? Oh, well, Polly has been dealing with all that side of things. She's a little belter. Nothing fazes her.'

'Evidently,' Juliette murmured.

'Ah, so there you are at last, I want a word with you, Douglas.'

We all sat up like meerkats hearing the hunting call of a hawk. It was Lorna, who had appeared round the side of the house, clutching a new straw handbag with a sombrero embroidered on the side and the price tag hanging down from the handles.

The only one who didn't seem startled was Doggie.

'Glass of wine, dear?' he said. 'Beer? Dubonnet and lemonade? No, we haven't got any Dubonnet, or any lemonade come to think of it. I don't know why I said that.'

Lorna looked a little less composed than she had. 'I would like to talk to you, Douglas. In private.'

'When I get home, I think,' Doggie said.

'I think we should go home together,' Lorna said.

I felt suddenly sorry for her. 'Would you like to sit down?'

Lorna threw me a look. 'No, not really.'

I tried again. It must have been very unsettling for the woman, being on her own in a strange country and not having any support.

'Perhaps a cup of tea, then? We have proper tea bags.'

'No, thank you,' she said.

'Coffee? Jaffa cake? Glass of water?' Kim said. 'Oh, no, I forgot. I've eaten all the Jaffa cakes.'

'I just want to speak to Douglas,' Lorna repeated, 'on my own. I have a flight home booked for tomorrow morning.'

Doggie stood up and pulled his sunhat off, carefully smoothing down his wispy hair.

'Well, I will be flying home as arranged, and then I will be going to stay with Vince for a few days.'

We all gasped. Vince looked a bit awkward and held up his hands.

'It was Doggie's idea, not mine. It's no problem as far as I'm concerned,' he said.

'Then would you like a lift to the airport tomorrow morning, Lorna?' Bruno said. 'It would be no trouble.'

'I have a taxi booked,' Lorna replied, glaring at Vince.

'For heaven's sake, don't look her in the eye,' Kim hissed.

Doggie sat down again.

'You can't do this, Douglas,' Lorna said angrily.

'I'll be back home in time to sort the oil delivery out,' Doggie said, 'and don't worry about washing the recycling bins. I'll do that when I get back. I just need a few days to think things through.'

'Oh,' Lorna said, rather deflated. 'Well. I'll make cottage pie, shall I? It always was your favourite.'

'Steak and chips would be better,' Doggie said. 'I think my teeth can still cope with that. We can have a good chat then.'

'Fine. Right,' Lorna said, fidgeting with her straw bag.

'Are you sure you wouldn't like a cup of tea?' I said.

'I have things to do,' Lorna said, ignoring me, and turned on her heel.

There was a moment's silence and then I think we all let out a collective breath.

'Goodness me, Doggie,' Johnny said. 'That's two things in one day I never thought to see. Well, three things, if I think about it.'

'Oh, shut up, Johnny,' Juliette muttered under her breath, 'or I'll tip my wine over your trousers.'

Doggie started talking. 'I just got a bit fed up with it all. Never being allowed to have an opinion without being shot down in flames. Always picking the wrong television programme. I mean, I like *Midsomer Murders* and *Gardeners' World* as much as the next person, but that doesn't mean we have to watch them endlessly, does it? That or *Murder She Wrote*. Sometimes I want to see a Bond film or *Die Hard*, but I have to wait until Lorna's gone to bed and turn the sound down. It doesn't seem fair somehow. And if I want to occasionally have a burger, it's not the end of the world, is it? Lorna found a McDonald's wrapper in my car once. You would have thought I was dealing cocaine.'

'You can stay with me as long as you like,' Vince said kindly.

'Just a day or two,' Doggie said, 'time for her to calm down. Oh dear. Have I done the right thing?'

'Yes,' Juliette said. 'I learned my lesson the hard way. I wouldn't let anyone push me around like that now.'

'No, but... well, you know. I've always wanted her to be happy. I didn't realise at first that meant I had to be miserable. It just crept up on me. But you see, I like being married. I don't want to be on my own. I'd just like us to have fun sometimes. I like bringing her a cup of tea in the morning and cleaning out the gutters and helping her with things. It's my way of showing I love her.'

'You and your gutters. Have another beer, Dog, me old mate,' Johnny said, holding one out to him, 'we're back home soon. Plenty of time to sort things out.'

Doggie took it and sat for a moment with a beer bottle in each hand. He looked a bit lost.

'I feel bad, though. I've never stood up to her before now, and she did come all this way to find me.'

'You'll work it through,' Bruno said, clapping Doggie on the shoulder, 'sometimes we just need to clear the air. Get everything out in the open.'

He looked at me and for a moment we stared at each other, and then I started laughing.

* * *

We had a very late night.

The chaps said they needed to finish up their beer supplies, and at about ten o'clock, Sophia made them some sandwiches to try to soak up some of the alcohol. Doggie veered between feeling as though he had done the wrong thing and minutes later being sure he hadn't.

'It's been a lovely break,' he said, 'I can see why you like living here, Bruno. It feels sort of relaxed and fun. Perhaps it's the climate? Maybe it's just because we are on holiday?'

'It suits me,' Bruno said. 'I have a lot of friends here, the life is very laid-back. Other parts of the island are busier, but I don't go there. Any of you are very welcome to come and stay with me. I have a house on the coast, there are a couple of spare bedrooms.'

'Don't you ever get lonely?' Kim asked.

'No, I don't. I read; I write articles for the local paper. Sometimes I do guided tours for the holiday visitors. I cook, and I look after my garden. Which can be a losing battle in the heat of summer. And I travel too. I've been to a lot of the Greek islands.'

'Sounds lovely,' I said. Because it did.

The others started moving things around the table in a feeble attempt to make some space, and Juliette came out from the villa, triumphant as she had found two packs of playing cards. It was half past midnight.

'Poker,' she said, 'come on, you lot, let's play poker.'

Bruno and I left the card sharps to it, and found ourselves clearing away the debris together, taking the plates and glasses into the chaps' kitchen where it was obvious that the cleaning deposit would be well earned the following day by some poor cleaners.

'It's been fun,' Bruno said, trying to force more things into the dishwasher and close the door.

Most men seem to do that. They think they can jam in things any old how, as long as they can close the dishwasher door, it'll be okay.

'It has. I hope it all works out well for Doggie and Lorna,' I said. I was on the other side of the dishwasher door, rearranging some plates.

'I'm sure it will,' he said. 'Communication, that's the thing.'

I stood up and looked at him. 'I've messed around for long enough, haven't I? We need to talk, don't we?'

'We do,' he said, with a grin, 'like I said, get things out in the open.'

And he shut the dishwasher door, stepped towards me, and kissed me.

It was as though the years fell away, and I was back in that place and time when it had all been good between us. I felt quite wobbly in the knee department. And I don't just think it was the lateness of the hour or the quantity of wine I had consumed.

'Flipping heck,' I said, coming up for air.

He kissed the tip of my nose. 'You always were one with words.'

I kissed him back, enjoying the feel of his broad shoulders

under my hands, the scent of his skin, the faint rasp of his stubble on my cheek.

'We need to talk,' he said, his voice rumbling against me. 'I think when your friends have gone back home, you should come and stay with me for a few days. Doggie isn't the only one who needs time to think. And time to talk things through.'

'I don't know,' I gasped.

An automatic reaction. What had happened to my decision to be spontaneous, to accept chances and opportunities?

'Why not?' he said.

'No reason.'

'Well then,' he said, and he kissed me again.

'Well, it's about bloody time,' Juliette said as she came in with her hands full of empty beer bottles.

In bed that night, just before I fell into an exhausted and alcohol-tinged sleep, I thought of my life, how it would be when I did return home. My house was fine, easy to look after and maintain. The garden was a bit small, but I could walk to the shops or the park if I wanted to. I had friends, even more now that I was officially an Old Duck. I too could travel, see new places. This holiday had awakened a new confidence in me that I hadn't expected. Maybe I would go to Carcassonne, and Rhodes now that Sophia had invited me to stay with her.

Perhaps I wasn't too old to see the Pyramids, the Great Wall of China, or stand on the white sand of a beach in the Caribbean. I just needed to do some research, budget, and believe in myself. The day would come when I was too old to drive or travel. I might be ill or dotty. But – and this was the thing – I wasn't yet. I had time to do stuff, what had Doggie said – have some fun. Everyone needed that, didn't they?

And what about company? Now that I was retired, perhaps I needed to think about that too. I'd made some great new friends here, but it felt as though life was offering me more than that. Perhaps – and I felt rather tingly – it was offering me a chance to spend more time with Bruno. And I was beginning to like the idea.

16

The following day, no one was up early. I went downstairs, still in my PJs, to find some tea and found the kitchen looking like a disaster zone. I didn't remember making that much of a mess. But we must have done. I had an elusive memory of Juliette organising the kitchen in the next-door villa, and then deciding to bring the trays of empty wine glasses and plates over to our place instead, in a vague attempt at helping.

I brewed some tea in the biggest mug I could find, turned my back on the muddle and went to sit outside in the shade, because the sun was already high in the sky, and it was going to be hot.

Perhaps I needed a swim to clear my head? The shock of the water might be refreshing, but at that moment it felt too much of an effort to go back upstairs and change into my swimming costume.

Instead, I drank my tea and re-ran what had happened the previous evening. The way he had stepped forward. Taken hold of my shoulders and kissed me.

It had somehow felt inevitable. There was still that attraction between us both, wasn't there?

Bruno was older, of course, greyer, but then I still saw him as a young man. Could the same be true of his view of me? Did he still see me as the young woman with whom he had spent those years; slim, dark-haired, always up for some fun? Did he notice my wrinkles, thicker waistline, rather sensible shoes? Why, after all the time apart, did he still want to kiss me, just as I wanted to kiss him? Were we actually still the same people underneath the misunderstandings and challenges of all the years apart? Did we still recognise the spirit of the other person, as something we still liked?

Perhaps that was the case. We were still drawn to each other. We still shared so many memories.

'Oh, God almighty, someone turn the sun down a bit.'

It was Kim, in a dressing gown, a nightie patterned with Donald Duck, flip-flops and sunglasses, one hand to her forehead.

'I think my liver is too old for this sort of caper,' she said, 'never again. The last thing I remember was Johnny pouring shots of *Palo de Mallorca*. It was only after we were halfway down the bottle he realised we should dilute it with soda water. But then we didn't have any...'

'Tea?' I asked.

'You're an angel. Two sugars, please.'

I went to fetch it.

'So,' she said, when she had taken a few sips of her tea, 'fun night, wasn't it?'

'What I remember of it,' I said.

'Perhaps it's a good thing the chaps are going home today. I think we need a few days to recover from their – what shall we call it – malign influence.'

'No. I don't think they were that,' I said, 'they were just mischievous.'

'Well, I have the mischievous headache to prove it. No sign of anyone else?'

'I've not heard anything.'

Kim sighed. 'This tea is wonderful.'

'So what are we supposed to be doing today? According to your spreadsheet.'

'Oh, that went out of the window days ago, I haven't really bothered looking at it,' Kim said, 'and that's their fault. We didn't get to the pearl factory, or the caves of someone or other. Or take the bus to Palma for the day.'

'But we have had fun, haven't we?'

'Oh, gosh, yes. There have been times when I haven't been having arguments in my head with Stewart, which has been such a relief.'

'Are you still doing that?'

Kim sipped her tea thoughtfully, her eyes on the horizon.

'There were times when I mentally planned all sort of things. Marvellous speeches I would make, truths I would tell the new wife. Wishing her luck, telling her she would soon realise what a mistake she had made. But now I'm beginning to see I can spend my time and energy on better things. Because I was glad to see the back of him. He was like an albatross around my neck. Holding me back from my own life. Spending all our money. I read on a website there are five stages of grief after bereavement, but seven stages after divorce. The two additional ones were fear and guilt. Well, I did feel fear for a bit after Stewart left, but I never felt any guilt. I looked after that man so well, and I realised that sometimes you have to be done. Not angry. Not sad. Just done. And I am, and this holiday has made me realise that.'

'I don't suppose he felt guilty,' I said.

Kim laughed. 'I bet he didn't. So did you get through the

different stages after Bruno left? Juliette did tell me what happened.'

'It depends, was that a divorce or a bereavement?'

'A bit of both?'

'I think I got to acceptance, after a few years,' I said, 'which is why it's been hard, seeing him again. Realising I still like him.'

'Are you the same person you were all those years ago?'

'No.'

'Well, I predict he isn't either. Can you condemn someone forever, for something they did thirty-nine years ago? Unless it was murder or drug trafficking or international arms dealing. Obviously that would be different.'

I laughed. 'I suppose not. Anyway, I think Juliette has enjoyed her time here.'

'Are you talking about me behind my back?' Juliette said as she stumbled out onto the patio.

'Yes, of course,' I said.

'Good, I don't want to be ignored.'

'As if we could,' Kim said, finishing her tea.

'So you and Vince are having a thing,' Juliette said, 'and from the evidence of my own eyes, Denny and Bruno are too.'

'Are you?' Kim said, swivelling to look at me.

'I saw them last night. Snogging in the kitchen,' Juliette said, 'it was like a student party all over again.'

'You didn't tell me that, Denny! How marvellous,' Kim said. 'The Old Ducks ought to start up a dating agency. For the more mature lady who is a bit confused by life.'

'Well, that's all of us,' Juliette said. 'I was thinking about all the daft things I have done over the years. And it all boiled down to *been there, done that and then I did it again because I never learn*. And I feel that now I have learned. To allow myself to be happy, to trust someone. I mean Matthew, of course. It's a shame it took quite so long, but good things are worth waiting for.'

'Unless it's cake,' Kim said.

Juliette nodded. 'True. When I think back to being married to Gary, it's like I was a different person. And the arguments we had. Just awful. But then someone told me, arguing with an idiot is like playing chess with a pigeon. No matter how good you are, the pigeon is always going to poop on the board at some point and still think it's won. Now I think I should go and have a shower to wake me up. Or perhaps a dip in the pool. It does look quite inviting.'

'I don't have the strength to go back upstairs and wrestle myself into my swimming costume,' Kim groaned.

'Then there's only one thing for it,' I said, pulling off my dressing gown.

A moment later I jumped into the pool, making the others scream as I splashed them with water.

'Oh, well, these PJs look like silk, but they aren't. I got them in Primark,' Juliette said.

I had to give them their due, they were both in with me a few seconds later, all of us splashing about in our nightwear and making one heck of a din.

'I see those pesky teenagers are back again,' said a voice, and Doggie shambled through the gate between our gardens. He was dressed in an unusual combination of football shorts, a fairly smart shirt and tie, and a tweed cap.

'Morning, Doggie, how are you feeling this morning?' Kim called, pulling at the hem of her nightie which was ballooning up rather embarrassingly.

'Old,' Doggie groaned, 'and in need of some water.'

He went back through the gate, and we heard him grumbling and muttering to himself for a few seconds.

'Good end of term party then,' I said.

'I hope they get packed and cleared up in time to leave,' Kim said.

'They don't have to leave until this afternoon. Most of their stuff is now in our kitchen by the looks of it,' I said.

'I was trying to help,' Juliette said, 'I don't think I did. Actually, I don't know what I was thinking. Perhaps we'd better wash it all up and take their stuff back? How many glasses did we have when we started?'

'I'm assuming eight?' I said. 'Or sixteen?'

'Well, we have about a hundred and fifty on the kitchen table by the looks of it. Come on, we'd better get out and start clearing up.'

We spent the rest of the morning washing up glasses and cutlery and trying to sort them into which ones belonged in which house. Then we put all the bottles, cardboard and cans into a box, and Bruno drove it all down to the recycling place just outside the town. It was rather embarrassing to see just how much there was.

'It's lucky the police didn't come round, they might have thought we had opened an unlicensed bar,' Sophia said. 'Perhaps we should cut back a bit. I feel quite liverish.'

'We have been a bit like teenagers on a break,' I said, 'but it doesn't happen very often, I think once in a while will be okay.'

'Right, I think I have it. These glasses are ours, and those belong next door,' Juliette said. 'And some of that cutlery must be theirs too. Unless this villa was expecting twenty guests to cram in here.'

'I'd come back here again,' Kim said, 'it's lovely, and so near the sea and the shops. I wonder if there will be other people in the next-door villa when they go? It will be odd not to have them in there, just through the gate.'

'When you get home, I am sure Vince will be beating a path to your door, cheer up,' Sophia said.

Kim sighed. 'I hate the end of holidays. And I dread to think what state my house will be in.'

'If your kids have made a mess, make them clear it up,' I said.

Kim pulled a face. 'No point, they wouldn't do it properly, and then I would end up doing it myself anyway.'

'Now don't play the martyr,' Juliette said, 'stand over them and make them do it, stop making it so easy for them.'

'I know, you're right.'

'If Doggie can stand up to Lorna, you can tell your kids what to do,' she added.

'Yes, that's true. Well, I'll see...' Kim twisted the cloth she was using to wipe the kitchen table. 'And I just feel a bit confused about Vince. And I don't know really what to think. And I have a lot of concerns, about – you know – intimate, private stuff. What if I take my clothes off and he laughs?'

I grinned across the worktop at her. 'What if he takes his clothes off and you laugh?'

Juliette went to put an arm around her shoulder and murmured reassuringly.

'Let's have a cup of tea and you can tell me all your worries, Kim. I'm really good at listening in complete confidence. I'm also very good at not listening properly, and I'm excellent about then telling everyone else what you tell me and asking their opinion.'

Kim tutted and shrugged her off. 'Thank you so much. I wish there was a book, or an instruction manual to deal with this sort of thing.'

Juliette laughed. 'Don't be daft. And when did any man ever read an instruction manual?'

Kim nodded. 'That's true. Stewart built a bookcase once, and when he was finished there were three bolts and a shelf left over. And he said it was the manufacturer's error. Books were always sliding off that bookcase. I bet Vince would have done it properly.'

I found the Hoover and plugged it in, hoovering up all the dust and debris which had settled over the last few days. I hardly ever had to do that at home, perhaps once a week. Because no one ever made a mess there. Which was a bit sad.

'So what are we going to do once we have waved the men off this afternoon?' Juliette said brightly. 'Let's have something to look forward to.'

'Let's talk about your wedding plans, and what you need us to do,' Sophia suggested.

Juliette's face brightened. 'Oooh, yes, I'd like that. We could sit out here with factor-50 sunscreen – oooh, no, face packs on, I brought some with me, and we can drink sensible cups of tea for a change.'

'Perhaps we'll need some cake too,' I said.

'Need? Or want? Or both?' Kim said.

'I'll go out later and get some from that fantastic bakery two streets away,' I said. 'Then we can have a nice, quiet time, making helpful suggestions about the seating plan and deciding what we would like to wear. After all, we are bridesmaids, we are supposed to be supporting our bride, not just flirting with the neighbours, offending local nuns, and seeing how much wine we can get through in twenty-four hours.'

Kim was initially indignant. 'I wasn't flirting... well, yes, I suppose I was. I didn't know I could still do that, not at my age. I mean, I'm not much to look at, I'm not exactly Helen Mirren, am I?'

Juliette patted her on the back. 'Well, I don't expect Helen

Mirren looks like that all the time, not when she's pegging out the washing or emptying the Hoover bag.'

'And Vince did say he liked the smell of new cars, didn't he? Perhaps you could buy some leather trousers?' I suggested. 'They would drive him wild.'

Kim rolled her eyes. 'No, Denny, probably not. Right, which are our plates, and which are theirs?'

There was a knock on the patio doors and Johnny appeared, looking as bouncy and cheerful as ever.

'Morning, ladies. We wondered if you would like to come over for a last get-together. Ah, that's where all our glasses are. I remember now.'

'Take these, Johnny, and we can bring the rest,' Juliette said, handing him a tray loaded with crockery.

'Righty-ho! Leave it to me,' he said and trotted off.

Seconds later, there was a loud shout and the crash of splintering china, and we all looked at each other.

'Oh, for heaven's sake,' Juliette said, 'we could have saved ourselves all that work.'

* * *

An hour later, Vince came back and invited us over to their patio, where there was an odd assortment of things laid out on the wooden table.

'We've been clearing out the fridge and there is some stuff needs finishing up, so we thought we could make a brunch party of it,' he said.

There was some serrano ham and cheese, open but still in the packets, a loaf of sliced bread, some dishwasher tablets and half a bottle of olive oil. A carton of orange juice, several bottles of water, some biscuits, a bowl of fruit and half a bag of sherbet lemons.

'Mmm, I'll have a ham and dishwasher tablet sandwich,' Juliette said.

Doggie looked as confused as ever.

'I don't think you should eat the dishwasher tablets, we just wondered if you wanted any of them. Those sweets were mine, I love a sherbet lemon, even though they do rip my palate to shreds. Lorna says I'll get diabetes so I can't take them back with me.'

'Ah, welcome, everyone,' Johnny said as he bounded on to the patio. 'Sorry there aren't any plates. I think I found all the bits, but no bare feet, eh? Bruno has gone to buy some more; he says they are from the big supermarket in town. Bruno to the rescue, eh? He won't be long. Now then, help yourselves.'

'Any news of Lorna?' I asked.

Doggie rolled his eyes. 'Her flight took off an hour ago. She rang me from the airport. I couldn't tell if she was angry or not. Anyway, it will be good to leave her to cool down for a few days.'

'So you really are going to stay with Vince?' Juliette said.

Doggie nodded. 'Actually, we have a lot of fun planned. First, we will get his cat back from the cattery. I like cats, I always wanted one, but Lorna refused. She said it would do its business in the flower beds. The way I am feeling at the moment, I might too. And then he needs help creosoting his fence, which is a task I always enjoy. And he was interested to hear about the things I found when I was clearing out my gutters, so we thought we would have a go at his. It's only a bungalow, so it won't be difficult.'

'Well, just be careful,' I said, 'you don't want to fall off and turn up to Johnny's wedding with your neck in a brace.'

'And if you come and visit, I want things to be nice for you,' Vince beamed at Kim.

'Yes, it's a truth universally acknowledged that women are always irresistibly attracted to men with clean guttering, aren't we?' Juliette murmured.

Johnny handed over a sheet of paper torn from a notebook.

'This is where we are getting married. That's the postcode so you can put it into your sat-nav, and this is Polly's number.'

'You're sure she won't mind? I'd be a bit twitchy if Matthew suddenly started adding to the guest list,' Juliette said, and then her face brightened, 'but I want to invite the four of you, and Polly too if she wants to come, so that's five, to our wedding in June. Doggie, I leave it up to you whether you bring Lorna or not. Write your phone numbers and email addresses down on some paper and I'll sort everything out. We are just having a buffet on the lawn, in a marquee, so there will be plenty of room. It would be a proper meet-up for us all.'

'By the way, we are all vegans,' Johnny said, rolling up a piece of ham and stuffing it in his mouth.

'Very funny.'

* * *

Shortly after that, Bruno returned, bringing with him several boxes of crockery to replace the things Johnny had broken.

He grinned at me. 'Bit of an accident, good job I knew where it came from.'

'You have saved the day,' Johnny beamed. 'Make yourself a sandwich, there are a few bits and pieces left over, well, there's some cheese anyway.'

'I'm fine,' Bruno said, 'now, is everything packed up? It's a good job you booked a late check-out. You have to be out of here by three at the latest if we are going to get to the airport in time. Let's start loading up the car.'

Typical women, we went and helped them. Clearing away the last few things into the dishwasher, hoovering and wiping dust and smears off the surfaces. Meanwhile the others were bringing an assortment of cases and bags downstairs, and Bruno was doing a sort of luggage jigsaw in the back of his people carrier. At last they were all packed and ready to leave, and I'm sure all of us were rather disappointed to see them go.

Bruno drove them away just after two o'clock, and I watched sadly, wondering if this was the end of it, or whether I would see Bruno again. After all, vague suggestions had been made but nothing definite arranged. Then they came back five minutes later because Doggie had forgotten his electric toothbrush.

'It's very quiet now, isn't it?' Kim said after a while.

We were still sitting around the patio table, the gate firmly closed between the two gardens. I had been given a notebook and pencil, and Sophia was leafing through a bridal magazine Juliette had brought with her. Juliette, meanwhile, had her head back, eyes closed, and her Ducks-on-tour hat pulled low over her brow.

'I'm exhausted,' she said. 'I need another holiday to get over this holiday and we still have two full days to go.'

'Perhaps we should take it a bit easy,' Kim said, 'relax a bit more. That's what holidays are supposed to be all about, aren't they?'

'I sometimes think life would be a lot easier if everyone occasionally just had a glass of milk and a nice slice of cake and then had a nap under a blankie for an hour or two,' Juliette replied.

'Well, I've enjoyed it,' I said, 'it's been enormous fun. And it's made me think about what I am going to do next.'

The others turned to look at me and Juliette pulled the brim of her sunhat up so that she could look at me.

'If Bruno asks again, I'll go out to dinner with him before we leave, if you lot don't mind, and see what happens. But of course he might not ask.'

'Good,' Kim said, 'and then if it all goes wrong, you can forget all about him. Like I did with Stewart.'

Everyone laughed at this.

'You are joking, of course?' Juliette said, gasping for breath. 'You never stopped talking about him, and wondering what he was doing.'

Kim tossed her head. 'Well, I'm not now. I've realised I have been wasting a lot of time and energy on him. It's not my circus, not my monkeys. I certainly won't keep going to Tesco when I think he will be there. He usually goes on Sunday mornings.'

'That would be a great start,' I said, 'and what about Vince?'

'Oh, Vince goes to Sainsbury's, ah, I see what you mean. Well, we are going to go together to Johnny's wedding. He asked if I would like to sit with him, as his plus one, and I said absolutely and what colour tie would he be wearing so I could coordinate with him.'

'Not exactly playing hard to get, are you?' Sophia said.

'Well, no. But I'm not hard to get, as it happens. I just want someone to be kind to me, I don't ask for much more than that.'

I thought about this and realised that was actually all any of us wanted. For people to be kind to us and to each other. And kindness seemed in short supply these days.

17

We decided to spend the last days of our holiday relaxing, drinking a lot of tea and taking things a bit easier.

A team of cleaners sorted out the next-door villa in record time. They came in a van, armed with brooms and buckets and efficient-looking trugs of cleaning products and we didn't hear them make a sound.

Another family came into the villa next door the following morning. A German couple with a little boy, who – like the cleaners – didn't seem to make any noise at all. They even went into the pool for their afternoon swim quietly, and the gate between the two villas stayed closed.

'I hope the boys all got home safely,' Kim said, that morning, 'I hope Vince and Doggie are okay.'

'I'm sure they will be having a fine old time. Living the bachelor high life,' I said. 'Late nights, playing beer pong, challenging each other on the PlayStation.'

Sophia frowned. 'That doesn't sound like either of them.'

'No, it doesn't, does it,' Juliette sighed. 'I expect they are having early nights and sensible meals after a happy day cleaning out Vince's gutters.'

'Oh dear, I hope they will be careful,' Kim said, worried.

'Perhaps they are eating a takeaway out of the foil containers and watching all the *Die Hard* films in sequence with the sound turned up,' I said. 'Yippee ki-yay!'

'I hope so. Poor old Doggie,' Kim said. 'Are there any biscuits to go with this tea?'

'Not the sort of biscuits you want,' I said, 'there are some very nice cookies, though.'

Kim shook her head. 'I wanted a chocolate digestive, or a custard cream. Or a hob-nob.'

Juliette snorted. 'You said nob.'

'Oh, for heaven's sake.'

'What about this?' Sophia said, handing over the bridal magazine she had been reading. 'There's a whole section here on bridesmaids' dresses. Apparently this season's colours are burnt orange, brown and black.'

Kim took a look and pulled a face. 'It's not Halloween, is it? Those models are about six feet tall, and a size eight. I'm only five feet three. And those dresses are stretch velvet. Can you imagine what I would look like in that dress? Either a pumpkin or a car tyre. And I need something with sleeves unless you want to be knocked out by my bingo wings. And I'm not standing on the edge of the photographs after what you said about it being the worst place.'

'Very needy today, Kim,' Juliette said, 'are you turning into a bridesmaid-zilla?'

'I'm just saying,' Kim said. 'I don't mind not being an attendant, if it makes things difficult.'

Juliette sighed and peered out from under her sunhat.

'Kim, don't be daft. It wouldn't be the same without you, bingo wings or not. I'm not looking for models, you're not there for decoration. I want my best friends there with me. To celebrate. That's what it's all about. I want everyone to see that older women can be happy, and how much you have meant to me. That's what we Old Ducks value more than anything, isn't it? True friendship. We'd do anything for each other, wouldn't we?'

'Absolutely,' Kim said, looking a little tearful.

'Great,' Juliette said, 'how many kidneys have you got?'

Kim laughed and slapped her on the arm. 'You are awful. I'll wear whatever you like then, even if I do look a bit shorter and fatter than everyone else. Perhaps I should go back on that cabbage soup diet when I get home, although it was disgusting. And I don't think Vince would like that, it had some unwanted side effects which weren't at all romantic.'

'He likes you just the way you are, and so do we,' I said.

'It will be what all weddings should be,' Juliette said, 'a celebration of love, optimism, friendship, and family. Not a fashion show.'

'That sounds lovely,' Sophia said, 'and that's what it will be.'

'Just not yellow,' Kim added.

We went out that afternoon to stroll around the little town. It was busier now that Easter was coming closer and presumably the school holidays were starting.

We had lunch at another restaurant overlooking the sea, where we ordered club sandwiches, which turned out to be as big as any meal we had ordered before and came with fat triple-cooked chips. So much for being disciplined.

Then we sat and talked about the wedding, and what Juliette wanted.

'It's going to be very informal. Matthew's first wedding was huge, in a cathedral. There was an arch of military swords and everything. And most of the men were in blues, and then there was a reception at the mess in his barracks where one of the waiters poured champagne all over his boots. And of course my first wedding was a quick dash down to the registry office, with Gary's mother crying at home and refusing to come, and two witnesses dragged in off the street. I think one was a secretary who had gone out to buy some Tipp-Ex, and the other was just opening up a burger van down the road. Terribly romantic, I think you'll agree.'

'No, not really,' I said, 'but this one will make up for all that. I would have come to your first wedding if you'd asked me.'

Juliette patted my hand. 'I know you would. It was all a bit of a rush, and of course back then for some members of my family it was still a bit of a disgrace. Thank heavens times have changed.'

'I'm sure you will be very happy,' Kim said. 'What about the food? And flowers?'

'We have a friend who is a caterer, and she is doing the buffet. I'm not messing about with table plans, a lot of Matthew's friends are on their second or third wife, and it makes life a bit difficult. As for flowers, Matthew has some lovely roses in the garden, and I just want some of those on the tables. I don't need a bouquet. And by the way, the vicar is very precise about not throwing confetti in the churchyard unless it's biodegradable. And no rice, because the birds eat it and raw rice isn't good for them.'

'We'll cook it first then,' I said, 'and throw that at you in big handfuls.'

'Very funny,' Juliette said.

'And you'll be Lieutenant Colonel and Mrs... what?' Sophia asked. 'You never did tell us.'

'Belvoir. But it's pronounced Beaver,' Juliette said.

There was a moment's silence, and Kim blinked a bit.

'You're going to be Mr and Mrs Beaver? Like in *The Lion, the Witch and the Wardrobe?*'

'Yes, I know,' Juliette said, rolling her eyes, 'that's what I thought when he proposed. I'm going to be Mrs Beaver.'

'I love it,' I said, chuckling, 'and somehow it seems to suit you.'

'We could club together and buy you a sewing machine as a wedding present,' Kim said.

'Please don't. Just be there, wearing something pretty,' Juliette said, 'just decide for yourselves what you want to wear. I'm not responsible for the weather, Matthew is. Now, look, we have been twenty-four hours without alcohol, I think we should have some champagne, don't you? And then later on we can have a go with those face packs I brought with me.'

We spent the rest of the afternoon packing up, cleaning and putting the furniture back where it belonged. We had a meal of leftovers at lunch time, some salad, chicken and fruit, but Sophia still managed to make it delicious.

'This has been the best holiday ever, even better than Rhodes. I'm really sad it's nearly over,' Kim said, 'and I'm so glad I came. I was thinking of making an excuse and not coming because Simon and Gemma always seem to be needing something, but then I thought to hell with it. If they had the chance to go on holiday, they wouldn't give me a second thought.'

'Well, I'm glad you did too, and don't be miserable, we will all be meeting up again in June for the wedding. And this time Anita is coming, so all the Old Ducks will be there,' Juliette said.

'Excellent news. Now come on, what about these face packs you promised us?' Sophia said.

Juliette disappeared into the house and returned a few minutes later with some sachets in her hand.

'I have four, all different sorts. I am sure they are all the same apart from the colour.'

'Do you remember fuller's earth?' I said. 'We used to use that as a face pack in a sort of goo, it was like plaster of Paris. And as it set it used to get hot. And if you moved your face it cracked.'

'It's a miracle we have any skin left,' Juliette agreed, 'I'm sure this is far better. And after that I can tidy up your eyebrows, Denny. They are looking a bit wild.'

We dutifully smoothed the face packs on. Mine was green – apparently avocado. Juliette's was pink and smelled of strawberries, Kim's was white and coconut, and Sophia's was blue and smelled of oranges.

'It says on the back you can simply peel them off,' Juliette said, 'in about fifteen minutes, so we won't be clogging the sinks up with a load of mud.'

'Feels quite nice, actually, although I can't drink my champagne very easily,' Kim murmured through stiff lips.

'Do what I always do; use a straw,' Juliette muttered back, 'and just chill.'

We lay in the shade, waiting for the timer on my phone to go off.

Kim wasn't very good at relaxing in silence.

'Have you noticed, the models who advertise this sort of thing all look like teenagers? And they all have flawless complexions to start with?'

'And when they've finished, they still have very skilfully applied make-up on,' I added.

'And even ads for cosmetics for people our age don't use people our age. They are always about thirty. Perhaps thirty is old in model years?' Juliette said. 'Like dog years.'

'What does that make us then?' I asked.

'Tortoises. Or I read there is some sort of whale that lives for two hundred years,' Sophia said.

'You'd need a lot of face pack for a whale,' Juliette said thoughtfully, 'and would you know if it made any difference?'

'I don't think it would. Apart from anything else, it would all wash off, wouldn't it?' Kim said.

We all started giggling, holding on to our faces with our fingertips so as not to dislodge the goo, which was starting to set.

'While we are waiting, let's do your nails, Denny. They don't look like they've been done for ages,' Juliette said.

She rummaged in her capacious make-up bag and came out with some turquoise nail enamel and manicure tools.

'I love this colour, it always makes me feel optimistic,' she said. 'In fact, we could all have matching nails to go home with. To remind us of all the fun we've had. I might have enough left.'

Juliette did some brisk filing and cuticle pushing while I winced bravely and then she tried taking the lid off the nail polish. Which had obviously been around for a while. She struggled and grimaced, her face mask starting to flap around the edges even more.

'Bang it on the table,' Sophia suggested.

Juliette did so and tried again. Suddenly the bottle opened and in one smooth movement flipped out of her hands and onto me.

A splodge of turquoise nail polish splattered over my shirt and onto my trousers in a rather Jackson Pollock way.

'Oh, God, I'm so sorry,' Juliette gasped, dabbing at me with a tissue, 'we really ought to get that off. Anyone got any nail varnish remover? I've only got these silly little remover pads because I couldn't bring the bottle on the plane.'

'Well, we wouldn't have been allowed to either,' Kim said.

'No... well... we could always try washing them, before it sets.'

'You know that's not going to work,' Sophia said.

'Kitchen scourer?' Juliette suggested. 'I'm so sorry.'

'I'll go and take them off anyway,' I said, and hurried off upstairs, trying to make sure nothing smudged onto the floor. Who knew if it was even possible to get nail varnish off polished stone floors? I bet it wasn't.

In my bedroom I peeled off my shirt and trousers very carefully. There were beautiful white towels in the bathroom, I didn't want to get any turquoise varnish on those.

Then I wiped some random smears off my fingers, and a couple off my legs. How had such a small bottle of the stuff managed to spread so far?

I found a free sample sachet of some exfoliant face wash which I'd had for years, at the bottom of my bag, and scrubbed diligently away at my stained clothes for a few minutes, and then I bundled them up, ready to put into the washing machine, managing in the process to smear a dab of blue across the sink. Mercifully, that wiped off quite easily.

Then I put my bathrobe on – good job I hadn't been wearing that because it belonged to the house and felt quite expensive – and went downstairs. No one seemed to be around.

'Hello, where are you all?'

After a few minutes, everyone reappeared from their rooms.

'What do you think?' Kim said, holding up her face towards me. 'Do I look young and vibrant?'

I realised they had all peeled off their face masks.

'The timer on your phone went off, sorry, we should have given you a shout. But it's quite easy, it all peels off in one piece,' Juliette said.

I pulled at the loose edges of my face mask and felt some resistance. It didn't feel very smooth at all, in fact it seemed a bit stiff.

'Go on, just ease it off, do you need some help?' Sophia asked.

'No, it's okay, it's coming,' I said.

It peeled off the lower half of my face and then the bit over my nose and then it seemed to be stuck.

'I can't get the top bit off,' I said, starting to panic.

'Come here, I'll do it,' Juliette said, and gave it a tug.

The whole thing came off with a rather odd, stretching noise, like sticky tape being pulled off the roll.

'Ow!'

'There, all gone, apart from some bits,' Juliette said happily. Then, 'Oh dear.'

'Oh dear what?' I said, panicking. 'What do you mean, oh dear?'

Kim came and took a look. 'It'll be fine, you're not to worry.'

I put my hands to my face, which didn't feel *silky smooth and reinvigorated*, it felt oddly dry and rough. Not the result I had been expecting at all.

'I think you left it on a bit too long,' Sophia said.

Then they all came to peer at me.

'What?' I said.

The three of them looked at each other.

'You know I was going to tidy up a few stray hairs on your eyebrows? Well, I don't need to do that any more. I think some of the face pack got stuck. In the wrong place. Sorry. But you're not to worry.'

I got hold of Juliette's hand mirror and took a look. And gave a scream.

'You've pulled off one of my eyebrows!'

'Only some of it,' Juliette said.

'I look like a boiled egg!'

'No, you don't. Honestly, it will be fine. You just need to draw them in while it grows back,' Kim said. 'Anyone got an eyebrow pencil?'

Sophia leaned forwards. 'Is that someone at the front door? I'm sure I can hear knocking.'

'Well, they'll have to knock,' Juliette said. 'Let's ignore them.'

'But it might be an emergency,' Sophia said.

'What sort of an emergency? A Tsunami warning, or one of General Franco's sea planes has crashed?' Kim said. 'Or perhaps it's the neighbours? Maybe they have a flood in the bathroom, or a problem with the induction hob. It took me ages to work out how to use it.'

'Someone should go,' I said. I took another look in the mirror, found my sunglasses, and put them on. 'But not me.'

Yes, there was someone knocking again at the front door.

At last Sophia went and answered it. After a few minutes she returned, looking very alarmed.

'It's the police. And a nun.'

We all exchanged horrified glances, wondering what to do. In the end, we edged up towards the door, and Juliette opened it wide enough for us to see a very young-looking policeman in a blue uniform, and a very old nun who had a face like thunder.

She jabbed a finger in our direction.

'*Esos son ellos!*'

'What's she saying?'

Juliette looked rather panicky. 'I have no idea, we did shopping and travel in my Spanish classes. We never covered being arrested.'

The young policeman stepped forward.

'You are the ladies on the beach?'

'Possibly,' I said carefully.

'The ladies with no...' His hands sketched out a female form and he blushed scarlet under his cap.

Kim hissed behind me. 'Shut the door. Deny everything.'

'*Esos son ellos!*' the elderly nun repeated. 'It's them.'

'We're very sorry,' I said.

The policeman and the nun looked at me curiously for a moment and then I remembered my missing eyebrow. My face felt hot, too. I hope it didn't look like a guilty blush.

'*Lo siento*,' Juliette added quickly. 'Sorry. *Mucho*.'

'Aha!' the nun said triumphantly as though we had confessed and admitted our guilt.

'What are we going to do?' Kim wailed.

'*Arrestalas*,' the nun said with another shake of her finger.

'I think she wants us arrested,' Juliette said. 'Sophia?'

Sophia shook her head. 'I know some Greek, but I haven't picked up much Spanish.'

The young policeman shuffled his feet.

'I am from Kidderminster. I know nothing,' Kim put in helpfully.

'Ladies in the newspaper,' he said at last, 'I have some... um... *preguntas*.'

Kim's nostrils flared. 'I most certainly am not pregnant. I may have put on a few pounds...'

Juliette interrupted. '*Preguntas* means questions. He wants to ask us a few questions.'

'Well, he'll need a court order and a warrant,' Kim said. 'And he needs to read us our Miranda rights. And he'll do that in Spanish, won't he, and we won't understand. But that's good, when we are in court we can claim diplomatic immunity.'

'Kim, this isn't *Miami Vice*,' I said, 'calm down.'

'*Error. Lo siento*,' Juliette said with an ingratiating smile. 'Mistake. God, I'm sweating. What are we going to do. *Dondé es el gato*, by the way?'

The nun narrowed her eyes.

'*Tenían sombreros. Con patos.* Hats. And ducks.'

She looked past us and pointed at the coat hooks where our team yellow hats were hanging ceremoniously in a row.

'*Así.* Like that.'

'Busted,' Juliette murmured.

'Well, you did say they would help us stand out,' Kim said.

The policeman fingered his walkie-talkie. Perhaps he felt he needed back-up.

'Can I help?' said a familiar voice.

It was Bruno. Of course it was. Thank goodness.

I sighed with relief. 'This nun wants the policeman to arrest us. Because of the skinny-dipping thing and the photograph in the paper.'

Bruno chuckled. 'Right, go inside and put the kettle on. I'll see if I can clear this up.'

Bruno started talking to them both and the policeman's face relaxed a little. We scurried into the kitchen and sat on the bar stools.

'Should we get out the back way and make a run for it?' Kim said. 'Oh, gosh, what will my kids say?'

'Policemen always go round the back,' I whispered, 'we'd open the patio doors and there would be another one with a gun.'

'You both watch too much television,' Juliette said.

Sophia put an arm around Kim. 'It'll be okay. I'm sure it will. Perhaps I will put the kettle on.'

We sat doing what any British people would do under the circumstances, drank tea, and ate some digestive biscuits Kim had found in her case.

We could hear the reassuring sound of Bruno laughing, the policeman sounding quite chatty and then the nun talking at speed.

After ten minutes, Bruno came into the kitchen.

'I think I've sorted it,' he said. 'I've told them it was a mistake, that you are very sorry. The sister says she will forgive you on one condition.'

'What?' Kim squeaked. 'I don't want to end up in a Spanish prison. Waiting for a call from the embassy.'

'You make a donation to the convent. Apparently they have been collecting all this week.'

'We know,' Juliette said, 'they've had a lot of money out of us already. Three times. Still, an Old Ducks' holiday isn't complete without the threat of arrest.'

Bruno shrugged. 'Well, it's up to you, but I'd be inclined to go along with it. They say it will go towards repairing the fence and putting up bigger signs.'

We all turned to look at each other and then hurried off to find our purses.

* * *

'Thank heavens you came along when you did,' I said a bit later when we had abandoned our tea and opened a bottle of wine.

'It was something and nothing,' Bruno said, 'anyway, I was hoping to see you.'

I pulled my bathrobe a bit tighter and put one hand casually over my missing eyebrow.

'We were having a pampering session. With some organic, vegan free-range face packs that Juliette has brought. Three of us have silky, clear, revitalised skin. One of us doesn't.'

'Not that you need it, of course. What else are you doing?'

'We were just discussing Juliette's wedding. What she wants us to wear, that sort of thing.'

'Great. Super,' he said.

It seemed the other three had tactfully slunk away to leave us to talk. I realised I felt a bit wobbly. Almost arrested, well, that was a new experience. Not one that had been on my bucket list.

Was it possible to buy false eyebrows, in the same way that Juliette bought false eyelashes?

I'd only seen that in films, and they were usually attached to crazy people.

'Did your friends catch their flight okay?' I said, trying to sound calm.

'As far as I know. No one has told me any different. Why did you think you needed a face pack?'

'You obviously haven't properly appreciated the mystery that is woman,' I said. 'This is the sort of thing we do. Did you want something in particular?'

'Well, you did say you would come out with me for a drink, or dinner, before you went home,' he said. 'It would be a shame to keep your revitalised complexion all to yourself, wouldn't it?'

'I did, didn't I?'

'So?'

I tried to get my thoughts into some sort of order, and coordinating with my mouth.

'We are going home tomorrow, and I really don't want to go out looking like this. I think we might be having a takeaway this evening, a last get-together before we all go our separate ways. We've finished up all the chicken and the other stuff. Although there is some bread left. For toast in the morning. If anyone wants it. Otherwise we will just chuck it away and get something at the airport.'

For goodness' sake, why was I talking such nonsense? I pressed my hands to my cheeks, which now felt dry and rather hot.

'What time is your flight?'

'Late morning.'

'So what about tomorrow evening?'

'No, you don't understand. My flight is tomorrow,' I said.

He nodded. 'Do you remember what I said the other day? What if you didn't get on it? What if you stayed on for a few more days? Would you be missing anything in particular? Took a later flight.'

Missing anything in particular? Took a later flight?

I stared at him for a few seconds, until I realised my mouth had dropped open. I closed it. There was a strand of avocado goo trailing around my mouth and I daintily picked it out.

'I have some hanging baskets that probably need watering,' I said.

'I'm sure they will be fine.'

'Took a later flight,' I said.

'They do exist,' he said, with a grin. 'Would it be that bad?'

'Stayed on for a few more days,' I said.

'What I mean is, why don't you stay on, come back with me to my house. It would give us the chance to actually talk to each other. There hasn't been the opportunity this week, with other people around. And there have been times when I thought you wanted to talk to me, but of course it wasn't possible. Well, I'm trying to give us both the opportunity, and this seems as good a chance as any. I don't want to leave it for another thirty years.'

'Thirty-nine,' I said.

'Thirty-nine,' he agreed. 'So what do you think?'

'It's a great idea,' said a voice behind me and I turned to see Juliette, Kim and Sophia hiding rather unsuccessfully behind a door frame.

'I'll sort out which are your bags and put them in a different pile,' Kim said.

'And I'll make sure you've got everything,' Sophia added.

'And if you haven't, I'll take it home and let you have it at the wedding,' Juliette said.

'It's all sorted, Bruno,' Juliette said cheerfully. 'Our taxi is coming at eight o'clock tomorrow morning, and we'll push Denny out if she tries to get in. You can come and get her any time after that.'

I looked at her, unnerved by the way things were turning out so unexpectedly.

'That's great,' Bruno said. 'I'll see you tomorrow. I would kiss you on the cheek, but I don't want to ruin anything.'

And he walked away. I think his shoulders were shaking with laughter, but I wasn't sure.

Sophia saw him out and then the three of them came back to stare at me a bit more.

'What have you done?' I said. 'I've only got one eyebrow. I need time to think about it.'

'You've had nearly four decades. I would have thought that was more than enough time,' Kim said.

'I'm taking charge, I'm good at that. We've watched you two skirting around each other for long enough. You need some time on your own to work things through. I'm a great believer in that. Then neither of you will be part of a group, there won't be any disasters or distractions. And I've found an eyebrow pencil in my make-up bag,' Juliette held it out, 'so you can repair the damage. He'll never know.'

'But what will we actually talk about?' I said.

Kim snorted with laughter. 'I'm sure you'll think of something.'

'And if it all goes horribly wrong then you can get a flight home, you have the card for the taxi firm, and you never need to see Bruno again,' Sophia said.

'If that's what you really want?' Juliette added. She looked mischievous. 'But somehow I don't think it is. Now which one of us looks the most like Cindy Crawford?'

'Claudia Schiffer, that would be nice,' Kim said. 'Can you imagine how marvellous it must be to wake up every morning and see that in your mirror?'

'I bet she has her off days,' Sophia said.

'I bet she doesn't. I bet she could wash a muddy dog in the bath and still look marvellous,' Kim replied. 'I bet the dog is photogenic too.'

* * *

Well, I had got myself into the travelling frame of mind. My bags were just about packed, I only had a few things to put in at the last moment. So I was ready to deal with leaving in the morning, getting to the airport, security checks, taking off from Palma, landing back in Birmingham and going home. The whole pattern for tomorrow had been precisely laid out in my mind and now I had to think about doing something very different.

I woke up several times in the night, touching my missing eyebrow sadly, hoping it was growing back, and thought about going to stay with Bruno. Perhaps it wasn't such a bad idea after all.

18

The following morning, I knew something was wrong before I'd even woken up properly. Juliette had thumped on my door and come in without ceremony.

'I hope you're decent? Oh, my God!'

I struggled into an upright position; I couldn't seem to open my eyes properly and my face felt tight.

'What the rolling heck has happened to you?' she said.

She went across to open the curtains and came to peer at me more closely.

'What? What's happened?' I said.

'My guess is you were allergic to that face pack. You look like you've been in a fight.'

I went into the bathroom. My reflection showed she was right. Everywhere the face mask had touched was a livid red, and there was some swelling around my eyes which made me resemble a boxer after a losing match. Particularly with most of one eyebrow missing.

I made a strange wailing noise while Juliette patted me on the back and tried to reassure me.

'It's not that bad. Honestly. I knew someone once who had such an allergy to a moisturiser that her eyes swelled up and she couldn't see out for weeks. I mean, it went eventually. Do you feel okay?'

I started splashing cold water on my face and peering into the mirror to see if it made any difference.

'Yes, considering.'

'After that, the only moisturiser she could use was olive oil. And she couldn't go out in the sun with that on her face for obvious reasons.'

'Oh, God! What am I going to do? They'd never let me on the plane looking like this! I look like I have some terrible disease.'

'Kim has some antihistamines for her hay fever, perhaps you should take one of those? And then perhaps you need to see a doctor, or a pharmacist.'

I did a bit more distressed wailing, to such an extent that Kim and Sophia came to see what all the fuss was.

'Oh dear. Oh dear me,' Kim said, clutching at the neck of her dressing gown, 'that's not right. What did you do to yourself?'

'I think it was yesterday's face pack,' Juliette said, 'unless Denny went out in the middle of the night without any of us knowing and had a bar brawl.'

'Oh, golly,' Sophia said, 'what can we do?'

I splashed my face with more cold water, not liking the feel of my swollen, taut face under my fingertips. I looked in the mirror again, hoping it wasn't as bad as I'd first thought. It was.

'I'll go and do some research on the internet,' Juliette said.

'I'll get you my antihistamines,' Kim said, 'you're not allergic, are you? This hasn't happened before? You're not having trouble breathing, are you?'

'No. I don't think so,' I said, taking some slow breaths to double check.

'And I'll get you some ice in a tea towel,' Sophia added, 'it might help reduce the swelling.'

'Ice in a tea towel? I haven't sprained my face playing tennis,' I wailed.

* * *

'It says here on the internet it may take a few hours to a few days for the allergic reaction to go down,' Juliette said later, 'as long as you aren't having any problem breathing or swallowing you should be okay. You should see some of the pictures on Google! Sores and blisters and red weals. Absolutely awful. I bet some of them sued. You got off lightly.'

By then, we were sitting in the kitchen and Juliette had been diligently tapping away on her laptop.

'Avoid the thing that did it, don't scratch and try not to worry. Apparently stress can make it worse.'

I slumped on the worktop, one hand clutching the damp tea towel which Sophia had wrapped around some ice cubes against my cheek. The other was holding a cup of tea. At least my mouth still worked.

'Shall I ring a doctor?' Kim said.

'I don't think so,' Juliette said, 'it sounds like contact dermatitis. Don't use the allergen again...'

'Like I'm going to,' I said.

'...antihistamines, cold compresses or take a cold bath.'

'But it's only my face,' I said.

The three of them stood in a line, staring at me.

'I don't think it's as bad as it was,' Kim said.

I looked up. 'Is the swelling going down?'

'No, not really, but it's early days,' Sophia said kindly.

'Now I just want to get home and hide,' I said.

'There's not much chance of that,' Juliette said cheerfully, 'it looks pretty bad. Good job we have Plan B.'

I looked at her.

'Plan Bruno,' she said, 'now you'll have to stay behind until it all calms down.'

'Oh, yes, this is just perfect,' I wailed, 'going to sort out our relationship, or lack of it, when I look like this! I look terrible.'

'Oh, no, it's not that bad,' Kim said encouragingly, 'not really. You still look like you but with a fat face, and sunburn. And a missing eyebrow.'

I gave a despairing shriek.

Juliette closed her laptop. 'You're not to get stressed. That makes the brain think all sorts of stuff, and it can make it worse. Deep, calm breaths.'

Okay. Yoga, four-part breathing. In, count, hold, count, out, count, hold.

It was as though history was repeating itself. I'd done this the first day we arrived here.

'That's the way,' Sophia said, looking at her watch. 'It's half past seven. The taxi is arriving at eight o'clock. What should we do? Should we all cancel?'

'But we can't stay on here, there are going to be new people here later on this afternoon,' Kim said.

'You're right. Maybe we could find a B&B or something?'

'No,' I said, 'there's no need for that. We all know what I've got to do.'

At that moment, there was a knock on the front door. We all looked at each other.

'Oh, God, that will be Bruno,' I cried, 'don't let him see me.'

'That's going to be difficult, unless you put a bag over your head,' Kim said thoughtfully.

'Have we got any paper bags?' Juliette asked. 'I think we might have a couple of plastic ones, but then she might suffocate.'

'I've only got the paper bag my fridge magnets came in, and that wouldn't be nearly big enough,' Kim said. 'There might be a screwed-up one in the recycling. She has got quite a big head, that's why she had to have the biggest duck hat.'

'I can hear you, you know,' I said, 'I'm not in a coma.'

I gave a last, despairing cry and went off upstairs to my room.

Downstairs I heard the others talking in low voices, and then I heard the door knocker again.

'Well, someone has to answer it,' someone said.

There was a moment's silence and then I heard Juliette.

'Bruno. We thought it might be you. Now you are not to worry.'

I stood by my open bedroom door and eavesdropped.

'Really,' he said at last. 'Oh dear. Poor Denny. Does she need a hospital? Or a doctor?'

'No, nothing like that, but – well, when you see her, you'll understand.'

'Don't bring him up here,' I shouted down the stairs.

'You'll have to come down at some point,' Kim shouted back, 'the cleaners are arriving at eleven.'

I went and looked hopefully in the bathroom mirror. Perhaps the swelling had gone down a little bit, but I still looked as if I was wearing a shiny scarlet face mask. Well, that was just marvellous.

I gave a sigh, wishing my hair was long enough to pull over my face. But then I would have looked like 'Cousin Itt' from *The Addams Family*. All I would need was a bowler hat and some sunglasses over the top.

I felt like crying, but perhaps that might make things even worse. My eyes were red and puffy enough as it was, I never was a pretty crier.

I dressed and went slowly downstairs. The others were standing around in the kitchen and there was a big pile of cases and bags by the front door. The holiday really was over, and they were going to be leaving without me.

'Are you okay?' Bruno said. 'Juliette told me what happened.'

He wasn't laughing but there was definitely a hint of humour in his tone.

'Oh, you know,' I said, putting my hands to my face.

'Don't scratch,' the others shouted in unison.

'I'm not bloody scratching,' I said, 'I'm trying to hide.'

'Don't worry, it's not that bad,' Bruno said.

'Of course it's that bad!' I said. 'Just look at me, I look like I fell asleep on a sunbed and then someone punched me.'

'Are you sure you don't want us to stay?' Sophia said.

'No, I'll be fine,' I sighed, 'but perhaps I need some more anti-histamines?'

'I'll sort that out,' Bruno said, 'I have a friend who is a doctor.'

'You seem to have a friend who does everything,' Juliette said.

He grinned. 'I do. Now your taxi will be here soon, just make sure no one has forgotten anything. And I will take Denny off to recover.'

'Are you sure you're going to be all right?' Juliette asked, but she was already looking through her handbag, checking for her passport and plane tickets, I guessed.

'I will. Just give me a few days. I'll let you know,' I said, rather glum.

The other three started panicking at the sound of a car horn tooting outside.

'That must be the taxi. It's early.'

'Have you got everything?'

'What about the bathrooms? Has everyone checked?'

I stood in the hallway watching while Bruno helped the taxi

driver load all their bags into the boot of his car. He darted a look at me, and his eyes widened, so I slunk off back into the house, taking my balloon face with me.

The other three came to give me a hug, and reassurance that in a few days I would be as right as ninepence, which in decimal currency was about 4p. Hardly comforting.

'Right then,' Bruno said, after they had gone. 'Let's get your stuff into my car, shall we?'

I nodded. My eyes were watering at that point, and they stung a bit.

'You'll be fine,' he said kindly, handing me a box of tissues which had been left on the worktop. 'I'll look after you.'

'Just don't look at me,' I said.

'I'll try,' he said.

To be fair, he put all my bags in the back of his car without once looking at me, but I knew he was making an effort, which somehow made it worse.

'Perhaps I should sit in the back?'

'Then I would have to look at you. In the rear-view mirror,' he said.

I got into the passenger seat, put my duck hat and my sunglasses on, flipped the sun visor down and slumped in my seat.

'It will only take an hour or so to get there,' Bruno said.

'Okay.'

I was torn. I did like the idea of spending more time with him, but I didn't want to be doing so with my face the size of a watermelon. At least that's how it felt.

'Would you like some music on?'

'I don't mind.'

He switched on the car radio, which unfortunately at that

precise moment was playing '99 Red Balloons', a europop song I remembered from the eighties.

Bruno snorted with laughter and was tactful enough to turn it off.

'I don't think we need that, do you?'

I sank down even lower, at the same time trying to concentrate on the scenery.

We drove out of the town and along the coast for a while, passing the signs for Alcudia and then driving inland away from the sea.

'I've brought you a bottle of water, in case you need it,' he said after a few miles.

'Thanks.'

I held it against my face, wishing I could just tip the whole lot over myself.

Outside it was another absolutely glorious day and the road was flat and straight, leading us past agricultural land and farmhouses.

'There are olive groves here and oranges later in the year,' he said, 'it's a beautiful country. This is not the tourist area, it's been farmed like this for centuries.'

'I feel such an idiot,' I said at last in a small voice.

He turned his head.

'Don't look at me!'

He grinned.

'You're not an idiot, you were just unlucky. It could have been one of the others, or you might not have reacted this way at all.'

We travelled a few more miles, following a truck piled up with flattened cardboard which didn't look too secure to me.

'See the vines, over there, that's the place I took my friends to visit, they do wine tours and tastings. It's very good, I think you tried some.'

Ah, yes, I remembered. All of us sitting around enjoying the warm evening, the wine flowing like – well, wine, and none of us had cheeks like a hamster after a corn-on-the-cob party.

The road was busier now, we passed roundabouts, furniture warehouses, car dealerships and huge supermarkets the size of aircraft hangars.

At last we reached a town where the streets were tree lined and shady, and then suddenly there was the Mediterranean in front of us again.

'We are nearly home,' Bruno said, 'just a little way out of the town and up in the hills. I have wonderful views, as you'll see.'

'How long have you lived here?'

'Twenty years. I was very lucky to find this place, I bought it for a song, but then I had...'

'Let me guess, a friend who was an estate agent?'

He grinned. 'You've got it.'

We turned off the main road and up an unmetalled track into the wooded landscape. We passed a couple of attractive white houses with undulating terracotta roofs, and at last we drove into a clearing, where there was a gravelled driveway in front of a picture-perfect stone house. The black-painted shutters were closed against the heat of the sun, but I caught a glimpse of a pool to one side, shimmering in the sunshine. The thought that I could perhaps plunge my face into it was very appealing.

'It's lovely,' I said.

'I like it,' he said. He pulled up to the front door and stilled the engine. 'It's not terribly smart, but I've done a lot of work on it over the years. Now let's get you settled.'

The front door opened into a cool, tiled hallway, with a white archway leading to a living room furnished with comfortable-looking sofas and chairs. On the other side was a beamed dining room which contained a wooden staircase.

'We'll leave the kitchen and everything else for now,' he said. 'Come and see the views.'

He threw open some patio doors and I followed him out onto a shaded stone terrace where there was a long wooden table and chairs. There were stone pots of flowers spilling out over the wall, and the sounds of birds in the trees that surrounded the back of the house.

Below us, the blue sea sparkled in the sunshine, one speedboat cutting a white wake across the calm water. A breeze from the sea cooled my face.

'This is glorious,' I said.

I tried to remember what twists of fate had brought me to this place on that day with this man. It all seemed a bit unlikely, and yet there I was. He stood with his hands in his pockets, watching as the boat disappeared out of sight behind the trees.

'I love it,' he repeated. 'I wouldn't live anywhere else. I know it is a bit out of the way, and it still needs a lot of work. A new kitchen, for one thing, but it's peaceful, it suits me. I built this terrace ten years ago. I thought those views were too good to miss out on. I spend a lot of time out here.'

I tried to reconcile this with my impression of Bruno all those years ago, when he had been a student who liked rock music, real ale, and the company of noisy friends. Now it seemed he preferred solitude and, by the immaculate state of the house, cleaning. Something the Bruno of thirty-nine years ago had not been particularly bothered by. Still, I had changed, so why should I be surprised if he had too?

'Now let me show you to your room,' he said. 'I'll bring your bags up. You can have a rest if you like? Although I was going to make some coffee.'

'Coffee would be lovely,' I said, dragging my gaze away from the matchless view.

Was it my imagination, or did my eyes feel a bit less swollen?

I followed him back into the house and he showed me a room, where there was a large double bed with a wooden bedstead, a rather rickety wardrobe and a small shower room. There were French doors which I could see opened onto a stone balcony with another view of the sea. There were two chairs there and a small stone table with a mosaic top.

'It's perfect,' I said, wanting above everything else to dunk my face in a basin of cold water.

He brought my cases up and left me to unpack. I went into the shower room, filled the sink with water and plunged my hot face into it.

I held my breath for as long as I could. Was it possible to drown myself in a sink? Even accidentally?

When I had imagined having time alone with him, I hadn't factored in being allergic to a face pack. I suppose I'd wanted to feel attractive and interesting. To be the old me from all those years ago. The more time I was spending with him, the more I liked him, the easier it was to remember the couple we had been all those years ago. Now I was older, and my life had been very different from his. And I had a face like a tomato.

Would he care? He hadn't seemed to so far. Perhaps that was just men.

For such a long time I had wanted to get answers to my questions, perhaps let fly with some pithy comments before I stalked off. But I no longer needed to say those things that I had festered over for so long. I had reached the acceptance stage; I'd said that to Kim. And anyway, there was no question of me stalking off anywhere.

Coffee sounded like a good start, and I dried my face carefully, and peered at my reflection for a few minutes. Then I drew on a few tentative eyebrow strokes, but Juliette's pencil was blunt, and the lines merged into a horrible splodge. And the pencil was the wrong colour, so it didn't even match. I had the awful feeling I looked like Max Wall or Groucho Marx. I was definitely not okay to get on a plane without the other passengers shying away from me in alarm, but I did look a tiny bit better. I wished I had a hat with a veil. Which was ridiculous.

19

I took my time unpacking and getting my things sorted out, then I dunked my face into the cold water again and stayed there as long as I could, coming up spluttering and gasping for breath.

After I had touched up my eyebrow, I went downstairs and I found Bruno sitting on the terrace with a cafetiere of coffee and a tin of biscuits.

'Ah, there you are. Feeling okay?'

'Not bad, thanks,' I said, 'a bit of a headache.'

'My friend Juan called by. He's the doctor I told you about. He did want to see you, but I said you weren't really up to receiving visitors. He left these tablets – one a day – and some ointment.'

How embarrassing was this? To be left some ointment by a total stranger.

'Thanks,' I said, grabbing them off the table.

'He says to get in touch if it gets worse, or if you have any trouble breathing.'

'I'm fine thanks, honestly, no problems.'

'Good. Have some coffee. By the way, what happened to your eyebrow?'

'Juliette said you wouldn't notice,' I wailed.

'Sorry. I won't say anything else.'

I sat with him, carefully positioning my chair slightly out of his eyeline, and stared out at the view, which was glorious.

I wondered what Bruno was thinking. Was he trying to find something for us to talk about that didn't involve my red, swollen face and my dissimilar eyebrows? Or the many daft things I had said and done in the past.

I'd fallen off some platform boots once when we were on our way to a summer concert in the park. I'd wrenched my ankle and had to take the boots off and carry them, and underneath I had been wearing Christmas socks, because they were the only clean ones left in my drawer. Bruno had found me a stick from somewhere and I'd limped along beside him like some old soldier back from the Boer War. And on another occasion in the days when cardboard mugs at takeaways had just become a thing, I'd tipped a whole chocolate milkshake over myself because I hadn't fastened the lid properly. And I had been wearing a white Laura Ashley dress at the time. Complete with milkmaid frills around the bottom.

And then there was the time when I had fallen down the stairs in our house and landed on the bag of groceries at the bottom, smashing a dozen eggs in the process.

Not to mention the day I had...

'I wondered what you'd like to eat this evening,' he said at last.

Phew. He hadn't been thinking about that sort of thing at all.

I forced myself to think.

'A salad of some sort? I like those,' I said.

'Chicken? Caesar?'

'Perfect,' I said.

'More coffee?'

'No, thanks, this is fine.'

'Biscuit?' He held out the tin towards me.

'No, I'm good, thanks.'

I wondered how the Old Ducks were getting on and looked at my watch. They should be at the airport by now, checking in their luggage and hurrying into duty-free to pick up some last-minute purchases. I felt a pang, not being there with them. I'd sent an email to cancel my flight, but would there be a string of increasingly annoyed announcements over the loudspeaker system, asking Denise Lambert to please come to the gate as the flight was closing?

I almost wished I smoked at that point; it would have given me something to do other than drink coffee.

We watched a helicopter overhead, a small one, not an official police sort. Perhaps a private owner, going home from work and avoiding the traffic. I wondered where he lived. In the town, perhaps, or in one of those sumptuous white villas on the coast. An attractive young wife was probably waiting for him, with a dry martini. And he would have brought her flowers. I bet she had two matching eyebrows.

'How are you feeling?' Bruno said at last.

'Not too bad. A bit foolish.'

'No need for that, it wasn't your fault,' he said.

'No, I suppose not.'

He flicked a glance across at me. 'I think the swelling is going down. Perhaps the antihistamines are working.'

I touched my face. 'Don't look at me! Yes, I think so too.'

There was another long silence, and I watched the helicopter circle around and suddenly return at speed in the direction from which it had come.

'I expect he has forgotten the present for his wife,' Bruno said.

I nodded because smiling was a bit difficult.

'I was just thinking something like that. I expect he is a

captain of industry, coming back from a conference, and he's left her flowers at the office.'

'Or he didn't remember to buy her any in the first place and his secretary didn't remind him.'

'And he knows she will be furious, so he has gone to try and find a landing place and a florist.'

'He'll be lucky,' Bruno said.

Then we watched a cruise ship, moving slowly across on the horizon, gleaming white against the blue sky. I wondered about the people on board. Were they enjoying themselves? I'd never been on a cruise; it might be fun to try one day.

'Did I ever buy you flowers?' Bruno said at last.

'No, I don't think you did,' I said.

'Not even once? For your birthday?'

'Nope.'

'That was bad of me. I should have done,' he said.

I don't suppose he had ever really known when my birthday was in the first place.

'It's 17 February,' he said at last. 'Am I right?'

'Yes, you are. What a good memory you have. And you are 18 June.'

'Aquarius and Cancer,' he said, surprising me.

Men didn't usually know that sort of thing, did they?

'You were certainly good at going into your shell,' I said.

'You weren't so bad yourself,' he replied.

We sat watching the sea for a bit longer, and I wondered if I would get away with going upstairs, for a nap. Or just some time away from this atmosphere which was slowly building between us.

'I want us to talk about what happened,' he said at last, 'but for now, can we just get to know each other again?'

'Of course,' I said.

This was what I wanted. To be at ease with each other again, to feel that friendship, that companionship that had once meant so much to me.

'Good. Look, why don't you go and relax? Have a shower or a nap maybe. There are plenty of books in the house, there is television, some comfortable corners where you can read or think. There's a Wi-Fi password on your bedside cabinet if you need it. I'll get some late lunch sorted out and I'll give you a shout when it's ready. What do you think?'

'Sounds great,' I said.

'And then this afternoon, I need to go into the village, pick up a few things for this evening. You could come with me if you felt up to it.'

I was already on my feet.

'Perfect, but I think I'll stay here for now.' I touched my face. 'You know. I don't want to frighten the horses.'

'Okay. I can see it's a bit difficult for you.'

Hmm, wasn't it difficult for him too? Perhaps men thought about this sort of thing differently.

I made my way back upstairs to my bedroom.

I had a long, cool shower and then sat in a comfortable chair on the little balcony outside my window. From there I could still see the sea, occasionally catch the breeze on my hot cheeks.

I could hear Bruno downstairs, making meal preparation noises. The occasional clink of a plate, cupboard doors being opened and closed. A tap being turned on and off. It was strangely relaxing.

When we had been together all those years ago, Bruno hadn't known one end of a kitchen from another. Our house share had been pretty basic. Landlords in those days filled their rental houses with cast-offs, mismatched china, and leftover furniture.

There had been none of the regulations that applied these days. And from what I knew, student expectations were higher.

There had been a broken gutter above the back door that he kept promising to replace but never did. When it rained heavily, the kitchen floor would get flooded. My wardrobe had to be kept shut with a scrap of cardboard. If someone turned the tap on in the kitchen when someone else was having a shower, there would be howls of anguish as the water in the bathroom ran cold.

I sighed; and yet none of that had mattered, it was just part of being a student. It was – we all agreed – better than being in the hall of residence, with a small single bed, a sink in a cupboard and only four showers for the whole floor.

How long ago it all seemed.

I logged onto the internet. There were several emails and messages from the Old Ducks, presumably sent while they were waiting at Palma airport.

Juliette: We've checked in and got rid of our bags. Are you okay? I'm sure the swelling will go down soon. Kim said she had a friend who had the same thing, and she had terrible, weeping blisters and had to go to hospital. It took months for it to sort out. You're not that bad, are you? I'm so sorry about the eyebrow. What are you doing? Send me pictures. Is the house nice? What are you doing????

Kim: We are about to board. I wish we didn't have to go home. We quite fancy a cruise next time. What do you think? My friend had a bad reaction to some face cream once, but she was okay in the end. What's the house like? Are you doing anything exciting?

Sophia: I'm about to board my flight home. Lovely to meet you, I hope you are feeling okay. Good luck with Bruno. See you at the wedding.

Juliette: Kim says I shouldn't have told you about her friend and the blisters. And there were only a few. It wasn't that bad. I'll be in touch about the wedding. Kim wants to wear something shroud-like and black and I've told her she can't. See you soon!

* * *

We sat on the terrace in the shade, and had lunch, a Caesar salad and crusty bread. Bruno had a small glass of white wine. I had water because of the antihistamines. And at last the difficult atmosphere between us seemed to thaw a little. It didn't exactly feel like old times, but at least we began to relax in each other's company.

He talked about an article he was writing for the local paper, about new places for tourists to visit in the area and events which were lined up for the summer.

A floral display in the village square, an outdoor concert, a food festival, a football tournament for the local schools. There was going to be a Fiesta, to bless the fishing boats in the harbour. I felt almost sad that I wouldn't be seeing any of it, although I would have given the football a miss.

'And you,' Bruno said, 'what will you be doing? I suppose the wedding will be the biggest thing this summer. It sounds like it will be fun.'

'Will you be there?'

'Well, I've been invited,' he said, with a wry smile.

I thought about the possibility of seeing Bruno in a sharp suit, perhaps a crisp white shirt and a tie. When I'd known him, I don't think he had owned a tie.

'I'd like you to be there.'

'Good,' he said, standing up to clear away the plates. 'Coffee?'

'Tea if you have it,' I said.

He returned a few minutes later with coffee for himself, tea for me and a bowl of grapes.

'I think I've made it the way you liked it. Not too strong, milk, no sugar?'

'Perfect,' I said.

'After this I will pop into the village, pick up a few things, and I have a couple of errands to run. Is there anything I can get you?'

Some tranquilisers?

'Nothing, thanks.'

He left about half an hour later, his car throwing up dust from the dry road. I stood and listened to the silence of the house. I was sure I hadn't imagined the renewed feelings between us. Which one of us was going to crack first and make a move?

I was. I was going to take a chance, trust my instincts and tell him how I felt. Because I knew if I didn't, I would regret it forever.

20

The evening was a pleasant one, with a warm breeze coming in from the sea, bringing with it the faint scent of the pine trees and hot sand.

'This is so beautiful,' I said. 'I can see why you have been here for so long.'

'I can't imagine living anywhere else,' he'd said. 'Life's too short. What is it like where you live?'

I shook my head. 'Nothing like this. I have a house in an area that used to be a bit rundown, but in the last few years it's been improved. I am not far from a station, there are shops and buses nearby. It used to be very convenient for travelling into work.'

As I said the words, I remembered the noise, the roulette possibility of finding a parking place outside my house, the occasional fast-food rubbish thrust into my hedge. Up until then I had been reasonably satisfied with my house, but now there was a nagging doubt at the back of my mind. Would I prefer to live somewhere tranquil, like this? Not a bigger house, because I didn't need that, but a place where the air was clearer, the traffic less intrusive. Without the bustle, the noise, the constant battle to get anywhere.'

'And now you have retired?'

'It's still convenient for lots of things. And these days Birmingham has so much to offer. Theatres, the cinema, museums.'

Oh, boy, that sounded dull.

'Do you go to theatres, the cinema and museums?' he asked.

'No, not very often,' I admitted, 'but sometimes with friends.'

Bruno chuckled and shook his head. 'You would have had to be drugged to get you into a museum back when I first knew you.'

'Actually, I still would if I'm honest,' I said.

He grinned at me.

The swelling around my face had gone down even more over the course of the day, so I hadn't taken any more medication. I was beginning to think I had been lucky after all.

On the strength of this, I allowed myself a small glass of red wine to go with the platter Bruno had produced for our evening meal. All sorts of different types of cheese and cold meats, wrapped in waxed paper, from the local delicatessen. There were tiny, sweet tomatoes in a bowl, slices of sourdough bread, a pot of unsalted butter, plump purple grapes.

'And what do you do for fun,' he said, 'you know, in your free time or at weekends?'

'I don't know, nothing much. I'm going to have to think about it. I've been so wrapped up in work I haven't allowed myself much free time, and it's been hard, getting used to not being there. Weekends – well, there are always household things to do. Sometimes I meet up with friends. I like decorating when the mood takes me. Why, what do you do?'

'I read, I cook, I paint. I write. I used to do some language coaching occasionally, but I haven't done any lately. I have a lot of friends in the area, we socialise, have meals at each other's houses. I spent last summer island hopping in Greece. I have made it my mission to enjoy life. Savour it. Make the most of it.'

'No regrets?'

'Yes, of course I have regrets,' he said.

There was a little silence between us then.

Unusually for me, I didn't say anything, just sat and twirled the stem of my wine glass. And then I stopped doing that because the wine slopped over the edge. I mopped up the spill with a tissue.

'Do you remember that time when you spilled a bottle of wine down the stairs? The whole thing,' he said, watching me. 'You and Hillary were trying to do some dance routine.'

'"Stairway to Paradise",' I said, 'we'd been watching *An American in Paris*. It was snowing outside.'

'That's it, we never did get the stain out. The landlord threatened me with legal action for weeks afterwards. I gave him fifty quid in the end. It didn't seem worth the hassle of going to court and explaining how filthy it was before we even moved in.'

'That was a disgusting place, wasn't it?'

'It seemed all right at the time,' he said.

I sat back in my chair and sighed.

'Everything was funny then, wasn't it? That's what I remember of the old days...'

Bruno tutted. 'Listen to you; *the old days*.'

'Yes, but the awful house we rented. Landlords would never get away with that now. At least I hope they don't. We never seemed to have any money, even though we had student grants and no loans. Having to walk everywhere because we spent all our money on beer, and hardly anyone had a car except you, and we were saving our money for trips away. I was thinking about that time on the boating lake the other day, when I dropped the oar and we had to be rescued.'

'That lad was so furious, wasn't he?' Bruno chuckled.

'And we had chips on the way home. Out of the newspaper. I don't think they are allowed to use newspaper any more. Which is a shame in my opinion. I think a bit of printer's ink made all the difference.'

I remembered that so well, the cold night air, my damp feet, the hot, vinegary smell of the chips which had burnt my mouth. We had walked back to our house, cold but happy. Laughing, nudging each other off the pavement, scrabbling for the last chip. And then later, leaping into bed, warming our icy hands on each other. I'd felt that I was in the right place at the right time with the right person.

And since then? What had taken the place of that? Nothing that was anywhere near as good. Over the years I had lived a more disciplined life, keeping to deadlines and organising my department. Checking and double checking everything. Eventually my weeks could have been interchangeable. The demands of relationships and holidays had sometimes felt irritating. Which was unbearably sad.

'And the bits of crunchy batter that were left over. What were they called?' Bruno said.

'Scraps. At least that's what we used to call them when we were kids. I expect they are against the law now; they probably contravene all sorts of by-laws and health warnings.'

'You do make it sound like another age,' he sighed.

'It was. My mother was still doing conversions from decimal money in the eighties when we went shopping. *Five shillings for a bar of chocolate! That's disgusting.*'

He laughed.

'And your parents? Are they still around?'

'No, sadly. What about your mother?'

Ah, yes, his mother. I'd tried to phone her once, about three months after I left university and Bruno still hadn't returned. But I had chickened out when she answered, my mouth dry. That gruff *Sí?* at the other end of the line. And then a louder *Quién está ahi?* Who is there? For some reason she had always terrified me, and my ability to ask her the questions I wanted to in Spanish was nil.

'No, she died over twenty years ago.'

'I'm sorry to hear that. So we really are the older generation now, aren't we? The ones at the top of the heap. In the direct line of fire.'

'Will we be on the old people's table at the wedding, do you think?'

'No, because most of the guests are going to be old people. That's the beauty of it.'

Bruno chuckled. 'Perhaps there will be just one table of younger people, and I bet you anything they will be behaving impeccably. Not throwing food at each other and setting fire to sweet wrappers like we used to do. Remember that dinner we went to, to celebrate the bicentenary of the university being founded? We really were awful, weren't we? You were wearing a long dress, green and white. I remember you looked lovely.'

I sighed. 'Until the zip split and I had to get an attendant in the ladies' cloakroom to sew me into it with a mending kit she had. And one of my friends – Caroline – broke half the heel off her shoe in a grating and had to hobble around all evening. So glamorous.'

He laughed, a lovely happy sound that I remembered so well. 'You are funny. That was the thing I remember so well, how we made each other laugh.'

And yet...

'Would you like a little more wine?'

'I would,' I said, holding out my glass towards him.

* * *

I went to bed soon after that, it was still early, only nine o'clock. But I was feeling worn out. Perhaps it was all the stress of the day, perhaps it was the lingering effects of the medication. Anyway, I retreated to my room, washed my face again and dunked it into another sink full of cold water. Then I applied some of the healing unguent that Bruno's doctor friend had left for me. It smelled like eucalyptus. Then I dabbed on a few more strokes of eyebrow pencil so I didn't frighten myself in the morning. After I had done that, I realised it was a bad idea and I would probably rub it all off onto the pillowcase in the night.

Then I fired up my laptop and caught up with the world. Nothing much seemed to have changed in my absence. Celebrity girls were still being photographed in revealing swimsuits in St Barts. Young men were still having brawls outside pubs and being arrested. Minor royals were still having dinners in fancy London restaurants.

I wondered how the Old Ducks were getting on, they should all be safely back by now.

I hoped Kim hadn't found too much to worry about when she got home. That Juliette and Matthew were enjoying being back together again. That Sophia had made it back to Rhodes and Theo.

I tried to imagine what it was like for her to have a partner, a lover who was also a friend, who gave her space. My relationships after Bruno hadn't been like that at all. There had always been a neediness, an imbalance for one person or the other.

What nice women the Old Ducks all were, the value of friendship had passed me by on that sort of level. Where we could exchange views, be rude, laugh at ourselves and each other and not damage the underlying affection. I would be seeing them again soon at the wedding. Which would be exciting if I could just find something suitably bridesmaid-ish to wear.

I sent them all a group email, telling them all about the day's adventures, describing the house and the views and reassuring them I was improving already but I needed to find a way to sharpen Juliette's eyebrow pencil. Then I attached a few photos and sent it off into the ether.

I sat looking at the screen for a moment, listening to the email whizz off. How amazing technology was. To be able to do that with just a few keyboard strokes. Life might have been very different all those years ago if I had been able to do that when Bruno went off to Italy.

Young people wouldn't understand the sort of problems we had faced back then. With only what they now called snail mail. No mobiles. Extortionate charges and delays to phone calls abroad. Even party lines, shared with another house. And you always knew when someone was listening in because there used to be a faint crackling noise, or the sound of someone's breathing. I for one was not going to reject the advances in technology, even with the potential problems it also caused.

* * *

I slept like the proverbial log that night. It was quiet; from my open window there was just the breeze sighing through the pine trees, and occasionally the sound of the sea, although there weren't of course many waves.

The bed was comfortable, my face had stopped hurting, and Bruno and I had actually been able to have a conversation without it making me feel as though I wanted to make some excuse and leave. Anyway, there was nowhere to go, I didn't have a car and I could hardly steal his. Not that I would, but the prospect of driving where everything was on the 'wrong' side, including the steering wheel and other vehicles, was very off-putting.

I tiptoed downstairs just after seven o'clock the following morning, and made myself a big mug of tea. Bruno had helpfully left the proper tea bags on the worktop by the kettle, which was kind, and then I went back upstairs and opened the bedroom curtains.

Sitting up in bed I could see the sea, which was beautifully framed by some wisteria which had grown around my window. It was just coming into bloom, much earlier than I would have expected, but then again, the weather here was kinder to some plants. The purple cones of blossom were already sending out a lovely scent, and I felt a delightful burst of optimism for the day ahead.

I wondered what we would do. I went to have another look at my swollen face and was delighted to see some further improve-ment. The eyebrow pencil had indeed transferred itself to my pillowcase, and I turned it over guiltily. By then I'd had a reply from Juliette, apologising again about eyebrow-gate, and telling me she was going shopping for her wedding outfit that day.

Nothing too out there, perhaps a nice dress and jacket? My friend's sister got married again the other day, for the third time, I've just been sent the pictures. The bride is seventy and wore a big white meringue dress and a long veil. And she had eight bridesmaids in a sort of egg-yolk yellow. Shall I do that? What do you think?

Hmm, I couldn't see Juliette doing that at all, and after every-thing Kim had said about yellow, she'd go mad. Still, each to their own.

I wondered then what I would have chosen if I had ever married.

Back in the days of big Princess Diana dresses with bows and puffed sleeves, I'd thought she looked marvellous. It was the era of lace and romanticism and Laura Ashley country frocks, with wicker baskets which snagged your tights. Then came big shoulder pads, big hair and tightly fitted power suits. I suppose that was one of the good things about fashion these days, you could wear what you liked and usually no one would comment. Well, you could if you were young.

I found an article on a newspaper website, headlined *What to wear if you're over sixty*, accompanied by some of the most dreary garments I had seen for a while.

Where did they find these things?

Evidently the message to us older gals from some twenty-something fashion expert was that if you really have the nerve to be seen in public, try not to be too noticeable. Damn cheek. Juliette had the right idea. Wear what you like, what you are comfortable in and to hell with other people's opinions.

Having clicked on that article, it meant that a lot of other related advice started to appear on my feed. Insurance schemes for the over-fifties with the promise of a free pen. Whoop de doo! Funeral plans. Lifestyle tips for the over-sixties, where the illustration was of an old crone, hobbling along with a stick and a sweet smile.

And yet look at the Old Ducks, we were all in our sixties, some of us would be seventy soon. And none of us were considering giving up and hiding so as not to outrage the younger generation with the sight of us. We were still planning and thinking about life, still learning, still prepared to try.

Perhaps the fashionistas couldn't bring themselves to deal with actual older people? Women with real lives and real figures.

And surely very few women would be able to afford £1,700 for a coat?

* * *

I heard Bruno going downstairs some time later. It must have been about eight-thirty. He never had been an early-morning person, so that hadn't changed. As a student at weekends, he had been capable of sleeping until midday and then having an afternoon nap as well. I'd once told him he was half-cat.

I could hear him moving about downstairs, the gentle sounds of cupboard doors closing, a chair scraping on the stone floor. He was making coffee, perhaps. It felt comfortable, safe to know he was there. I had thought that before, hadn't I? That Bruno made me feel secure.

I got up, had a shower, and dressed. Hmm, those navy-blue linen trousers had a bit of an old lady vibe. Perhaps I would wear a maxi dress instead, and some white trainers. I still wasn't cool enough to pair a long dress with Dr Marten boots and I probably never would be.

In the end, I found my red jeans, a white T-shirt and a stripy cardigan. Juliette would have approved. In future I would make an effort to be colourful. There was definitely too much grey and navy-blue in my wardrobe. Was that my choice or because that was what the fashion industry thought we wanted?

Downstairs I found Bruno sitting at the dining room table, with a cafetiere of coffee. He looked up.

'How are you feeling? I know I'm not supposed to look at you, but after all, you're not an Egyptian queen, and I think you look much better.'

'I feel better too,' I said.

He filled a coffee mug for me. I took an appreciative sip. The coffee here tasted so much better than what I was used to at home. Perhaps I would try when I got back and not rely on giant jars of instant.

'So shall we go out somewhere?'

I suppose the thought did cross my mind that if I was well enough to go out, then I would be okay to fly home. Except at that moment I really didn't want to.

At home it was cold, windy and there was an 80 per cent chance of rain. Here it was going to be warm and sunny with a 0 per cent chance of any precipitation. Perhaps I would hang on for a little bit longer.

'Yes, I'd like that, nothing too taxing in case you were thinking of a day's hiking,' I said. 'Where do you suggest?'

'There is a beautiful walk, down by the harbour. There are a lot of boats there to look at, and plenty of places to eat with a view over the sea. I remember you always liked that, eating outside. And don't worry about any hiking, I learned my lesson a long time ago. I remember taking you to the Brecon Beacons once. It didn't go well. I seem to remember a lot of complaining and sulking.'

I laughed. 'And I was even worse than you.'

He laughed too and topped up my coffee.

'Did you sleep okay?'

'Excellent, thanks, I was very comfortable.'

'Would you like some breakfast, or shall we get something when we are out?'

'I can wait,' I said.

He nodded his agreement.

We carried on chatting and the conversation became easier. Me asking him about the area and the people he knew. Him asking about my job, my life up to this point. What we had both been doing in the intervening years.

He had been back to England many times, visiting old friends, he had even been to a twenty-year university reunion. One which I could have gone to as well, and who knew; we could have met there. But I had been in Stockholm on a conference. I don't think I had even responded to the email invitation. Never even considered it. I began to wish that I had. Perhaps we could have... what? Saved ourselves a lot of time and wasted years apart?

I looked at his hands, strong and brown, cradling his coffee mug. There was a little scar across one thumb, and I had an almost irresistible desire to reach out and touch it.

The more time I spent with him, the more I remembered how much I had loved him, more importantly how much I had liked him and still did. So there was nothing wrong with renewing an old friendship, was there? I would just see how the day went and play it by ear. I thought that with my new Old Ducks' attitude to life, my brain would think of things I shouldn't say, but I would probably say them anyway.

21

———————

Just before midday, we drove down the hillside again, and even though it had been a short time, I had the feeling that I had been away for ages. Like when I had been in hospital with appendicitis for four days a few years ago. By the time a friend came to collect me, it felt I had been away for weeks. The world going on without me, while I ate strange meals and learned to stand upright again.

The scenery that day was stunning, the sky clear and blue, and the sun shone down on the little town, the sea sparkling all around us.

We parked in a tree-shaded square and walked down a pavement lined with palm trees, their new leaves starting to unfurl above us. We went towards the little marina where dozens of boats were moored. It was still the Easter holidays so there were families with their children, tourists like me, locals standing around smoking and chatting in Spanish, a couple of older ladies with shopping bags taking a rest on one of the benches.

There was a small playground with swings and a slide, a few cafés and restaurants, with chairs and tables set out under white gazebos, and menus written up on chalk boards, neat apartment blocks with balconies where couples were drinking coffee and admiring the view.

'This is lovely,' I said at last.

'And no scree slopes to scramble up,' Bruno said with a grin.

'I was awful that day, wasn't I?'

'It wasn't your finest hour,' he admitted, 'but you did warn me beforehand.'

We stopped at a café where Bruno was warmly greeted by a large man in a white apron, and we were shown to a table by the edge of the water.

'Now don't fall in,' Bruno said.

'There's a two-foot-high wall,' I said, 'I'm not likely to clamber on top of that, am I?'

'It wouldn't surprise me,' he said, 'if anyone was going to, it would be you.'

'I'm all grown up now and far more sensible,' I said.

'Which is a shame,' he said.

We grinned at each other.

I felt a little jolt of something inside me. I did still love him. I thought I did, and at that moment I knew. In fact, I don't think I had ever stopped.

As it was lunchtime, we ordered a pizza to share and it was borne aloft in triumph to our table by Bruno's friend, who turned out to be the owner, Santiago.

'A beautiful pizza for a beautiful lady,' Santiago said gallantly, before he placed it on a metal stand between us.

'Santiago has run this place for years, and his grandfather and father before him,' Bruno said, 'but his son has left to work in Madrid, so he doesn't know who will take over. Perhaps he will sell up when the time comes.'

Santiago nodded his agreement and for a few minutes stood next to our table, his hands clasping and unclasping in front of him as though they were unused to having nothing to do.

'Children, you know what they are like. One minute I am a hero to my son, the next Papa is an old fool who knows nothing. My wife says I need to wait a few years and then maybe he will realise I did know a few things after all.'

He wandered off back to his kitchen, picking up a couple of empty plates on the way.

I levered off a large slice of pizza; it was fantastic. The edges crispy and slightly charred, the filling delicious.

Of course, I didn't know what children were like because I had never had any. Nor had Bruno. Perhaps that was a shame. Or perhaps the world was full enough.

We sat and ate, watching the boats bobbing in the water, a couple of them setting out to sea.

'Do you wish you had children?' Bruno asked sometime later.

'Maybe,' I said. 'Do you?'

'Yes,' he said, 'I would have liked children.'

'Why didn't you have any?' I said. 'Not that it's any of my business. You don't have to tell me.'

He pulled a face. 'Wendy and I were never going to last long enough to make good parents, you know that already. And even back then, I knew being a parent lasts forever. Not just until they leave home or have their own families. And after we divorced, I had a few partners, perhaps one or two might have... but I never met anyone I wanted to have children with. Not after you.'

The last mouthful of pizza was suddenly like a stone in my throat, and I swallowed hard, washing it down with a gulp of water.

'Really?' I said at last.

Bruno nodded. 'Of course. You know that. We were going to

have three sons, called Curly, Larry and Moe. After the Three Stooges. It was all planned out for us.'

I gasped, putting a hand to my mouth in shock. Ah yes, I remembered now.

We had been at a party somewhere; it had been fancy dress. I had been in my Laura Ashley finery as a milkmaid, Bruno had adapted a striped bath towel into a poncho and come as Clint Eastwood, a chocolate cigarillo clamped between his teeth before it started to melt, and I ate it.

We had been sitting in the ramshackle conservatory, where holes in the glass were stuffed with plastic bags to keep out the rain, drinking beer out of paper cups. All the cushions on the seats were slightly damp, so I had been sitting on Bruno's knee, and we had all started talking about the future, in that drunken, unrealistic way that students did. Where we would be in five years, in ten years?

'Well, I predict you two will be married and living in some beaten-up old farmhouse. With an Aga, and a load of socks drying on the rail. And a disgusting old dog asleep on the floor,' someone said.

'Dogs are not disgusting,' someone else said, 'and Benny will have a hoard of kids, running wild in bare feet and shorts even though it's snowing.'

'Three kids,' someone else chimed in, 'boys.'

'Curly, Larry and Moe. The Three Stooges.'

'I'd forgotten,' I said, slightly breathless, as a pain clenched at my heart. There was perhaps a small piece left of me that was truly young, and in that moment it shrivelled, as I thought about what might have been.

Just for a moment I could see those phantom boys, with Bruno's dark curls and sparkling eyes, maybe the youngest one with my colouring, a bit quieter than the other two. Wandering about with a stick in his hand, looking at a leaf, a ladybird.

'I wonder why they saw us living in such squalor,' I said, trying to sound light-hearted.

I took a drink of water and a deep breath to steady myself.

'Back then, all we needed was each other. We didn't need fancy cars, or showy houses with expensive furniture, did we?' he said.

'Oh, God, Bruno. What happened?' I said and it was almost a cry.

He reached his hand across the table and covered mine. It was warm and reassuring.

'We just lost each other somehow,' he said. 'I was too busy with being abroad, you were too busy with finals and then work. I should have tried harder.'

'I should too,' I said. 'I was hurt and then annoyed and then bloody-minded and now it's too late.'

'No,' he said, 'it's not too late. Too late for those memories, but not too late.'

'Oh, Bruno.'

I felt rather odd. Sad and confused. And I didn't think I could eat another mouthful of pizza, even though it probably was the best one I'd ever tasted.

'I think I need a glass of wine,' I said.

He smiled. 'Me too.'

He called a waitress over and she brought us a small carafe of red wine and two glasses.

Bruno poured some out and raised his glass towards me.

'Here's to you, and to us,' he said.

I clinked my wine glass with his.

'I didn't think there was an us, not now.'

'There's always been an us, Denny,' he said, 'you know that.'

We sat in silence for a while, drinking the wine and looking out at the boats.

I watched a young couple walking hand in hand past us. He was tall and slightly messy; she was cute in the way young women who are becoming aware of the power of their beauty are.

Don't waste this, this moment, this chance, like I did, I thought, watching them as they strolled away.

Life was offering me a second chance at something. It was up to me how I dealt with it. And there was no guarantee that this time it would work.

If you want a guarantee, buy a toaster.

* * *

We drove back up the hillside, the air through the open windows cooler here, and went into the house.

'I think we need more wine for this,' Bruno said with a rueful smile, and went to fetch a bottle and two glasses.

We went out onto the terrace, beautifully cool in the shade. I sat on a wicker settee, he sat in a chair next to me.

'So,' he said at last, 'who wants to go first?'

'Do you remember, Bruno? Do you remember how we were? How we just fitted together perfectly.'

'Yes,' he said. He took a sip of his wine. 'Of course I do.'

22

THIRTY-NINE YEARS EARLIER

We met up at freshers' week, both of us in the same hall of residence, him on the top floor, me on the second. Each of us with our own small room, crammed with books and record players and portable black and white televisions if we were lucky.

There had been an instant attraction between us, even at the Freshers' evening where we had first locked eyes across the baying mob of students, while five people tried to eat three cream crackers and then whistle the national anthem.

In the days that followed, we had casually sought each other out for weeks, we had made each other laugh. Eventually we had become *Benny* to our friends, part Bruno, part Denny. We had gone on to share a rather dilapidated house together with three of our mates. Jason, Hillary, and Tommy.

Those were days of laughter, saving to go on trips away, not really needing money, because walking, being together with Bruno, making love in our uncomfortable bed had all been free.

And then, as the months whizzed past, I was about to start my third year with finals at the end of it, and Bruno was going to Italy for his study year. We were going to be apart, thousands of miles apart, and I still couldn't quite believe it. I felt as though I was in a film or a play, watching other people deal with the shift in their lives, and yet of course I had always known this would happen. That no matter how much we enjoyed each other's company, that one day... Like my sister's husband, like my mother, like my father, Bruno would leave, and I would be left behind. I wouldn't be needed any more.

It was the last day before he left. We had woken up to a sunny morning, the sunshine filtering through the inadequate curtains. I was somehow annoyed; it would have felt better if it had been raining.

'I still can't believe you're going,' I'd said.

I snuggled closer to Bruno's warm back and kissed him in that sensitive spot he had between his shoulder blades.

I looked at the silly bedside clock we had, with Snoopy on the front, leaping into the air with the joy of another new day. It was nearly midday. We had planned to meet up with some friends for lunch at a new and very popular wine bar that had opened up in the town. Such places were unusual in those days, and Tommy had made the booking weeks ago. At this rate, we would miss them. I don't think I really cared. This last day was all about endings, not beginnings.

Bruno took one of my hands and kissed it.

'I'll be back. I'll write. I'll ring when I get the chance.'

'You'll be having too much fun. You'll forget me,' I sulked.

He turned over and pulled a face. 'Don't be daft. I am going over there to study, you know. And I won't know anyone.'

I tried to imagine how I would feel the following day, when he had gone, and I was still here. I simply couldn't get my head around it.

In two days' time, it would be the start of the new term, my final year at university. All that lay ahead was work, revision,

projects, more work, and exams. I would still be in our terrible
little house share with the leaking conservatory, the fridge with
cartons of milk with pencil lines drawn on then, the plastic boxes
of food on specific shelves and *This is mine, don't eat it, Jason*
written hopefully on a paper label.

Meanwhile Bruno would be in Italy, in Naples. Spending a
year studying at an ancient university, living with an Italian
family. Probably seeing streets filled with Renaissance buildings
and unbearably cute trattorias where wine came in glass carafes
and cost pennies.

I had never been there, but to me Naples meant pizza, Vesu-
vius, Pompeii, and Herculaneum. Wonderful honey-coloured
stone houses, where flowers spilled out of window boxes. The Isle
of Capri would be just visible in the mist across the bay, a
winding road along the Amalfi coast, the verges filled with lemon
trees and pretty local girls in colourful clothes, probably leading
photogenic donkeys. I had no idea why the donkeys mattered. Or
the girls. Bruno and I had been together for years, we were inseparable. Surely I trusted him by now. Didn't I?

'I am feeling sorry for myself,' I'd said. 'I know you are going
to have such a great time, see Italy, meet new people, learn such a
lot. And I'm excited for you, really I am. But I'll be stuck here with
nothing to do but work.'

'Well, you won't have me to distract you,' Bruno said, 'I expect
you to get a First, and be hailed in triumph.'

'I'd rather be going to Italy like you,' I said.

'Oh, come on, Denny,' he said, shifting around to face me, and
putting an arm around my shoulders, 'you've always known I
would be going, I'll be back at Christmas, and I'll bring you something special.'

'You'd better,' I said, swallowing down my tears, 'What time
is it?'

He looked at his watch. 'Twelve-thirty, we are going to be late. Come on, we should get dressed. The others will be waiting for us.'

He got out of bed and went into the shower, while I lay thinking about tomorrow, and torturing myself with the thought of not seeing him for months.

We hadn't really been apart for more than a few days since we had met. We had written to each other when he had gone home to Barcelona for the first half term. Me telling him my news and trying to make it sound more interesting than it was.

He had sent postcards; it was a joke between us that he liked to find the dullest, most boring pictures he could find. I received one with a photograph of a dreary industrial estate and another of a roundabout with badly coloured cars. They made me laugh for some reason; it was another thing we had shared.

I'd met his mother twice when she came over to visit him, and both times – head to toe black – she had fixed me with a hard stare, not happy about her only son taking up with a girl who dressed in bright, clashing colours, micro skirts, baggy linen dungarees, and ripped jeans. She had poor health, apparently, bad circulation which meant her hands were always cold. I should have been kinder to her, reassured her that I loved Bruno, that I would take over where she left off. I'd moved all my things out of our shared room, and slept in the box room during her visit, hoping to fool her. No wonder she hadn't approved of me.

I could have tried harder, lengthened my skirts, taken the ribbons out of my hair, not worn the fingerless lace gloves, but I had been too sure of myself back then. Perhaps arrogant. But Bruno didn't seem to mind, and that was all I cared about.

Bruno came back into the room and sat on the edge of the bed while he put his socks on.

'Come on, you lazy mare. You need to get dressed.'

'Okay,' I said, rolling over, my face buried in the pillow that smelled of Bruno's shampoo.

Perhaps I would keep the pillowcase, not wash it, scenting out the last of him when he had gone.

'If you don't hurry up, I'll go without you,' he warned.

He had wandered around the room we shared, picking up his shoes, finding his jacket, checking for his wallet in the pocket.

I watched him that day, in the wine bar. Sitting across the table from me, eating without a care in the world, while I had picked and pushed at my salad, hardly joining in with the conversation and our friends who were there too.

'I'm so jealous,' Hillary had said, sounding perfectly cheerful. 'You're off to Naples while we are left here freezing our socks off while you lounge in the sunshine.'

'I'll be back at Christmas,' he'd said, careless and carefree.

'I wouldn't,' Jason had said, 'you'll be having far too much fun. And those Italian girls are gorgeous.'

'I have a gorgeous girl already,' Bruno had said and winked at me. 'Absence makes the heart grow fonder.'

'Out of sight, out of mind,' someone said.

It was Al, a loudmouthed drama student, who liked to think he was destined for Hollywood greatness. Which eventually he wasn't because he'd ended up managing a shoe shop in some huge out-of-town shopping mall. I don't know why he was there that day; he wasn't a particular friend of any of us.

'I promise you, that's not me,' Bruno had said, nudging my foot under the table.

'I don't care,' I'd said. 'Bruno can do what he likes.'

'Now there's a free pass, if ever I heard one,' Al had said with a rich chortle.

'Oh, do shut up, Al,' I'd said.

'I don't like to make any promises to my girlfriends,' Al said, 'it keeps them keen.'

'Which is why you're here on your own?' someone had shouted, laughing.

'I'm not on my own, I'm just keeping my options open,' Al said defensively.

* * *

'Will you keep your options open?' I said later, as I watched Bruno loading his cases into the back of the taxi that evening.

He was travelling to the airport for an early-morning flight the next day, planning to snooze on a seat in the departures lounge until his flight was called.

He'd looked confused. 'What are you talking about?'

'What Al said. He's keeping his options open.'

Bruno had sighed. 'He's an idiot, why are you taking any notice of him?'

'Perhaps he's just saying what all men think?'

'No, he's not. You know Al's a loser, a waste of space. He's far too interested in himself to ever give any relationship an opportunity.'

'You might change,' I said, a foolish, cold feeling falling over me, 'once you are out there.'

Bruno had stood up. 'Will change? How?'

I'd shrugged. 'I don't know.'

'Look, Denny, what's got into you? I'll be back at Christmas. I'll write, I'll phone you if I get the chance. You could fly out and see me. It's only a year, not even that because I'll be back in June next year for good. And then...'

'Then?' I'd said.

'Then I thought, you know, we need to think about the future now, Denny. It'll be all right.'

I'd wrapped my arms around myself. The evening was suddenly cold.

What had my real father said to me when my mother left him all those years ago? Exactly the same thing. The same words.

We need to think about the future now, Denny. It'll be all right.

After the divorce from Juliette's father, who had been my second step parent in five years, my mother had disappeared into the night with a used car salesman from Bromwich. I'd gone back to live with my father and I hadn't really seen her much since then, other than for awkward meetings in over-decorated hotels for lunches neither of us wanted. She had been glamorous and cheerful, expensively dressed and coiffured. I had felt awkward all the time, waiting for her to say something derogatory about my father, who I adored. Asking snide questions about Juliette and her hurried marriage.

Bruno was still talking, trying to reassure me, and, I thought, perhaps himself.

'You'll have graduated, I'll be here for my last year, then I'll graduate too. Think about… you know, maybe – if you wanted to, I don't know – getting a place together. Just us.'

Why didn't I just say yes? That would be amazing.

'We might have changed our minds by then. Let's wait and see how we feel.'

What a stupid thing to say.

The taxi driver had slammed the boot shut, and then done it again harder when the catch didn't work.

'I see,' Bruno had said.

He'd taken me in his arms then and kissed me goodbye.

I'd watched the taillights of the taxi disappearing and then I had gone back inside and sat on the edge of the bed, wanting to cry but not being able to.

That felt like the end of it, then. Our glorious summer days of warmth and happiness were over. He was going and I would be left behind. He would go his way and I would go mine. I had no trust in myself, I had to finish university, find a new path without him. Maybe he would return, but it would never be the same again, and I had the awful feeling it was all my fault.

I'd written, apologising. Trying to explain how upset I had been.

And then at Christmas, after I had counted the days off on a wall calendar, Bruno had not returned. He had sent me a post-card from Milan, a picture of an unremarkable square, wishing me a happy Christmas and telling me he was going back to Barcelona, his mother was unwell, and he wanted to see her. Reasonable, of course, and I understood perfectly. And I still didn't cry.

23

'I loved Naples,' Bruno said, 'it was so exciting. I'd never really been anywhere like it before. Everyone was so friendly and welcoming. The family I was staying with had a special room prepared for me, with its own bathroom. They had five children, but only one was still living at home. Pietro. He was the baby of the family; his mother adored him. Even though he was what you might call a wrong 'un. Always getting into trouble, staying out all night, bringing girls back after hours, and heaven knows what else. But he was fun.'

'Then what happened?'

Bruno settled back in his chair and stared at the sea.

'I enjoyed the university, the lifestyle. It seemed so much better to be living in a country with good weather, where you could rely on it to be sunny and warm, where you could plan outings and not have to have a rain contingency. I got swept up in it all, I suppose. I wanted to write and tell you all about it, but every time I tried, it sounded as though my life was one long, sunny party. And you were back at home working hard for finals. So in the end I just sent you postcards.'

'Two,' I said. 'I had two.'

'I sent more than that, I know I did. Then that first Christmas my mother was ill, I went home to see her. And then back to Naples, and I think I had got to the place where I hadn't contacted for you for such a long time that I was embarrassed. And I missed you so much. Every day I would wonder where you were, what you were doing. I know that sounds ridiculous. And you didn't write to me.'

I sat forward. 'Yes, I did, and it came back, not known at this address.'

'I moved out of the Italian family's home just after Christmas, into a flat above a bookshop, I did leave them a forwarding address. Perhaps they lost it. I was sharing with three other exchange students. I can't tell you how terrible it was. The roof leaked, the electricity went off at odd times, the only entrance was a stone staircase on the outside of the building. And the time went past so quickly. I travelled around in the holidays, Milan, Florence, Rome. Such wonderful places, but every time I wished you were there with me.'

'I do too,' I said, 'it sounds wonderful.'

'And then before I had to come back to do my final year, that summer, I went back to Barcelona. My father had died, and despite the way he had behaved, my mother wasn't coping very well. He might have been an arrogant sod who flitted between women over the years, but she had never looked at another man. So I got a job in a restaurant until it was time to go back to university for my fourth year. What were you doing?'

'I got a First in my finals, you said I had to, and was offered a job. And I started the following week. By the time you got back, I had left,' I said, 'and I never heard from you again.'

'I'm sorry,' he said. 'I can see now it was unforgiveable. I did ask around to try and find out where you had gone, but our friends had scattered and the office wouldn't tell me. Student confidentiality, I suppose.'

He leaned forward to top up our wine glasses.

'After university, I moved to Spain and then France and then to Italy to teach, and I did some travelling, and eventually I met Wendy and got married and divorced. And then I went back home for a bit, and I worked there. I stayed with my mother until she died. Then I got a job over here, and I've been here pretty much ever since.'

Bruno stretched his long legs out and turned to me.

'That's about all. I've talked for long enough. Now tell me what you did for all these years.'

I sipped my wine and thought about it. All those years ago. Some memories as bright as torchlight, others dim, and half forgotten.

'That first Christmas after you left, I went home to my father and his usual domestic chaos, which was made worse by the fact that he was packing up the house where I had been brought up and moving. He was going to live in Leamington Spa with some woman he had known for ages. Fiona, a friend from the gardening club who had come to mean more to him than just the occasional tray of seedlings. He assured me I was always welcome to stay with them, there would always be a bed for me there.'

'And did you go? I mean to visit him?'

'A few times,' I said. 'He wasn't well for a long time, and the house was cheerless and filled with her belongings. I felt a bit of a spare part, although Dad seemed happy. Which was the main thing. That Christmas before he moved, Juliette came round to the house on Boxing Day with her baby daughter to see me. She didn't look like herself at all, she looked tired and stressed, she'd been angry about something, but she wouldn't tell me what. Of course it was Gary. And nothing was the same any more.

'Then I went back to university and did nothing but work. I'd sent an airmail letter to your address in Naples and received no reply. Two months later, as I said, it was returned to me. Not known.'

'I swear I did leave a forwarding address,' Bruno said, 'and I suppose you had moved too. I guess that's why you didn't get my cards.'

'Probably. I expect they would have been sent on to Dad and Fiona. Anyway, that summer I graduated, but Dad couldn't attend because of his ill health. My actual mother hadn't come either because she was on a cruise around the Canaries with the car salesman. Terribly apologetic, she had sent me flowers when I had no vase to put them in, I told myself it didn't matter.'

Bruno touched my hand at the point. I let it lie there, covering mine. The feel of it was warm and welcome.

'That's awful, that no one came.'

'Juliette wanted to be there but then there were the unexplained problems she was having with Gary, things that had flared up, he was changing jobs, her daughter wasn't sleeping. I'd got a job starting the following week, and worked sixteen-hour days, making myself indispensable, important, promotable. Three years later, I was headhunted for a better job in London. I bought a tiny flat and then a larger one. Finally, before the housing market went completely crazy, I bought a little terraced house in a dodgy area which suddenly became fashionable. I made money on that and then the office was relocated, and I moved to a place in the Midlands. Life went on. I was fine. Wasn't I?'

'It sounds very lonely, actually,' he said.

'I was okay. I had friends and a social life. I did financial stuff, worked my way up. I had a few partners, I had some holidays with them, I bought a nicer house, I retired. It doesn't sound terribly interesting, does it? Being able to condense a life into a few sentences.'

'But you were happy?' he said.

I shrugged. 'Yes, and sometimes no, like most people. I did try and contact you, in the early weeks. I even phoned your mother once.'

He looked surprised. 'She didn't say anything to me.'

'No, nor did I. I just put the phone down. I always did find her rather intimidating and of course I didn't know enough Spanish to hold any sort of conversation with her. Particularly not "Where is your son and why haven't I heard from him?"'

'I'm sorry,' he said again. 'I don't know what else to say. I never met anyone who was half as important to me as you were. We lost so much time together, and things could have been so different. These days, with social media and the internet, it's a lot easier to stay in touch and to find someone.'

'Actually, I think it's almost impossible to hide,' I said.

'I think perhaps back then we were too alike, Denny,' Bruno said after a while. 'Both of us knew what it was like to lose parents at a young age, to see how even their marriages could go wrong. I suppose both of us were guilty of not trusting very much. Of taking that final step. I was just as bad as you were.'

The afternoon light was gradually fading as the sun dipped into the sea. A glorious sunset was developing in front of us, all shades of apricot and rosy pink, a couple of vapour trails from planes criss-crossing the sky.

'What restless creatures we are,' I said, looking up at them, 'I always think that when I see planes flying overhead. People travelling all over the world. Holidays and business. Arrivals and departures. Partings and reunions.'

'Would you like to travel more, now you are retired?'

'Yes, I think I would. I've spent such a lot of time in offices and conference rooms. And a lot of them don't have any windows. I'd like to go somewhere where there are wide-open spaces and endless views. Mountains and valleys. Where I can fill my lungs with air and my head with new ideas.'

'You need to see Montana,' he said, 'I went over there a few years ago. It's beautiful.'

I gave him a look. 'I bet you have a friend who lives there?'

He laughed. 'A distant cousin, actually, who married a rancher. They have five sons. They could ride before they could run. They live miles from anywhere, in a big house with a swimming hole. And in the winter the snow covers the windows.'

'Sounds wonderful.'

'I think you'd like it.'

There was a long silence then, and I tried to imagine it.

'Tell me how you are feeling,' he said.

What did I feel? A mixture of excitement, relief, insecurity.

'Do you know, I have thought about this moment for such a long time. First I thought I would be emotional if and when we ever met up again. And as time went by, I thought I would be furiously angry. Or shocked, or perhaps sad. And then one day, it must have been after I had an invitation to that twenty-year reunion weekend that I didn't go to, it prompted me to have a clear-out and I found those two postcards and some photographs. And I threw them all away. And I think I had finally got to the state of mind Kim mentioned to me the other day. I was done. Not angry, not upset, just done. And then that day, all those years later, there you were. Out of the blue. Standing in front of me, and inside I was a mess. And you said I didn't seem bothered.'

'But you were?' he said, sounding rather unsure of himself.

This was the moment to be honest. To say the things I needed to say.

'Of course I was,' I cried. 'If I had been standing up, I might have fainted! I had been in love with you. No man ever made me feel the way you did. And I put it down to remembering it wrong, or just first love, or something. But yes, I was bothered, as you put it.'

'I was too,' he said. He turned towards me, his expression earnest. 'I didn't sleep at all that night. I kept looking at this.'

He pulled out his wallet and reached into one of the slots, pulling out a tiny, much-creased black and white photograph. He stood up, came and sat next to me on the wicker settee and handed it over.

It was one of those snaps, originally a line of four, taken in a photo booth. Me sitting on his lap, a huge grin on my face, Bruno looking up at me, revelling in my happiness. My hair was long and tousled over one shoulder. A flower clip in my hair. He had been trying to grow a beard. We both looked so young, so care-free. So cheerful.

'I remember this,' I said at last, my voice rather shaky, 'that was our first holiday together. When we went to Paris. We were waiting for the ferry.'

'And we got there too early, and there was terrible chicory coffee at some café which we couldn't drink.'

I stared at the little photo again, remembering how I had felt. We had been at the start of an adventure, I had been thoroughly, completely happy.

'And you kept this picture all these years? I don't think Wendy would have appreciated that if she had known.'

He shook his head. 'I didn't know I had it. I found it in a box when we were splitting up just before the divorce. And somehow I couldn't throw it away. I just couldn't, Denny.'

He turned to me then, the wicker sofa creaking as he put his arm around my shoulder and looked at me properly. And I forgot about my missing eyebrow and what I looked like. My reticence, my doubts. My habit of running from this sort of struggle.

I was going to do what I had promised myself; I was going to say the things I wanted to and I wouldn't consider 'the worst that could happen'. Because at that moment, I knew the worst that could happen was not telling him how I felt.

If I didn't go after what I wanted, I would never have it. If I didn't step into the future, I would stay in the same place forever, and if I didn't ask for something, the answer would always be no. And I was going to do all those things.

'Oh, Bruno,' I said, 'I still love you. I don't think I ever stopped.'

And at long last I cried.

* * *

We sat out there for hours as the sunset faded, the evening sky turned to indigo blue, and the stars came out.

I shivered once and he went to fetch me a pale throw the colour of a robin's egg, which he wrapped around me with such care that I cried again, so much that he went to find me a box of tissues. And we both laughed at my easy tears, which in the past had been so difficult to shed.

We talked about everything. What we had done with the intervening years, the places we had seen, people we had known, and at last, as the thinnest of new moons rose over the inky sea, we went to bed.

24

I woke up the following morning, my cheek resting on his shoulder, his other arm across me.

For a while I lay still, not wanting to disturb him. It had been such a long time since I had woken up next to him, been able to watch him sleep, his dark eyelashes fluttering with the ends of a dream, perhaps. After such a long time, I had wondered whether the magic between us would be missing, or at least lost some of its magic. But no.

The feel of his skin against mine was just the same. The scent of him, the familiarity, the security of his arms around me. It was almost as though we had never parted.

But of course, at that precise moment, I needed the loo.

I slowly slid from under his arm and out of bed. Then I tiptoed across to the door and back into my room, where I went to the bathroom and then pulled on my dressing gown. What should I do next? Go back to bed? Make some tea?

In the end, I went downstairs and pulled two matching mugs out of the cupboard. Tea for both of us because I wasn't sure how to make coffee with his complicated machine. And anyway, it would have taken too long, and I wanted to be back with him.

Upstairs he was still asleep, the curtains across the open window moving slightly in the breeze from the sea.

I put his tea on the bedside table next to him, and there, unbelievably, was the same Snoopy alarm clock he'd had in university. They obviously made things to last in the old days.

'Hello,' he said, looking up at me with a sleepy smile.

'Hello.'

He stretched his arms above his head. 'Sleep well?'

'I think so. I've brought you tea,' I said. 'I didn't know how to use your coffee machine.'

'I'll show you later, if you want?'

'Okay.'

He propped himself up on his pillows and sipped his tea.

'You've still got that silly clock,' I said.

'It broke down a couple of times. I had it mended. I always liked it, I didn't see any reason to replace it.'

He reached out an arm towards me and I got back into bed beside him.

'Denny—'

'Bruno—'

We both started talking at once and laughed.

'I need to go home,' I said.

'I know. I was wondering when you would say something like that.'

'This is different, Bruno. I'm not running away this time, I need to get back to make sure my house is okay, and then there is Juliette's wedding. I need to find something to wear, and also see if she needs any last-minute help with the preparations.'

He nodded. 'Of course.'

'So will you come too? She did invite you.'

Bruno laughed. 'Nothing would keep me away. How could I resist visiting a church called St Botolph's Without? And what exactly was St Botolph lacking, I wonder?'

I felt a little spark of pleasure. 'St Botolph will be glad to see you, and Without just means it was built outside the old town walls, not that St Botolph was missing anything. You could stay with me if you wanted to. And Juliette's booked me a room at the local pub for the night of the wedding, you could share that, if that's not too forward of me?'

'Ideal,' he said, 'and I think it's a bit late for that. Not after last night.'

I could feel myself blushing.

He reached out, took my mug and put it on his bedside cabinet. Above the rim, I could just see the clock and Snoopy's smiling eyes.

'Now come here, let's talk about this "being too forward" business.'

I spent another week with him because the flights home were fully booked with returning holidaymakers, and I didn't really want to go. We spent those days talking and laughing and exploring the countryside together. I bought silly souvenirs and even found a shady hat that fitted me.

Being with him and my time with the Old Ducks had made me feel better about myself and the possibilities ahead. I had wasted so much time being busy with and then missing work, worrying about the future, that I had been forgetting to enjoy the present. To see that the future didn't have to be a scary, lonely place of uncertainty and emptiness.

Eventually we went on the internet and found a seat on a

plane going back to England. Part of me was sad that my time in Mallorca was coming to an end, but another bit of me was excited that I was starting a new phase in my life.

I had the time and the freedom and the courage now to do the things I had always wanted to do. Go on a cruise, perhaps, see more of the world, explore the UK too. There were so many parts of it I had never seen, even at my age. I wanted to try.

Bruno drove me to the airport the next day, both of us a bit sombre. There were banks of cloud massing over the sea, and the forecast was for rain, in a way it seemed appropriate.

Our parting was brief, sad, and yet positive. He had said he was coming over in June for Juliette's wedding. There was a lot to look forward to. I needed to remember that.

The bustle of the airport was the same as when we had landed, a lot of people trundling cases behind them and hurrying through to departures, while other people who had obviously just arrived looked for tour reps and coaches, their faces excited because they were at the start of their adventure.

I hoped Mallorca worked the same sort of magic for them that it had for me. It was a wonderful place, and I wouldn't hesitate to return.

* * *

Back home, everywhere seemed cold and dull, the damp streets filled with traffic and impatient pedestrians. Buses, their windows running with condensation and people hurrying home from work. I stopped at the local supermarket and picked up a few essentials, feeling as though I had been away for weeks.

But as I opened the front door, pushing aside the pile of post and flyers and fast-food menus, my house was just as I had left it, warm, comfortable, and pleasantly familiar, and I was glad to see it again.

I spiked the film on top of a ready meal, shoved it into the microwave and ate it, with a glass of supermarket merlot, in front of the television, where the news seemed unchanged from when I had left.

The previous evening I had been sitting out on the terrace, eating *Panceda* olives, then lamb *empanadas*, which we bought, still warm, in the local market. They looked like a wonderful pork pie which we enjoyed with a colourful salad and a bottle of perfect *Sió* red wine, produced locally. If I closed my eyes, I could still remember it, the taste of ripe plums and spices, in a rustic green glass.

And yet that evening I was content. I was happy to be back home, to see all my familiar things around me, the chair that was so comfortable, to know how everything worked and where everything was.

But I wasn't the same person who had left here, in just a short time I had changed. I was able to see my way through at last. I would not be forgotten or overlooked. I would make an effort to stop being afraid of what could go wrong, I would start to be positive about what could go right. Every day, from now on, would be a chance to get my life right.

25

TWO MONTHS LATER

At last it's the weekend of Juliette's wedding. I have found a lovely dress in pale blue, with a sequinned border around the neck which gives it a suitably celebratory feel. Even better was the fact that it was reduced in a mid-season sale. How was June mid-season?

Since I left Mallorca, Bruno and I have been communicating properly and often, talking on the phone and exchanging emails about our daily news. How easy it is these days to keep in touch. It makes the difficulties we had all those years ago seem ridiculous.

I'm expecting him to arrive at my house this evening. He's getting an afternoon flight and will be with me by seven o'clock. I am so excited I can't really concentrate.

He is going to be staying with me, then tomorrow we will travel together to the wedding and stay the night at the pub next to the church. It is all arranged and booked. I have bought some new underwear, which like all glamorous things is slightly uncomfortable.

The day passes in a fever of re-packing my bag, cleaning, and tidying and generally being nervous. I have new towels in the bathroom and extra milk in the fridge. I bought that before I remembered he drinks coffee black. It seemed ages, not just a few weeks, since I have seen him.

Juliette reports that she has everything in hand; the marquee is up, the tables and chairs have arrived, and the caterers are coming on Saturday morning ready for the early-afternoon wedding service in the local church. The florist has already been to leave long white boxes of roses and greenery in Matthew's house. It seems she has changed her mind about not wanting any flowers.

Kim and Vince (who seem to now be an item), Anita and her husband Rick will be travelling together to the church, Sophia and Theo will be arriving tomorrow morning. It is all so exciting.

But then, as I sit in the kitchen buffing up my wedding shoes (which are pale blue with bows on the back), no one seems to have heard from Bruno. In fact, for two days when I rang him his phone went straight to voicemail, and my last email went unanswered.

'I expect he is on the plane and his phone is turned off,' Juliette said reassuringly on the phone to me yesterday evening.

'Not all this time, surely? It's less than a three-hour flight.'

'I'm sure he will be there. And isn't it marvellous, the weather looks promising. Happy the bride that the sun shines on, eh? Although I don't care if it snows, actually. When are you arriving?'

'We'll probably be at your place about nine-thirty-ish. So make sure there is something for me to do.'

'Matthew has been marvellous organising everything, it's all done. I'm sure that's his military training. You just have to calm me down and help me get ready. I'm staying in the Rectory while he goes off to stay in the pub down the road with the General and a couple of brigadiers. I expect they will be having a stiff sherry or two. I shall have a bottle of bubbly so we can celebrate while I get ready.'

'Sounds wonderful,' I said.

'Must go, Matthew has just made me a cocktail before he disappears for the night with Bertie and Spotty. I've no idea what their real names are.' At that point, she turned away to speak to someone else. 'What's that, darling? A Hanky-Panky? Well, colour me surprised! I'm going to reek of gin tomorrow. Must go, Denny, lots of love, see you tomorrow.'

I go to bed at eleven-thirty and Bruno still hasn't turned up at my house. There are no phone calls or messages either. I consider ringing the police or phoning around all the hospitals, perhaps he's had an accident?

In the end I don't, heaven knows the police and hospitals are busy enough without random people ringing them up on the off-chance their university boyfriend is there. And with patient confidentiality, they wouldn't be able to tell me anyway. And is he still in Mallorca or in England? I don't even know that.

I think I almost sleep with one eye open, waiting to hear a knock on my front door, but nothing happens.

And then the possibility dawns on me, just after five-thirty in the morning, that perhaps Bruno has done it again. Just gone. He'd made promises to keep in touch before and look how that turned out. Maybe he has chickened out, had second thoughts, decided all this raking up the past is a bad idea after all.

I go quite cold at the thought and feel small and rather foolish.

I lie in bed as the dawn creeps through the curtains and ponder this.

And then I dismiss the idea. He wouldn't do that. He couldn't, not after how much we had talked it over and come to understand the other person's perspective. But he might. But surely he wouldn't?

The possibilities rattle round my brain for an hour or so, and then I get up, shower and dress in some new jeans, a T-shirt, and a warm fleece, because the morning is still chilly.

I mess about for a bit, wiping the kitchen worktops and making tea which I don't drink. I'm too nervous. I check my watch. Seven-thirty. I will wait until eight to see if Bruno turns up. Perhaps his plane has been delayed? Or crashed? I switch my laptop on and check the news. No, there is nothing anywhere about that.

At eight o'clock, I make a decision, and pack my bags into the boot of my car. Then I dither for a bit longer. I'll give him another ten minutes.

Ten minutes pass.

Oh, well. Right. It is time to set off. I have Juliette to consider, my matronly duties await me. And I can't wait, because Bruno or no Bruno, it is going to be a memorable day.

* * *

The sky brightens up during my journey and by the time I reached the Rectory where the reception is to take place, the morning sun is burning off the dew on the grass in little curls of steam.

The marquee is, as Juliette said, on the lawn, gleaming white in the sunshine. There are several vans parked on the driveway which I negotiate, finding a space around the side of the house where my car will be out of the way.

Inside there is a great deal of noise and bustle. There are

caterers in the kitchen, a florist organising a huge display of roses on the hall table, and several young people in regulation white shirts and black trousers, carrying trays of crockery, cutlery, and glassware out to the marquee.

I know Juliette is somewhere in the house because I can hear her playing the piano.

I wander down a hallway and find her sitting at a grand piano, her hair in huge foam rollers. Her fingers, long and delicate with impeccably manicured pink nails, are on the keys.

'There you are!'

She turns. 'Ah, my matron of honour, if I'm not much mistaken. Thank heavens. I've had no one to talk to since last night. It took an age to get Bertie and Spotty out of the house. They kept banging on about regimental dinners they had been to and how badly behaved they had all been. There better not be any of that food-throwing nonsense today. I warned Spotty he would be on a charge if he did, and he just laughed so much he fell over into the flower bed. Let's just say drink had been taken.'

For the first time in years, Juliette's face is make-up free, and without her trademark lipstick, she somehow looks very different. More vulnerable, I suppose.

'How are you feeling? Excited?' I ask, hugging her.

'I am, but I also want to get ready, and I've been advised not to, in case I spill something down my dress. That would be good, wouldn't it? A bride with a big coffee stain on the front of her frock.'

I look at my watch. 'It's only nine-thirty so I wouldn't suggest opening the champagne just yet.'

'The others should be here soon anyway, and then we will,' Juliette says. 'Come on, let's go upstairs, at least I can put my face on. I'm sure Bruno can find some chairs to move or something. Or he could just walk down the road to the pub and have a snifter with the three amigos.'

'He's not here,' I say.

Juliette stares at me for a moment.

'What do you mean, not here? I thought he was getting to your place last night?'

I shake my head. 'Nope. No sign of him.'

'You're sure?'

'Well, I didn't actually check behind the dustbins, but yes, pretty sure.'

Her face collapses into sorrow, and she comes to give me another hug. 'Oh, Denny!'

I shake my head. 'It's fine. It's what he does, isn't it? I thought I was the one with the commitment issues, but apparently it's both of us.'

'No messages? Emails?'

'Nothing. Not for two days now.'

Juliette purses her lips. 'You wait until I see him again. I'll give him a large chunk of my mind. And despite my age, there is plenty left to go round. He'll be sorry.'

'It's okay, Jools. I think I would have been more surprised if he had turned up, all things considered.'

'But...'

'Come on, I want to concentrate on you. This is your special day. Let's go upstairs and think about your hair and make-up. I can't get used to seeing you without lipstick. We need to get ready.'

Juliette takes a deep breath. 'What we need is to open that champagne.'

* * *

About an hour later, Kim, Vince, Anita, and her husband Rick arrive, followed shortly afterward by Sophia and Theo.

There is a great deal of laughter and chatter and catching up to do. Anita is positively fizzing with excitement, and desperate to change out of her tracksuit into her bridesmaid's dress. Rick is lean and quite handsome in an Anthony Hopkins sort of way and is obviously more interested in the garden than anything else. He goes off after a few minutes to explore.

Kim and Vince seem very much a couple and stand like children holding hands while introductions are made and details of everyone's journey compared. Vince has replaced his broken glasses with some new ones which are much more flattering than the old ones, and he keeps sending proud looks at Kim in a way that is very endearing.

Theo is tall, silver haired and utterly charming. I can see why Sophia was so taken with him.

'I am glad to see the magic of the Old Ducks has worked again, and brought us all together,' he says, 'and pleased to meet new friends.'

'I'm delighted to meet you, Theo. I've heard so much about you.'

Theo gives a little self-deprecating smile. 'Oh dear.'

'No, all good,' I say.

'I am going to take Rick and Theo to the pub down the road in a bit. We can dump our bags there and we need to get out of the ladies' way so they can make themselves even more beautiful,' Vince says with a fond glance at Kim which makes her blush, and then his eyes light up with a familiar zeal. 'I saw a great spotted woodpecker as we came up the drive. *Dendrocopos major.* Do you know they can bash their beaks into a tree trunk at forty beats a second?'

'I feel like that sometimes,' Juliette mutters.

'No Doggie and Lorna?' I ask.

'They are on a river cruise, at the moment. Amsterdam to Basel,' Kim says. 'I don't think any of us saw that coming.'

'Marvellous,' I say. 'And Johnny and Polly?'

'In Florida, taking the grandchildren to Disney. They must be boiling,' Vince nods. 'By the way, where's Bruno? I thought he would be here by now?'

'No idea,' I say. 'I thought so too, but he's not.'

Vince's brow crinkles in confusion, and he pushes his new spectacles up his nose.

'Have you tried phoning him?'

'Don't be daft, Vince, of course she has,' Kim says. 'Now you chaps disappear, we have a bride to attend to. And don't forget the wedding is at the church at midday. It's up the little lane by the side of the pub so you can't get lost. We'll see you there.'

* * *

Upstairs, Juliette is sitting in a comfortable armchair still in her dressing gown, looking thoughtfully at her wedding outfit, which is hanging on the back of the door in a white cloth bag.

'At last!' she says, brightening up as we come in. 'I can open the champagne. Has everyone arrived? Have they gone to the pub?'

'Everyone except Bruno,' Kim says. 'I'm going to give him a piece of my mind when I see him.'

My heart does another little plunge of disappointment.

'I'm going to do that already,' Juliette says firmly, 'you can just hit him with a stick.'

We spend the next hour in Juliette's bedroom, drinking champagne and catching up on each other's news.

Kim sits in a comfortable chair by the window, holding her

champagne glass at an angle and squinting at the garden through the bubbles.

'This is like a school reunion, only better, because only the nice people have turned up. The ones you hoped to see. And not Sue, who was a bully who used to sit behind me in maths and tie my plaits together. Do you know, she once knotted my plaits around a netball goal post. I was out there for ages.'

Juliette nods. 'Or Linda somebody who was at school with me. I had a favourite pencil once, from Chessington Zoo, and she deliberately broke it in half. Still, that was the visit when my parents told me they were getting divorced, so it wasn't really a happy memory.'

'It's so lovely to see you all again,' I say, 'it seems ages since we were all together in Mallorca, doesn't it?'

'So where are we going next?' Anita asks. 'And this time I'm definitely coming.'

We discuss this topic for a while and Juliette tops up everyone's champagne.

'You're going to be swaying down the aisle at this rate,' I say.

I'm trying to focus, to concentrate on being here with my friends and being a part of such a special occasion, but there's a little nagging worry at the back of my mind. Where is Bruno? Why isn't he here?

'I am a very happy woman,' Juliette says, raising her glass. 'Let's have a toast; to the Old Ducks.'

We chink glasses together again and then we start to get ready.

By midday, we are all very presentable. It seems we didn't need fashion advice from twenty-something experts to scrub up well.

The four attendants are in knee-length dresses. I am in blue, Kim in pale peach, Anita in pink and Sophia in lavender.

Juliette, meanwhile, has twisted her hair up into a sophisticated chignon held in place by the enamelled hair pin she bought
in Pollença and is wearing a cream dress and matching coat
which show off her shapely legs.

'Well?' she says, standing in front of a cheval mirror and
angling it so she can see herself properly. 'What do you think?'

We all give happy sighs of approval. She really does look
wonderful. No ugly old lady clothes or shoes for any of us, just
five friends who are ready to party.

'You look perfect,' I say, feeling rather emotional. 'You're going
to knock Matthew's socks off.'

Juliette finishes her glass of champagne and then re-applies
her lipstick.

'I keep thinking I'm going to be nervous, but then I'm not,' she
says.

Kim looks knowing. 'That's the champagne.'

'I think it's because I'm so happy. I'm marrying Matthew, and
you are all here to celebrate. I can't wait to get started.'

She picks up a small bouquet of cream roses and stands to
attention.

'You look wonderful. I thought you didn't want any flowers?'
I say.

'Matthew arranged for them to be delivered. I'm not
complaining,' Juliette replies with a happy sigh.

'The car is here,' Sophia says, looking out of the window. 'Are
you having anyone to give you away?'

'No, I thought that's what you four were there for,' Juliette
says. 'You walk into the church, and I'll trot along behind you.'

'What about the flower girls?' I ask.

'They are meeting us at the church. And they are going to go
in first so they will be corralled by you behind them, and Melissa
can scoop them up at the front before they run off. I wanted them

to get ready here, but Melissa said she would have more chance of getting them dressed in their room at the pub. Otherwise they would be running riot apparently. They had a big argument about which one of them was going to hold the bag of rose petals to throw after the ceremony so in the end I had to get them one each. Bless them.'

'They sound like a handful,' Anita sighs.

'They are lovely, but a bit – shall we say – spirited,' Juliette says, teasing a stray curl back behind one ear. 'Still, that's what they said about me at school, and I turned out okay.'

'Come on then,' Kim says, 'if we are all ready. The car is waiting. All aboard the Skylark.'

We go downstairs, like a phalanx of guards around Juliette in case her stilettos snag on the carpet and she plunges to her doom. Although what use Kim and I would be if she landed on us, I'm not sure.

Safely at the bottom, we teeter out of the house on our unfamiliar shoes and make our way to the grey limo which is waiting to drive us the very short distance to the church. In fact, we could have walked it in ten minutes, but apparently the photographer ('Jeremy, but call me Jez') insisted. He told Juliette it would make for good copy, whatever that meant.

She told us he had admitted to her that he was more used to writing articles for the local paper about football, but he was also Matthew's godson and needed the work.

Anyway, he makes the required approving comments as the five of us wedge into the limo, and we set off at a very stately pace, Jez powering ahead of us on his Vespa scooter, his camera bag slung over one shoulder.

As we get to the gate, he tries to adjust the strap of his bag and wobbles violently, nearly ploughing into a rhododendron bush before righting himself.

We all gasp in horror, watching him, wondering if we are going to have to scoop him up and take him to A&E, and then let out a collective sigh of relief.

'So exciting,' I say. 'I can't believe we are doing this, even now.'

'Me neither,' Juliette agrees. 'Golly, I'm really hungry. Anyone got any biscuits?'

'I had some Jaffa cakes in my case, but I left them at the pub,' Kim admits. 'Vince calls me his little Biscuit Buddy because I always have something in my bag for emergencies. I tried some strawberry ones once, but they're not the same.'

Next to me, Juliette takes a deep breath and puts one hand to her forehead.

'Are you nervous now?' I ask, squeezing her hand.

'No, it's this blooming hair pin, it's digging into my head. I wish I could ditch it.'

'Oh, we're here, well, that didn't take long,' Kim says cheerfully.

We all pile out again as Jez gets his camera out and starts clicking away again, making encouraging comments as though he's Lord Litchfield.

'Lovely, ladies, the camera loves you. Chin up, lady in the salmon.'

'It's pink blush,' Anita says, outraged.

Juliette looks surprised. 'I thought it was orange. Oh, well, whatever it is, you look lovely. I told you I was a bit colour blind.'

Through the open door of the church we can hear the organ playing 'Sheep May Safely Graze' and the low hum of conversation.

A sprightly gentleman in an impeccably cut suit comes to the church door, winks at Juliette, and gives two hearty thumbs up.

'It's all right, Spotty, you can tell him I'm here,' Juliette says with a grin.

And then, behind us, we hear a car pulling up. We turn to see a taxi, the passenger door opens and with the help of the driver, Bruno gets out.

I think my jaw drops as I watch him limping up the path towards us because he has a leg in plaster and is on crutches. I am torn between delight and relief at seeing him and concern as to what has happened. At that moment, two small girls come cannoning out of the church door, nearly skidding into Jez, who does some impressive juggling with his camera.

Bruno gives us an apologetic smile.

'Sorry about this, everyone. Better late than never.'

'Bruno! You're here! What happened?' I say.

My heart is thumping so hard with a mixture of shock and relief.

He kisses my cheek. 'I'm fine, I'll explain later. Go on, I think it's your cue.'

Juliette clears her throat, sounding nervous for the first time.

'Come on, troops. What was it Sharpe used to say, *chosen men to me*. Well, come on, chosen women, let's go.'

I feel rather emotional, hearing her say that. I am one of the chosen women. I am not alone; I am part of a wonderful support group. I have friends, I have myself, and maybe I have Bruno too. Life feels suddenly very different from the dull, unexciting place I had anticipated.

From inside the church, we hear the 'Wedding March' start, and the flower girls storm back in again, hurling handfuls of rose petals at each other. Kim, Sophia, Anita, and I follow at a more elegant pace, although Kim gets her heel caught in a grating for a moment.

She hisses, 'Oh, *arsington!*'

We all giggle. I hope no one hears her.

Juliette follows on behind us and we walk forward into the church. This is it.

At the head of the small nave, I see Matthew, proud and perfect in a dark suit. His best man, who I guess is Bertie, is holding onto a dog lead. And there is Matthew's Border terrier, Maurice, with a big white bow on his collar and a small cushion tied on his back; he is acting as the ring bearer after all. When the dog sees Juliette, he gives several short barks and starts worrying at the ribbon around his neck and everyone laughs.

26

'You won't believe me,' Bruno says, 'the reason why I was late. I'm almost too embarrassed to tell you.'

We are sitting at a table in the marquee. Juliette and Matthew went back to the Rectory in the limo, and the rest of us walked back through the lane, the summer air warm and still and scented with the wildflowers in the hedges.

The picture-perfect marquee, decorated with glorious arrangements of cream roses and greenery, was waiting for us, the smart line of waiters holding trays of champagne and canapés.

The wedding went off perfectly, apart from Juliette's twin flower girls, who had to be taken away howling at the end because one had used up all her rose petals and the other had some left.

'Well, tell me anyway,' I say, 'everyone is going to be sitting down soon.'

Bruno takes a deep breath and then laughs.

'I was cleaning out the gutters.'

'What?'

'I know, and after all the things we said to Doggie about being careful and what a daft job it was. And then one day, at the start of this week, I didn't have anything to do. I was missing you, and I looked up at the gutters and realised they were full of pine needles. So I got the stepladder out.'

'You twit! You didn't?'

Bruno nods. 'I did, and I was getting on quite well, and then, well, I fell off.'

'And broke your leg?'

'I'm afraid so.'

'Why didn't you tell me?'

'I had my mobile in my pocket, and I landed on it. Smashing it. Which meant I couldn't ring you to explain, or anyone else for that matter because all my contact details were in there. I had to hobble inside to get to the house phone. It's a very long time since I've had an address book of any sort. So I couldn't ring anyone. It's taught me a lesson. Technology might be good, but everyone needs a back-up.'

'And are you all right?'

'Wounded pride, I suppose, and this.' He taps the cast on his leg. 'I didn't even know the address of this place, I just remembered the name of the church, St Botolph's Without, and luckily there aren't many of those. I tried contacting the firm that rented out the villa, but you know what client confidentiality is like these days. They wouldn't tell me anything.'

Kim taps me on the shoulder.

'Vince thinks he saw a pair of willow tits in the shrubbery, we're going to look.'

'*Poecile montanus*,' Vince adds, rather breathlessly.

We watch them go for a moment, both of us, I think, a little puzzled.

'Anyway, apart from being completely daft, what have you been doing?' I ask.

'I painted the hallway and pressure washed the terrace. I've been writing, walking, trying out some new recipes. I'm hoping you will come back soon, and I wanted to show off.'

'I thought…'

I stop.

'You thought I had run off again, didn't you?' Bruno says with a grin. 'Well, now you know I didn't.'

I look around at the guests, all in their best, the lovely marquee where the rather extravagant floral displays are sending out a delicious scent. Juliette and Matthew are standing by the front door of the Old Rectory, glasses of champagne in their hands as Jez snaps away. In front of them, on the grass, Maurice is savaging the ring bearer's cushion accompanied by some hearty growling noises.

I am so happy I think I might burst.

'I'm glad you didn't run off,' I say at last.

Jez shouts into the marquee. 'Can we have all the matrons, please?'

There is a moment's silence and then Bertie gives a piercing wolf-whistle and someone else, I think it's Spotty, throws a bread roll at him, missing and hitting Jez squarely on the head.

Jez looks as though he is going to burst into tears. 'I say…'

'Take that man's name,' someone shouts.

It is hilarious and not what I was expecting at all. Several very distinguished-looking men, impeccably dressed, behaving like schoolboys. I wonder what they will be like when they have a few drinks inside them.

I stand up, smoothing down the skirt of my dress. 'I'd better go and have my photo taken, don't go away.'

Bruno catches hold of my hand and smiles up at me. 'I won't. Anyway, I can't get up much speed with this thing on my leg.'

I lean down and kiss him, and Spotty gives another wolf-whistle, and the fierce-looking woman with him whacks him with her handbag.

Anita appears at my elbow. 'Any idea where Kim is? The photographer wants her.'

'Last seen heading for the shrubbery with Vince,' I say. 'They were looking for a pair of tits.'

'What?'

* * *

We have endless photographs taken, various groups of people, all happy and smiling, and Maurice the Border terrier, relieved of his duties and very full of himself now that he has destroyed the hated cushion. It really is a joyous occasion. Even the two flower girls join in, after a small argument about on which side of Juliette they are going to stand. Then they are taken away by Melissa with promises of squash and a biscuit and are last seen heading under a table with handfuls of sausage rolls and crisps, pilfered from the buffet table.

Then at last we sit down, the vicar says grace and the buffet is declared open, much to Juliette's relief, as she had been heard loudly complaining she was ravenous, to which Matthew gallantly responded, 'Ravishing, my darling.' She was all smiles after that.

How wonderful for her to have found happiness at last, after the problems with her first marriage, her various relationship disasters. It really is lovely to see.

Then there are the speeches, and Matthew pays tribute to Juliette in affectionate and rather emotional terms, and Bertie stands up, is very funny and rude about his military friends who heckle him unmercifully, and then he makes up for it with some lavish compliments to Juliette and to us. So we all forgive him.

'And so it is indeed my pleasure to raise a glass to the happy couple, the wonderful matrons and the flower girls, wherever they are.'

'Under my table,' Melissa mutters at the table next to ours, 'and thank heavens they are asleep.'

As Bertie raises his glass, another bread roll hits him on the head.

'Now look here, Spotty,' he starts, 'any more of this and I will tell them about that time in Sandhurst with that wheelbarrow. Still, at least your aim has improved since then!'

Then, to cheers and applause, Juliette and Matthew cut the wedding cake with Matthew's sword.

As the evening darkens, and the lights in the marquee twinkle overhead, music starts playing and Matthew and Juliette get up from the table for their first dance. No simple shuffling from one foot to the other for them, they do a very skilful slow foxtrot to 'The Way You Look Tonight' and I don't think there is a dry eye in the house. When they finish, everyone stands up and applauds them, and Juliette sheds a few happy tears while Matthew, moustache bristling, looks proud.

Then there is a minor scuffle as Maurice finds the two flower girls under the table, snarfs up the last of their sausage rolls and then flees the marquee with a small shoe in his mouth.

So much has changed for me in the last few months, I realise as I look around the room. I have retired, wondered about my future, reconnected with Bruno, and made so many new friends. And out of this muddle of meals and wine and laughter and face packs I have learned to trust. To trust myself, to trust my friends, and also the only man I ever loved. Bruno.

Life holds promise now, I know I can achieve so much more than I had realised. And it was all due to the Old Ducks, their friendship, their support, and their optimism.

The dance floor gradually fills up with couples.

Anita and her husband Rick seem to be getting on well too, their heads together as they dance and chat about something. They make a handsome couple, moving confidently around the dance floor.

Kim and Vince are together out there too, flirting outrageously, her face alight with happiness and probably too much champagne. Vince's new glasses are reflecting the light from the canopy overhead. Who knows where that relationship will lead them?

Sophia and Theo are dancing, her head nestled under his chin, a happy smile on her face. It is perfect.

'I wish we could dance too,' I say rather wistfully after a few minutes.

'I don't think I can dance very well,' Bruno replies. 'In fact, I don't think I ever could. And certainly not with my leg in plaster.'

'No,' I say, looking rather regretfully at the other couples, who are smiling, moving around to the music with varying degrees of confidence.

Bruno puts one hand over mine. 'But I suppose you could always pivot me round on my good leg.'

I look across at him in the dim, twinkling light, his face so familiar now, his expression filled with humour. The way his eyes sparkle at me, we have so many new memories to share now, and who knows, more memories to make and perhaps a life to look forward to.

'Why don't we give it a try,' I say, holding out my hand towards him, 'and see how we get on?'

We move to the middle of the dance floor, and Bruno puts his arms round me. It feels so lovely, so right. Luckily the music is reasonably slow, and I do actually pivot around him, with some exaggerated hand movements that I've seen on *Strictly*. He laughs and staggers slightly, bumping into Spotty and his furious-looking wife, who doesn't seem particularly pleased that her husband is attempting a Charleston to 'I Left My Heart in San Francisco'.

'I'll take you dancing properly one day,' Bruno says, 'when I'm out of plaster.'

'I'd like that.'

The music is coming to an end, but I just want to stay there, with him, with my friends, with this lovely day.

Suddenly, as the music ends, Bruno gets his balance on his good leg, puts one arm around my waist and dips me back over it. My word, he must be stronger than I realised.

I look up at his face. Behind him, the roof of the marquee is filled with little lights like stars, and he is smiling. And then he kisses me.

There is a sudden burst of clapping and some whooping and cheering and I come to my senses and look around to realise everyone else has stopped dancing and they are applauding us.

In front of me, Juliette is standing, a champagne glass in her hand, which she tilts in my direction. Sophia, Kim, and Anita are there too, and they all cheer again.

'We knew you'd get there eventually!' she says. 'Here's to the Old Ducks and their 100 per cent success record.'

ACKNOWLEDGMENTS

As always when I get to the end of a book, I want to express my thanks and gratitude to so many people.

To all the great team at Boldwood Books, especially Emily Ruston, Nia Beynon, Jenna Houston, Isabelle Flynn, Ben Wilson and of course Amanda Ridout.

Huge thanks for all the support from Broo Doherty of DHH Literary Agency who is always there at the end of the phone when I need her.

Thank you to my family, who continue to give me the love and encouragement I have needed over the last, difficult months. I don't know what I would have done without you all.

To all the other Boldwood authors who are unfailingly supportive and positive.

To my bestie, Jane Ayres, who selflessly came on a research trip to Mallorca with me. What a great time we had. Here's to the next one!

And finally, to Brian, always loved. Without him, none of this would have been possible.

ABOUT THE AUTHOR

Maddie Please is the author of bestselling joyous tales of older women. She had a career as a dentist and now lives in Herefordshire where she enjoys box sets, red wine and Christmas.

Sign up to Maddie Please's mailing list for news, competitions and updates on future books.

Follow Maddie on social media here:

facebook.com/maddieplease

twitter.com/maddieplease1

instagram.com/maddieplease1

bookbub.com/authors/maddie-please

ALSO BY MADDIE PLEASE

The Old Ducks' Club

Sisters Behaving Badly

Old Friends Reunited

Sunrise With The Silver Surfers

A Vintage Vacation

The Old Ducks' Hen Do

Boldw∞d

Boldwood Books is an award-winning fiction publishing company seeking out the best stories from around the world.

Find out more at www.boldwoodbooks.com

Join our reader community for brilliant books, competitions and offers!

Follow us
@BoldwoodBooks
@TheBoldBookClub

Sign up to our weekly deals newsletter

https://bit.ly/BoldwoodBNewsletter

Printed in Great Britain
by Amazon

41640258R00178